THE DESIGNATED DATE
Drew Taylor

Taylor Made Publishing

Copyright © 2024 by Drew Taylor Smith

All rights reserved.

Ebook ISBN: 979-8-9910542-0-1

Paperback ISBN: 979-8-9910542-1-8

Hardcover ISBN: 979-8-9910542-4-9

No part of this book may be reproduced in any form or by any electronic or mechanical means, including information storage and retrieval systems, without written permission from the author, except for the use of brief quotations in a book review.

Without any way limiting the author's and publisher's exclusive rights under copyright, any use of this publication to "train" generative artificial intelligence (AI) technologies to generate text is expressly prohibited. The author reserves all rights to license uses of this work for generative AI training and development of machine learning language models. No part of this book may be used for training, included in, or reproduced in any form for use in machine learning, large language models, and artificial intelligence programs.

This book is a work of fiction. Names, characters, businesses, events, and incidents are the products of the author's imagination. Any resemblance to actual persons, living or dead, or actual events is purely coincidental.

AI was not used in the creation of this story or its design.

Scripture quotations are from The ESV® Bible (The Holy Bible, English Standard Version®), © 2001 by Crossway, a publishing ministry of Good News Publishers. Used by permission. All rights reserved.

Cover and Interior Design by Drew Taylor

Character/Object Art by Callie McLay

Edited by Leah Taylor

To the women who are complete messes and often wonder how
God could even love them.
This book is for you.
And He does.
Love you.
So much that He took your mess upon His shoulders on the cross.

Have mercy on me, O God,
>   according to your steadfast love;
according to your abundant mercy
>   blot out my transgressions.
Wash me thoroughly from my iniquity,
>   and cleanse me from my sin!
For I know my transgressions,
>   and my sin is ever before me.
Against you, you only, have I sinned
>   and done what is evil in your sight,
so that you may be justified in your words
>   and blameless in your judgment.
Behold, I was brought forth in iniquity,
>   and in sin did my mother conceive me.
Behold, you delight in truth in the inward being,
>   and you teach me wisdom in the secret heart.
Purge me with hyssop, and I shall be clean;
>   wash me, and I shall be whiter than snow.
Let me hear joy and gladness;
>   let the bones that you have broken rejoice.

Hide your face from my sins,
  and blot out all my iniquities.
Create in me a clean heart, O God,
  and renew a right spirit within me.
Cast me not away from your presence,
  and take not your Holy Spirit from me.
Restore to me the joy of your salvation,
  and uphold me with a willing spirit.
Then I will teach transgressors your ways,
  and sinners will return to you.
Deliver me from bloodguiltiness, O God,
  O God of my salvation,
  and my tongue will sing aloud of your righteousness.
O Lord, open my lips,
  and my mouth will declare your praise.
For you will not delight in sacrifice, or I would give it;
  you will not be pleased with a burnt offering.
The sacrifices of God are a broken spirit;
  a broken and contrite heart, O God, you will not despise.
Psalm 51:1-17 ESV

BEAT ONE

THE CHEMICAL EQUATION // "DON'T BLAME ME"

Prologue

Stone

Is a lie still a lie if I'm actively working to make it true?

"I want to meet the lady who was able to tie Stone Harper down!" Gracie Helms and my sister, Stella, smush their faces together to fit into the parameters of the phone screen. The two nosiest women on this side of the Mississippi River, if you ask me.

"One day, Gracie. I promise." I smile through the lie at the buoyant, short-haired blonde. I can't promise anything because Lucy May Spence won't give me the time of day despite all my advances. I've thrown everything at her—charm, wit, my handsomeness, and even a little money.

No, not like *that*. I meant to say I've offered to take her out to nice restaurants and have bought her little gifts and such.

She might be the only woman in the world immune to me. She's certainly the only one who has made me chase her this long, which is why with every passing day, I grow more and more agitated at the situation.

Excuse me. *Lack of* a situation between us.

Four whole months. Once I made my mind up at the Valentine's Day West Coast Swing Dance back in February that I wanted to get to know my now-permanent assistant more, I started to stop by Lucy's office at random for nothing more than a chat or to compliment her. That led to me asking her out to the occasional business lunch while scheduling work dinners for everyone just to spend a little more time around her. I wanted time with *her*, though, so lately I've started asking her out to private dinners...

But she hasn't said yes to one of those yet. Even with my blatant attempts to flirt and make my intentions known. She always has an excuse, the most frequent one being *you are my boss*. And the challenge is making me want her more...

"She's so pretty in her social media photos. Did you know her twin got engaged to the Crown Prince of Korsa yesterday? Of course you did. You were probably there. Why haven't we gotten pictures? Why do you two *not* post pictures together?" Stella asks without taking a breath, giving a fierce eyebrow raise in my direction. I know that look—the look of doubt.

I sigh, shoulders rising and falling dramatically, as if the reason is the most obvious one in the world. I've already concocted an explanation because I knew my sister would ask me eventually. "Because she's my assistant director and we haven't told everyone at the community center."

Stella's eyebrow still rides high as her gray eyes bore into me. "Scared people will accuse you of nepotism or something?"

"Yeah, he probably wanted her as his assistant just so he could keep her around him all the time." Gracie laughs, and I grin through tight lips. She's not wrong...

"No. Lucy is skilled with management and has proven herself capable of performing assistant duties such as planning events, which is her forte. That's why I merged the assistant director and events planning roles back in April when we started dating." Also not wrong. While I did want Lucy to work closer with me (more opportunities to get to know and flirt with her), she's also a competent woman who is phenomenal at event planning because of her creative soul. She's responsible for the Valentine's Day West Coast Swing Dance night that opened my eyes to just how downright tempting the woman is.

Then sometime in April I decided to tell my family I was dating her so they would stop nagging me about settling down.

"We're just teasing you, bud," Gracie claims, but my sister looks suspicious as she tugs her brunette ponytail tighter.

"We need to meet her soon, Stone. Or else we are going to think you're lying to us." Stella's pointed stare sends panic racing down my spine. Why in the world did I even tell my family I was dating Lucy? I'm regretting that decision right now, but ultimately, I was tired of hearing that I needed to settle down and stop going through girls like I was trying on new clothes. With Stella marrying Lucas over a year ago, all-eyes turned to me with the expectation that I was clearly next. Mama began to question me; Stella and Lucas straight-up told me I needed to start looking into settling down with someone; and Jared, Gracie's husband, began to try and to set me up with a myriad of women.

The easiest out, since I now live in Juniper Grove, which is six hours north of Dasher Valley, was to state I had a girlfriend. That led to me having to give them a name two months ago after they pestered me while I was home visiting for Stella's big announcement that she was going to forgo teaching the next year and run for Mississippi state representative.

Can you guess the name that spewed out of my mouth without a morsel of thought when they nagged me for my girlfriend's name?

Ding, ding, ding! Lucy Spence.

"I don't have plans to come home anytime soon, Stells. I'm busy with the community center."

Gracie whispers something into Stella's ear, and my sister's ice gray eyes brighten for a moment before she schools her expression.

"You could take a couple days off and road trip down to show us your lady friend. You haven't dated someone for this long since Lacey. Lucy is apparently special, and we want to meet her. Don't make me pull the Mama card..."

Disdain and discomfort stir at my sister's mention of my ex-girlfriend, Lacey Fraiser. But I shake the feeling off and narrow my eyes. "You wouldn't."

She smirks. "You used it on me to get me home for Christmas, remember?"

"Revenge!" Gracie hollers, pumping her fist in the air. Stella high-fives her and they let loose an evil laugh. Gracie's seven-month old son proceeds to scream in the background, so Gracie hands the phone to Stella.

"My dearest brother, you know that our lovely and caring mother is sick. You know as well as I do that her rheumatoid arthritis is disabling her with every day that passes. It would warm her soul to see her long-lost son that hasn't graced her doorstep in two long months. And lastly, you know how pleased she would be to meet the girl who has captured your heart."

I cringe as my sister bats her eyelashes, clasping her hands together underneath her chin. Regardless of her show right now, she's right about Mama. Every time I talk to her, she sounds tired. I know her new husband is taking care of her, but it still worries me. And Mama has been subtly pushing me to bring Lucy home; it's nothing compared to Stella's agenda, however. If that woman doesn't win come November, I'd be shocked. She's as tenacious as the kids at the Juniper Grove Community Center who play basketball like they're in the NBA. Maybe I should appease her for now.

"Okay, Seester," I say, using my own variation of sister as I have since I was a child. "I'll have to check my calendar, but what if I came home in September for your birthday?" As I say the words and watch a wide grin stretch across her face, I know something mysterious and unfortunate will happen between me and Lucy before then. And I'll get an earful about it while I'm home.

Man, I've dug a hole for myself with this lie.

"You're going to stay with her for three more months? This feels like a ploy for a 'breakup.'" Stella says. *This woman.* Too sharp and perceptive for her own good. She'll make an excellent politician.

"I plan to still be with her," I say nonchalantly, then I change the subject to ask how Lucas, my brother-in-law, is doing for a few more minutes before ending the call and kicking back with a beer and chicken wings.

Overall, I've got a good life going for me, even without Lucy saying yes to my advances. Though it'd be the icing on the cake if she would. I don't know what it is about her that is simply and utterly captivating. The primal need to experience her is something I'm slowly losing control of. It's impacting my dating life.

My real one that I keep on the down-low.

My phone lights with a notification—a message from a girl I dated in college at Juniper Grove University. I read it; she's wanting me to come over. But then Lucy's freckled face and hazel green eyes and messy curly hair pop to the forefront of my mind, and I wish it was her I was going to see.

What's with the hold this lady has on me?

I shake it off and shoot back a text to Gabriella, telling her I'll come over for a movie.

Might as well entertain myself, even if Lucy saturates my vision all night.

As I get ready to leave, my phone rings again, and I answer my buddy's call.

"'Sup, Tate?"

A nervous laugh proceeds his speech. "Hey, man. Glad I caught you. Julia and I decided to get hitched, and well, we aren't wanting a huge wedding, but I do need you by my side. We are doing a simple ceremony at the church in two weeks with a reception at Julia's parent's house to follow. You'll come down, right? I'm sorry it's not much notice. We just decided it was time, you know how it is."

I'm silent for a beat because I don't know how it is. How does someone *just decide* to get married? Isn't there supposed to be months and months of planning? There are women out there who don't want a huge barn-style wedding with the whole town present? I had wanted to marry Lacey, sure, but I wasn't prepared to hitch myself to her after two weeks. The engagement was simply supposed to be the next right step.

Key word: supposed.

The engagement never happened.

I swallow my thoughts. "Of course, man. Congratulations. I'm happy for you two. I'll be there. Text me the details."

After we chat a bit longer, and I lock up my front door behind me, a thought zooms by me like a baseball while I'm up to bat: I'm going home to Dasher Valley in two weeks for my buddy's wedding.

Strike one.

Which is a wedding my sister and Gracie will attend since Julia is Gracie's little sister.

Strike two.

And the two of them are going to want to meet my girlfriend.

Strike three.

Batter out.

Chapter 1

Lucy

My precious and well-intentioned friend, Karoline, gifted me a beautiful purple orchid three days ago while she was visiting from Nashville, and she emphatically told me that the man I was destined to be with would find me when it bloomed come early spring. I was content with the long wait since it's only June, but...

Frannie, my devil cat, ate it for breakfast this morning.

I'm doomed. Utterly doomed to a life of failed relationships.

Why can't I become a jaded cynic like my sister was prior to meeting and falling for a literal prince who is priming to become the next king of Korsa? Why do I still hold out hope for true love and a lifetime of swoony kisses, soulful conversations, playful antics, constant pursuit, and the consistent giving of one another when I've been shut down time after time by different men?

Is it too much to ask for? Does God even hear my prayers? Does He have any inclination to honor my deep-seated desires to be a wife and a mom?

Why can't I do what everyone tells me to do and stop looking? Don't they understand that it's IMPOSSIBLE for a woman who has grown up with romance at the center of her world to stop looking? I write romantic comedies for crying out loud, and I want to do it full-time. Romance is my Roman Empire. How do I simply stop looking?

So many questions with no answers in sight... Just me sitting here bawling to Taylor Swift while I wait until the last possible second to leave the comfort of my car and start another day that I desperately wish didn't exist.

Hadley, my best friend, gathered me, my twin who is across the world, and our friend Karoline, who resides in Nashville, on a group video call yesterday to announce that she was pregnant. And while she expressed her fears of becoming a mother (her mom was once a narcissistic raging alcohol and drug abuser), I quietly judged her for not thinking that motherhood wasn't the greatest gift in the world. I silently thought that I would give anything to be a wife and mom, and there she was, upset and scared over getting pregnant.

I'm sometimes an awful friend in the dark recesses of my brain. It's hard to balance feeling envious of those you love and would move mountains for and feeling utmost joy for their wins.

Even if they don't see their wins as wins.

At least it's Friday-eve. Though, to be honest, my weekend plans don't look too promising at this point. Just me, Frannie, and my new work in progress. It's the second book in my urban fantasy romance collection. I want to write them all before I begin publishing them. This book follows a vampire boss and event planner in Alaska. I haven't quite figured out the tropes, though I think I want to ship the two off on a fake date. Now, what reason does a male vampire need to fake date a human woman…?

I contemplate the question at hand as Taylor Swift sings about the pain of living alone (#relatable) and shoving her friends away because her brain is on dark-mode (#superrelatable). I flip the visor down and swipe the mirror cover to the left. Staring back at me is a puffy, red-faced raccoon.

There's another question: What's the point of dolling myself up every day when I end up crying because of loneliness stalking me viciously around every corner?

Snagging a tissue from my center console, I blot my eyes, then grab the translucent powder from my purse. As I press the pad to my face with gentle precision, I contemplate my life at twenty-six—single with no prospects, living alone in an apartment that's meant for two while my sister still continues to pay half her rent because I can't afford the entire payment on my own, and working full-time now at a job I know is going nowhere for me. And then the deluge resumes from my eyes.

Because all I want to do is write romance books and provide for myself on that income while awaiting my knight in shining armor.

He doesn't even have to wear armor. He can wear old jeans and flannel. He can wear a suit. He can wear a cooking apron. He can wear scrubs. He can wear sweatpants and a t-shirt. He can wear noth—*Don't go there, Lucy girl.*

Heck, he can be a shifter or a vampire or fae for all I care…

I just want a man who adores and loves me in the same way that I will adore and love him. A man who works hard and loves the

Lord. One who strengthens my relationship with Him instead of pulling me further away...

I've done a good enough job of that on my own.

I mean, really, God? Why are You withholding this from me and giving it to everyone else in my circle? It's because I've sinned, isn't it? It's because I've had sex outside of marriage. A lot. And now You're withholding love from me because I'm tainted. A big ole sinner...

No. I attempt to send the train of thought away, determined not to believe that about God. I can question and ask for a man, but I can't hitch a ride on the Devil's train by believing that my good God would withhold lifetime communion with a man after His own heart on the premise that I have failed to live in purity.

That doesn't mean the thought goes away, though. No matter how much I wish it would. Some thoughts are stationed for lingering moments due to a lifetime of believing them. Toxic church culture has a way of doing that to you.

My church is great, don't get me wrong, but they still don't make room for women like me. I have to hide my sins behind a stained glass mask because my type of sinning isn't the acceptable kind. It's not the kind people want to talk about.

It's the kind people say to "just try harder" to overcome.

I fully recognize God's design for marriage is perfect. There are so many positives of Godly marriage that I yearn for—the lifetime connection with a man who I know loves and trusts me, the spiritual leadership I'm desperately searching for, though I admit, that one desire is waning with every "Christian" man I meet who turns out to be more toxic than my non-Christian pursuits. Regardless, in my soul, I know that a man who is truly in communion with the Lord will love and cherish me. And then I could finally thrive. No more using sex as a means to keep a man interested in me, no more lonely nights, no more doubting God.

Glancing at the clock, I realize I have five minutes left to get inside Juniper Grove Community Center to start my work day. I blow my nose using the napkin I had dried my eyes with, then I flip my visor, turn my car off, and take a steadying breath before exiting my powder blue '74 Mercedes-Benz (that Grandma Netty gave me years ago when she decided she'd no longer drive) and walking to stand in front of the automated double doors that will welcome me to another day of work.

Another day of being bossed around by the World's Most Notorious Playboy.

You've got this, Lucy. You will make it through today.

Smoothing my pink plaid skirt down and double-checking that my white blouse is tucked in with the neck bow front-facing, I walk with soft heel clicks into my workplace with my head down as I fiddle with my silver ring on my left thumb.

Powder does wonders to soothe the redness, but the puffy eyes are still fully intact. No need to elicit questions that I don't want to answer from my coworkers.

Especially my boss, Stone Harper, said Notorious Playboy. I swear, that man has a new girl every month.

No.

Every week.

"There you are, Lucy May." Speak of the devil...

Without looking up, only briefly acknowledging him with a nod as I continue to make my way through the back offices of the community center, I state, "How many times do I have to tell you not to use my middle name?"

You might be thinking that I shouldn't talk to my boss like that. Well, you're wrong. Stone Harper deserves my stern coldness because he constantly teases me and uses my middle name when addressing me even though I've told him not to. The man is a natural flirt and can't seem to control himself, even as a director in charge of various employees. Except... I'm the only woman here who's within his age range. The other ladies are much older and married or widowed. They enjoy the lavish attention Stone gives them.

One would ask, is it a red flag that he disregards what I ask? Probably. But ultimately, he's not stepping on my boundaries, and I most certainly will not file a workplace harassment report. I'm kind of a covert fan of the way he innocently teases and flirts with me by using my middle name, which happens to be a part of my pen name, Lucy May. I secretly relish in his unwarranted attention. I could put a stop to him using my pen name if I *really* wanted to.

He, however, does *not* need to know that. I can only imagine how insufferable he would become. How much bigger that handsome head of his would get...

So why shouldn't I date my boss since he's all Flirty McFlirter Pants with me? I'll say it again: Notorious Playboy. Don't forget that, friends.

I mean, sure. I technically *could* date him if I wanted to. He would fit the jeans and flannel, suit, and sweatpants and t-shirt categories. (I've seen him in all varieties of clothes, and the man can pull off just about anything). But... I know better. I know better than to try and to date a player at this juncture in life. Like I said, I've dated many different types of men, and I've had my heart broken by believing I could change one.

Some special kind of woman will catch and hold Stone's attention one day, effectively tying him down, but it's not going to be me. I will not fall in love with my playboy boss. I won't allow myself the opportunity to even flirt with the idea.

As if you haven't been doing that all morning. Jeez, Lucy. Are you that desperate and starved for a man?

Yes, unfortunately. But I don't *want* to be. It's a battle. Every. Single. Day. *Stupid romantic heart...*

I'm tired of my brain mindlessly chasing and imagining "what if" scenarios over every encounter with a handsome man. It's only gotten worse since everyone in my life has abandoned me to their own romantic pursuits.

Okay, not really. But it feels that way sometimes.

Reaching my office, I open the door and walk into the plain room. There's a simple metal desk with a black mesh rolling office chair. My computer and monitor sit on a riser so that I'm able to stand and work when I need to. However, the bare white walls make this room feel like an asylum. I've deliberated decorating, but what's the use? I don't plan to be here forever. I do have a hanging now half-dead English Ivy in the corner by the window, courtesy of my sister, but that's it as far as personal things go. The rest of my desk is cluttered with paperwork I need to sift through and organize, a random collection of pens I should probably get a holder for (don't worry, my writer pens are residing inside a comfortable bookish bag), sticky note reminders galore, and a pink coffee mug for the much-needed post-lunch coffee break.

After setting my purse down inside the bottom drawer of the five-tiered metal filing cabinet that's on the wall side of my desk, I plop into my chair and turn on my computer for the day.

It flashes, and I drum my fingers on the keys while laying my head on my other hand as I wait for it to load. I lose myself in mentally curating Midnight Sun Enterprises, the fictional event planning company of my new urban fantasy novel.

"Having a morning, are we?"

I startle, noticing Stone standing in the doorframe. He's leaning against it with his arms and legs crossed; the baby pink button down dress shirt stretches across his chest and biceps, but I don't notice it.

Nope. I'm immune to his golden, shaggy hair, light blue eyes, tanned skin, and well-trained muscles. Good gracious, that man could model khaki pants for Hollister and my former teenage heart would burst...

Okay, I'm not immune. I'm not even unimpressed.

But I am smart.

Ish.

Ugh, fine. My playboy boss is hotter than the sand on the Mississippi coast in mid-July. Playing with him would leave blistering, bubbling burns.

He's also a little over two years younger than me at my ripe old age of twenty-six. I can't fall for a man younger than me... That's just not how things are supposed to work. I need a manly man, and manly men must be older than their women.

Says who? my brain taunts. But then Stone clears his throat, and I realize I've been ogling my younger, very manly boss for probably the past thirty seconds.

"Uh, what?" I ask in a bit of a daze. I turn the ring on my thumb, attempting to ground myself. Why is he in my doorway, again?

Get it together, Lucy May...

Great. Now *I'm* using my first and middle name.

He motions to his face. "Your face. It's all red and splotchy. Have you been crying?"

Curse it all. I'm ordering new concealing powder when I get off work. "No," I lie and shift my attention to the computer to log in.

Stone appears beside my desk and crouches down, resting one arm on the side. "If something's bothering you, you can talk to me. I know I'm your boss, but I do care about the mental health of my employees."

I glance at him with suspicion out of the corner of my eye, and he tacks on, "Even you, Lucy May."

There it is.

"Ha!" I snort in the most *attractive* way. But it's Stone, so I don't have to care. Because I will not date him. Are we clear? "You'd run screaming for the hills if you spent five seconds within my brain listening to my thoughts." *Because, buddy, Dark Mode has been activated. It's my only coping mechanism since everyone's left me.*

He stands up and sits on the corner of my desk, also known as the one clean area. "Oh, you think I can't handle a little bit of insanity?"

"I know you can't handle the likes of me." The words slip out unbidden, and I find myself leaning into his sphere, close enough that I can smell a peppery bergamot scent mingled with something that demands my pheromones recognize it at an animalist level. *Get it together, Lucy. Just because a man gives you attention does not mean you pursue it.*

Stone chuckles and shakes his head. "Try me. Say yes to dinner with me tonight at The Flats."

Did I mention Stone is becoming quite relentless in attempting to get me to go out to dinner with him? This all started four months ago after the Valentine's Day West Coast Swing dance we hosted.

A shudder runs down my spine at the memory of his hands on the small of my back, sliding down my arms, my waist, gripping my hands as he guided me in an admittedly sultry dance to "Put Me in My Place" by Muscadine Bloodline. Four months of increasing invites to dinners, movies, and other various activities.

"Is it a team dinner?"

"You know it's not, Lucy May. Say *yes.*"

I make the mistake of making eye contact, and my breath hitches at the sparkling blue color, emphasized by his dark, long lashes. He truly is a gorgeous man. One that is smirking to high heaven right now because he knows exactly what he's doing to me, but still breathtaking.

"I, uh," I stammer, then collect myself and tear my gaze away from him and back to my computer. He's just toying with me, and I'm not in the mindset to play. At least, I wasn't until my sister left me all alone. "No. You're my boss. I can't go get dinner with you."

He hops off the corner of my desk. "Suit yourself."

I ogle freely as he walks away, truly admiring the way he fills out those khaki pants. As he opens my office door to leave, he turns around and says, "Whoever you were crying over this morning, he isn't worth it."

Flabbergasted, I state, "How come you assume I was crying over a man?"

He shrugs with one hand on the door. "You date a lot. I date a lot. Both of us don't last very long. We might be more alike in our heads than you think, Lucy May."

Slack-jawed and processing, I mull over his words to the click of the door shutting.

"It wasn't over a man!" I shout, standing to my feet and splaying my arms out on my desk, the sudden and overpowering need to correct him taking over.

I hear the echo of his laughter on the other side of the door, then he cracks it open, peeks his head through, and says, "Ah, then it's the lack of a man. I see." He shuts the door again after a playful wink.

Fury burns and rages, and I finally know what seeing red feels like. How dare he? Where did he find the audacity? Just who does he think he is to call me out like that?

But, Lucy May... He was right. Stone Harper, the Notorious Playboy Boss, just saw right through you like you were Casper the ghost.

Chapter 2

Stone

She knows I love the game.

And she's made it the most drawn-out, entertaining fight of my life.

But not for much longer.

The blushes, the lingering stares, the cracks in her voice… I can tell her stubbornness is eroding; she should say yes to me by the end of the night if I continue to play my cards right.

At least I hope so. I've thought I was on the verge of having her before and was wrong. It's not that I see forever with Lucy; I know her dating history. She gets around as much as I do. We could have a lot of fun together, and I think she enjoys toying with me as much as I revel in making flirty advances toward her. I would stop if it looked like it was hurting her, but I don't miss the thrill in her eyes at our banter. It's all part of this cat and mouse game we've been playing.

Nothing serious will happen between us, but if she wanted to play with me, I wouldn't turn down the opportunity. As long as she agreed to my usual spiel: no feelings, no commitment, and if one of us begins to develop those pesky feelings or if the desire to commit dawns upon our souls, then we end it immediately.

Those rules would especially be vital considering I work with Lucy.

And maybe, just maybe, I can get her to agree to be my girlfriend for the weekend if I can convince her to go out to dinner with me. It's not like I can pull her aside at work and tell her I'm in need of a fake girlfriend.

I mean, I could, but it feels wrong. I should at least treat her to food first...

"Mr. Harper, Keaton Welch is on line one." My secretary, Jeanie, pokes her head through my door, pulling me from thoughts of winning over Lucy Spence.

I smile at the middle-aged, kind mother of three then glance at the clock. "Thanks, Jeanie. Will you tell him I'm in a meeting and that I'll call him back later?" I pause. "Why don't you go take your lunch break? Oh, and will you send Lucy in here?"

She grins. "Of course. Thank you, sir."

Jeanie's floating head disappears, the door clicking shut behind her.

I stand, stretching out my back after pouring over financial reports all morning long. The community center I opened here in Juniper Grove about a year ago is thriving as I hoped it would. While attending college in the area, I noticed the local kids didn't have a place to hang out, study, or engage in sports, especially the kids from lower-class families. I found an empty building, which used to be a factory, and had it turned into a community center using my earnings from stock trading and the money I had saved from *not* purchasing a ring five years ago.

I'm proud of what I've accomplished here. No, this endeavor doesn't make me a lot of money, but that's what working the stock market is for. Plus, I'll open more money-making businesses in the future. This was a heart project. When I was a child back in Dasher Valley, I wished I had somewhere to go to stay out of trouble and still have a good time. I plan to open a center down there next, especially if Stella wins a representative seat, but Juniper Grove was first because I used my internship class during my senior year of college to kickstart things in this town.

Three light knocks on the door inform me she's here.

"Come in, Lucy May," I say with a broad smile already taking over my face. She claims she doesn't like me using her middle name, but when I do, her cheeks redden, and sometimes, I catch her suppressing a smile as she rolls those hazel eyes into the back of her pretty little head.

When I learned she was a romance author mere months after I hired her, I ran to get my hands on her books. She has two completed series of romantic comedies published, but from her marketing, it looks like she has some urban fantasy romances coming out in the near future. I can still use those for my purposes. A direct line to her heart and mind to assist in my attempts to win her over? Yes, please. I adore that she uses her first and middle name as her pen name. It's so Lucy... It shows her constant battle between desiring attention while simultaneously attempting to hide herself away. The duality of her character is fascinating.

She steps into my office, her stubbornness already cemented in place. Her shoulders are pushed back, chin tilted up, and her hands are planted firmly on her all too delectable hips, which are on full display in that tight, pink plaid skirt she's wearing.

We match. Isn't that cute?

"What do you need me for, Mr. Harper?"

"If you won't go to dinner with me, then let me take you out to lunch." She narrows her eyes and purses her lips. "For official business," I add.

I have to leave to go to Dasher Valley for my buddy's wedding by tomorrow morning at the latest, and I need Lucy by my side if I want to keep up the "she's my girlfriend" charade with my family. If she doesn't agree, then I'm going to have to come up with something to appease my family, which will put Stella further on my case. Everyone who knows me knows that I would rather croak than to show up to a wedding without a date. (My sister's was the only exception because I thought I'd take a go at her New York friend, Hayden, which was shut down quickly. Turns out she was meant for the new president of the country, so that's kind of cool.)

Lucy rolls her eyes and cocks her hip out to the side. I take a steadying breath to keep my face from heating. I might be the ringleader of this game, but that doesn't make me immune to the hypnotic sexiness of this woman.

"This is becoming a weekly occurrence, Mr. Harper. It's impacting my work performance."

I lean against my desk and cross my arms. "So should we bump it up to twice a week so that you'll be *doubly* impacted? I didn't realize me pestering you for lunch and dinner was such a positive thing."

Lucy tugs at the bow tied in the front of her shirt at her neckline. The unbidden mental image of me reaching across the sea of distance between us and tugging the bow loose might be enough to undo me.

"I never said it had a *positive* impact."

"But you didn't say it was negative." I wink, and a rose petal flush paints her nose, cheeks, and forehead. I adore that when Lucy blushes, she does so with her entire freckled face. "Come on, one lunch. Just one lunch and I promise I'll stop asking you, okay?"

She thinks for a moment, pinching the bridge of her nose and closing her eyes. "Fine," she bites. I celebrate the moment in my head, but I know my thoughts leak through my smile. I've finally won her over, even if she isn't considering this an actual date. *She finally said yes...*

Lucy speaks again in that sharp tone. "But I'm picking the restaurant. And you can bet it will be an expensive lunch. Seafood. Lots of it."

I chortle, admiring this confident, bold, fierce side of her. "I would expect nothing less from you, Lucy May." *Now to get you to go to Dasher Valley with me tomorrow morning for the entirety of the weekend...*

Thirty minutes (and a fifteen minute bickering session in my truck) later, I'm seated across from Lucy at Perry's Seafood, a local restaurant known to bring the Cajun heat. This place is one of my sister's favorites to eat at when she visits me.

I thought I'd have three months to build a decent breakup story to tell Stella. To tell her that I was coming home alone for her birthday because things were over between me and Lucy. I'd start with slowly mentioning fights we had, then I would start creating stories that painted Lucy in a negative light, such as she flirted with other men in front of me or something. The killing blow would be that she cheated on me, so I could no longer continue seeing her.

Just like that, I could go home alone for Stella's birthday, and my "girlfriend" would be no more. My family wouldn't ask me about it because they never bothered to ask me about Lacey when that ended. I kept quiet, and they let me. Lucy would be the only other woman they think I've seriously committed to, and while they harass me about my flings, they've never gotten on my case when it came to Lacey. It would be the same with Lucy.

I'm a mastermind, right? Well, *was*...

The planned course of action will not take place since I'm going home in the morning, and that's clearly not enough time to build up a breakup. I also feel a smidge guilty over the thought of painting Lucy in such a bad light. I don't actually think she would cheat on a man. She might date a lot, but she's got a heart of gold.

Though that golden heart seems to be a little broken and bruised by the way she always has this crestfallen look about her lately when she thinks nobody is watching.

But I am always watching.

"Here's a plate of crab for the lady." A tall, tanned, and muscular man sets the plate down in front of Lucy, whose eyes widen. I'm pretty sure there's drool at the corner of her mouth.

You thought I was describing her expression toward the food?

Nope.

She's making heart-eyes at the man.

Maybe I'm not so far off on the assumption she'd flirt with another man in front of me...

But wait.

I'm not actually her boyfriend.

I'm not even her fake boyfriend.

Yet.

"I cooked this one myself, so if anything's wrong, let me know. We are trying out new recipes."

Lucy nods emphatically, twirling her hair around her finger. "Of course. It smells delicious. I'm sure it will taste even better."

And then the woman has the audacity to wink!

Flames of jealousy lick my skin to a blackened crisp.

The man sets down my order of crawfish etouffee and walks away, Lucy's eyes trailing after him.

When her gaze finally shifts and falls onto her plate, I clear my throat loudly, earning her attention.

"You okay?" She arches her brow and tilts her head.

"What's he got that I don't?" I try to sound teasing, but even I have to admit that I sound like a jealous punk. Not jealous of Lucy looking him over but jealous that she's in my presence doing it. *Cool it, Stone.*

Lucy rolls her eyes. "He's not my boss. And do you see this food he placed in front of me?" She gestures to the plate of crab. "Bet you can't do this."

I lower my voice and drop my gaze to her lips. "Say yes to dinner with me one night, and instead of taking you out, I'll take you *home*."

She gasps, those cute pink lips forming an "o." I shouldn't tease her like that, especially if I'm going to get her to say yes to going to Dasher Valley with me for the weekend, but I don't think I can help it. She's too tempting. And when her face flushes because of me, it makes me feel some type of way.

"To cook you dinner," I finish, satisfied with her reaction and also needing to redirect my thoughts. If she does agree to be my pretend girlfriend for the weekend, I'll have to set up careful boundaries for myself. She's my employee, after all.

Lucy scrunches her nose and knits her brows, but she doesn't respond, opting to focus on deshelling her crabs. She struggles pulling off the carapace, but man, she's cute when she's giving it her all...

"Let me get that for you." I reach over the table to grab her plate, but as my hands wrap around the edges, hers wrap around mine. *Our first touch...*

I never understood what people meant by electric touches until that very moment. It was as if the static we'd acquired over every single year of our lives was transferred as her fingers brushed against mine. *ZING!*

It's at the precise moment I'm imagining those petite fingers trailing down my chest that I'm pelted in the face with a plateful of crab. Salty juices run down my cheeks, mingling with salty tears, as my eyeballs cry out a desperate plea to escape from the hell inflicted upon them. I collapse back into my seat. My body tenses as crabs fall to the table with a hard plunk while others drop into my lap, the smell of butter and spicy seafood all encompassing. The plate must have fallen back to the table as I don't hear shattering.

"Stone! Er—Mr. Harper, here. Take this."

I grit my teeth and clench my fists on the table. "I can't see a thing."

"Oh, right."

Suddenly, coolness presses against my face, which I'm assuming is a napkin of some sort. She wipes off my cheeks, crossing the bridge of my nose with a gentle touch, before she moves lower. Involuntarily, I tilt my head as her fingers rest underneath my chin. "I'm so sorry about that," she says quickly, still wiping at my face. "I just reacted when your hands touched mine."

That I understand, I think to myself. Then I smile because it sounds like she felt the same *ZING!* I did.

"One second," she whispers, and the napkin disappears. It takes over ten quickened heartbeats pounding my chest before I sense her presence in front of me again. A refreshing spicy vanilla scent breaks through the sourness of the seafood.

"I'm going to wipe your eyes," she says. I nod, but that must have been the moment she was approaching because instead of receiving a cool, gentle caress like I was anticipating, I'm poked in the eye.

The curse that slips through my lips is perfectly warranted if you ask me.

"Gah, I'm sorry! But please, hold still, Mr. Harper." While Lucy does sound sorry, she also sounds amused. And though my eyes are burning and the right one is also throbbing, the way her voice sounds when it shifts to a command could bring the dead back to life.

The damp napkin presses against my right eye and moves in slow circles before she moves to the other one. It's as if I could see her directly in front of me, hazel eyes erring on the side of green, concentrating on the contours of my face as she works. I can imagine her lips parting or her nose scrunching up again. She's so close that if I just leaned in, I could finally educate myself on how those supple lips taste...

"Done. But you should probably go wash your eyes out before you try to open them. I can get someone to lead you to the bathroom. Maybe the chef guy from earlier?"

"No," I choke out, imagining my hands clutching the biceps on that guy. *No thank you.* Not the arms I want to feel up. "You can lead me to the bathroom just fine. But first, I think there are crabs in my lap." I smirk, unable to help myself once again. "You want to clean those off for me, too?"

I can practically hear the scowl as she says, "You can find your own way to the little boy's room." She mumbles about how she feels like a mother managing a toddler because of our two-year age gap, which triggers memories I'd rather not remember. So to cope, I joke.

Chuckling, I regress, though there's a slight bite to my tone. "Just messing with you, ma'am. Should I call you that? Since you're older and such?"

"Be my guest. It's good to respect your elders."

I laugh some more to not feel the *things* and then change the subject. "Thanks for wiping my face clean. I'll get the crabs off my lap, but at least guide my hand so that I can drop them back on the plate for you. These should be salvageable since they didn't land on the floor." I go to hold my hand up, but instead, I knock the bottom of the table. How many injuries will I walk away with from this lunch outing?

Silence.

"You want me to eat crabs that have been on your lap? Mm, no, don't think so."

"'Kay, then." I stand, the crabs falling to the ground. I feel the hard edge of the table against my hips, so this time, I swing my arm around to hold out my hand to Lucy. "Lead me to the bathroom, my fearless liege." That word is foreign on my tongue, but I've read it in one of her books, so I give it a try.

She snorts. "Are we in a situational twist? Am I now your leader?" As she's speaking, she wraps her hand around my outstretched wrist. Once again, electricity radiates from her touch, but this time, I'm prepared for it.

I grin toward Lucy, or at least I hope in her direction as my eyes are still squeezed shut. "I may be your boss, but you can order me around anytime you please."

She doesn't respond, but I can imagine her face flushing and her lips parting into that cute little "o" expression; she's unintentionally Pavlov-ed me to react with pleasure when I see it. Or even think she's wearing it, apparently.

My arm is yanked rather hard as she pulls me. I hip check a table and kick a chair as she drags me forward, not bothering to warn me of things in my path.

"We're here." She drops my wrist. "But I'm not going in there with you. Use your hands to feel around."

A wicked smile stretches across my face. "Can I start now?" I stretch my hands out in the direction of her voice, but she slaps them and redirects me until both of my palms are flat against a door. Not willing to push her further, mostly because a fleeting thought crossed my mind that I might have gone too far with that one, I enter the bathroom and do as she says, feeling around until I touch a knob on a sink.

I let the faucet run for about thirty seconds to make sure I didn't accidentally turn on the hot water, and then I set to work rinsing out my eyes. Once I finish and can finally open my eyes without the air stinging them, I cringe at my reflection in the full-body mirror by the door. I resemble a three-year-old who spilled his food down his shirt and then had an accident in his pants. The pink shirt I wear is now more of a dirty orange color down the front, and that bleeds into an unfortunate stain in an unfortunate area of my khaki pants. My hair has juices and pieces of crab shell from the few she managed to crack before I attempted to be a chivalrous man and help her. I wash my hair the best I can and dry myself off with a bundle of paper towels. What's a little water dripping down the front of my shirt when there's already other liquids there?

Confident that this is the best I'm going to look, I exit the restroom.

Lucy waits outside the door, her arms folded and a smirk across her face as two women with scowls stand behind her.

Nervously glancing at the signage by the bathroom, I realize the woman led me to the ladies' room...

The situation grates my nerves, and I grimace in an attempt to hide my disdain. *She* shoved the plate onto me. *She* poked me in the eye. *She* brought me to this bathroom. "A step too far, Lucy May," I say with a gentle but stern voice. My *boss's voice*.

She swallows, dropping her folded arms and clasping her hands in front of her. She hangs her head low, and I immediately regret using that tone coupled with what I call her to flirt with her. *Good going, Mr. Harper...*

"I'm sorry," she whispers, barely audible over the noise in the restaurant. Speaking of, how many people saw that incident? Did Lucy shoo them away silently when they came to help? "I promise I'll make all of this up to you. I got carried away in my frustrations."

"Why were you frustrated?"

She shakes her head. "It's nothing. You just... it's nothing."

"Tell me," I press.

"You just have a special way of irritating me, that's all."

Laughter escapes me despite our current situation. Briefly, I wonder if the way I irritate her is the same way she irritates me?

The best kind of irritation.

Irritation because of desire.

"But I'm really sorry," she tacks on sheepishly.

I sigh and step toward her. "It's okay. All's well. But can we go?" I sniff my shirt. "I stink."

She glances up at me through thick eyelashes, and I offer her a reassuring smile. She returns the smile and nods, then she scrunches her nose in that cute way that melts any remaining frustration from the crab incident. "Yeah, you do stink. This will be a fun ride back to work."

As we exit, I turn over a million words in my brain—a million different ways to ask Lucy to be my stand-in date this weekend. I already know if I ask her in the sense that I'm asking her out for real, she will say no and bolt as she has in the past. I need to approach this like it's all pretend. She will pretend to be my girlfriend this weekend, that's all. Nothing real. Nothing permanent. Heck, I don't want something permanent with Lucy. Yeah, she's captivating. Yeah, I think about her even when I'm with other women. Yeah, I think she's somehow written her name on my soul, but all that could go away in an instant. It has before. There have been a few women in my life who have made me feel this way, but those deep feelings end up dissipating. Usually once the high of the chase was over. That could happen with Lucy, too.

It *will* happen. Love never sticks around.

Simply put, it's smart of her to keep fending off my advances. Even if I didn't want to, I would still break her heart.

The thought of adding another crack into Lucy's golden heart sends a wave of anger over me. I glance at her, walking with her head tilted down and hands clasped in front of her as she matches me step for step.

I really don't want to hurt her.

But I also really want to *experience* her.

Maybe a weekend away playing pretend will put these feelings to rest so I can move on and not lose control when it comes to my pretty employee whose company I genuinely enjoy.

An all too familiar voice calls out my name. It freezes me in my tracks, and I'm instantly transported five years into the past to high school graduation night for Dasher Valley High where that same voice uttered words that completely derailed my life plans as I was down on one knee. *You're not enough for me, Stone. A real man...* That night I realized just how much pain my now brother-in-law, Lucas Grady, must have been in when my big sister left him for her career.

Something akin to horror flashes before my eyes as I realize I have no choice but to address her. I could have kept walking, pretending that I didn't hear my name, but now that I've stopped, I have to face her. I wonder if she has the man who *is* enough for her on her arm.

Lucy elbows me, ripping me from my nightmare.

Lucy...who is already my girlfriend in my family's eyes, though she doesn't know I've been using her as a shield against the desires of my family. The woman I want to play pretend with anyways...

I slip my arm around her waist and tug her close before leaning down to whisper in her ear. "Lucy, are you truly sorry for leading me into the women's bathroom?"

"Of course," she says, looking up at me perplexed while also trying to step backwards.

I tighten my hold around her.

"Stone, is that you?" The ghost of my past is now right behind us.

Once more, I whisper in Lucy's ear. "Play along."

As I bring my other hand to her waist, I spin her around, take a steadying breath, say a quick prayer that this won't go to hell in a handbasket like the rest of this day has, and then I turn around.

Sliding my arm back around Lucy and splaying my fingers across her hip so she doesn't attempt to move, I muster all the courage I can find and paste the biggest of smiles to my face.

"Lacey, it's good to see you." I nod once then shift my attention to the shorter, stockier, *older* man clasping her hand. "Jordan."

"Good to see you," Jordan says, stretching out his hand, doing an admittedly good job at not looking me over in my nasty crab-soaked state. I shake it with a firmness I didn't know I had. He turns to Lucy. "I'm Jordan Hopper."

She looks up at me with questions in her eyes. I relax a little, confident enough that she will play along with me. She takes that as the go ahead and grabs his hand, giving him her full attention. "Lucy Spence."

As soon as she drops his hand, I lock eyes with Lucy and tack on to her introduction. "My *older* girlfriend."

She physically stiffens at my side but makes no motion to correct me. In fact, I'm slightly amazed at her ability to not blurt "what the—" at the proclamation. Not letting me get away completely unscathed, she does tilt her head to the side and narrows her eyes. But as soon as the expression touches her face, it's gone. In its place a love-struck woman who adores her man...

At least that's what the sudden rounded eyes that sparkle and the perma-looking upturn of the corners of her lips look like to me.

She looks at me, then to Lacey, and she takes a small step to stand in front of my body as if she's my personal bodyguard.

My hands shift to her waist, and I do something I've often dreamed of doing....

Pull her hips into mine.

BEAT TWO

MEET CUTE // "SPARKS FLY"

Chapter 3

Lucy

My girlfriend.

The words bounce around my brain as if they were on caffeine. I won't try to dissect why he felt the need to say I was older; I can do that later. I had an inkling when he said to play along at the sound of another woman's voice that he might pretend to be my boyfriend. (Thank you, Romance Writer Brain. You've finally come in handy in a real-life situation.) But still, hearing those words curated a momentary flicker of questioning before I schooled my expression into something that comes naturally for me—a lovestruck fool.

I can allow myself to get lost in this fantasy for one small second. Tearing my gaze from my handsome just-for-the-moment boyfriend, I notice the slender brunette female is staring at him. I adjust myself so I'm blocking as much of his sullied clothes as I can with my petite frame, but then his hands find my waist, and he pulls me flush against him.

I won't deny I've had similar fantasies, though he was shirtless and, well, the stench of crab wasn't present.

Mentally shaking the image and focusing on *not* feeling inappropriate things, I reach out to shake the brunette's hand. "It's nice to meet you, Lacey."

She shakes my hand, but she's still looking at Stone.

Lacey drops my hand and says to Stone, "I didn't know you were seeing anyone. Usually you blast your women all over your socials."

His hands tighten around my waist as he nonchalantly says, "I've been having way too much fun with my Lucy May over the past two months to even care about posting."

My heart thumps and tingles race down my neck. Two months. So we've been together since April. Got it.

My Lucy May…

Why do I feel like I could live within those words rolling off his tongue every single day of my existence from here until the end of eternity?

I turn to face him with a sharp smile. "Oh, you…" I say, dropping my words off because I have no idea what I was about to call him. Devilish man? Handsome hunk of hotness? Silver-tongued snake? Roguish, redneck rake?

Any would suffice but may not be appropriate in this context.

Instead of attempting to speak again, I place my palm over his heart.

Which is buried not only under rib cage, muscle, and skin, but also a pink-now-orange shirt coated in crab juices.

I tap my fingers a few times before slowly bringing my hand back down to my side and balling it into a fist so I don't accidently rub the juices and stench onto my clothes. Then I turn back around to face the woman who apparently has a rich history with Stone.

"How wonderful," Lacey says, but something flashes across her eyes. Hurt? Sorrow? It's a similar expression to Karoline's when she talked about how much she hated that she *didn't hate* Mason. A look that says Lacey wished Stone would have been more than he was.

What did Stone do to this woman...?

Jordan lets go of her hand and slips his arm around her waist. Lacey places her hand on his chest, showcasing a big ole diamond ring glistening off the sunlight.

"Well, we should probably get going. Lunch plans," Jordan says. He looks concerningly at Lacey, and it swells an emotion deep within my soul—loneliness. How nice would it be for a man to read me the way Jordan read Lacey's uncomfortableness?

Like the way Stone read you earlier when you were upset at work? my brain so generously reminds me. Apparently, my internal thoughts are pro-playboy boss. But my conscious thoughts know better.

Jordan and Lacey wave goodbye as they walk away. I glance at Stone, who is donning an expression I've never seen on him before (and I've cataloged many of his facial contortions... for book research purposes and all). His eyes are a misty blue, cheeks sunken and lips rolled inside his mouth. Sweat beads from around the edges of his hairline as he runs his fingers through his styled honey blond hair.

"What happened, Stone?" I move to touch his arm but instantly retract my hand. He isn't mine to touch. He is my boss. He is two years younger than I am. I bet he hurt that woman in the past and now it's coming back to haunt him. Just like he would hurt me if I allowed myself to open up to him.

Don't make assumptions, Lucy.

Yeah? Well, I've been hurt too many times by making excuses for men. I'm not doing that anymore. I will believe my eyes instead of talking myself in circles to justify uncouth behavior.

"Just a girl from my past," he says, planting a smile on his face. "Let's go."

"Am I free from being your fake girlfriend now?" I reach to open the door of his truck, but his hand closes over mine. We lock eyes. An evil grin unfurls slowly across his face as I continue to ask my questions. "Also, why tell her I'm older? What's with that?"

"Don't worry about it." His voice is cool before warming to a mischievous tone that matches his face. "Hm. You were only my fake girlfriend for a span of minutes—" He gestures down his soiled shirt and pants with the hand that is not still resting on top of mine. Mercy above, his touch is absolutely electrifying. "—and all this requires more, I believe. That is, if you truly want to make up for dumping a plate of crabs on me."

My heart races as my nerves continue to fry like chicken strips at his touch. "Are you suggesting I continue to be your fake girlfriend for some reason? I'm sure there are a million other things I could do to make up for spilling my food on you…"

As the words escape my mouth, his sly smile widens and eyes twinkle and dance. Whatever dark mood that Lacey woman had him in has vanished. The predator has come out to play with his willing-but-unwilling prey.

Maybe this is a part of his dark mood, now that I think about it?

When I'm feeling dark, I like to pretend I'm a suave, confident, and sexy woman who is capable of toying with men and then disposing of them. *Not that I'd have the guts to do it in real life...*

Is Stone Harper actually a good guy disguising as a villain?

Why in the world am I so internally twisted that the thought turns me on...?

Get. Some. Help. Lucy, I mentally clap back at myself.

Stone moves closer to me, our bodies inches apart against the passenger door of his truck. He tucks a strand of flyaway hair behind my ear before leaning closer and whispering, "What are you offering, Lucy May?"

Even the putrid smell of drying crab juices can't keep my heart from beating quicker at his nearness.

A villain.

Stone Harper is definitely in his villain era.

No, not an era. He was most likely born this way.

Is he the truly evil kind or the morally gray kind?

Nope. Doesn't matter.

I shove him away as he laughs under his breath. I take a few steps back, but he doesn't follow. Instead, he opens the door for me. "Get in, Lucy. Don't worry, your virtue is safe with me. But I do require your fake girlfriend acting skills."

One: Little does he know my virtue is far from intact.

Two: Do what?!

I climb in the lifted F-150 and wait for him to settle into the driver's side before responding. "Why in the world do you need me to pretend to be your girlfriend? Can't you just go get an actual girlfriend?"

The truck roars to life as he gives me a cheeky grin. "I could, but the woman I want to make my actual girlfriend sadly doesn't feel the same way." His grin morphs into a playful pout as he shifts into gear, backing out of the parking lot.

He's not talking about me, right?

Of course he is. He's been after you for months. Don't act oblivious to it, Lucy. You know the signs.

I choose to ignore *the signs* because he doesn't actually want me *for* me. He wants me for his own satisfaction. If I ever said yes to him for real, it would purely be for *my* own satisfaction, but I'm trying to be better than caving to Loneliness's siren call of temptation. "What's the occasion? Will we be seeing that woman again?"

At the mention of Lacey, he tightens his grip on the wheel and presses his lips into a firm line. "I'm not sure why we saw her here, but yes. She will most likely be at the wedding."

"A wedding? You need me to be your fake girlfriend for a wedding?"

His voice is cold as he replies. "Yep. My buddy, Tate, is getting married this weekend. I need to drive down to Dasher Valley tomorrow morning to be there for the bachelor's party tomorrow night. Then the wedding is Saturday afternoon. We will drive back on Sunday."

"We? I haven't said yes," I state. He looks at me for a brief second. It's an expression I would imagine a fox, if it were human, would wear the moment it knew it had locked onto a rabbit. Or maybe it's the look a bird of prey sports as its talon close around a small puppy.

"Yes, we. Us. You and me. I hope you didn't have weekend plans. If you did, cancel them. I'm cashing in on the whole 'I'll make it up to you' right now."

"He didn't give you any more information?" Emma Jane asks, a certain joyous flair to her voice. I narrow my eyes at the ash-blonde barista who is currently sitting across from me in the empty café. I helped her clean earlier as we chatted before we sat down to talk some more. She's been my constant companion since everyone else abandoned me at the beginning of the month.

Ugh, fine. I know I need to quit thinking that way.

Karoline got married and moved to Nashville, and my sister got engaged and moved to a whole different country. They both call me frequently and check in on me and love me well from afar, but it's not the same. I also have my lifelong best friend, Hadley, but she's married and now expecting. I don't always want to pull her from taking care of Braxton and her pregnant self over my inconsequential, miniscule lack-of-love problems.

I'm thrilled Emma Jane came to work at this coffee shop-slash-bookstore, and I'm ecstatic she's single and intent on staying that way.

I take a sip of my vanilla latte. "He told me to be ready to go by six in the morning and to pack a pretty dress. That's all."

She rests her chin in her hand as she leans on the square, wooden table. "Hm. That doesn't give you much to go on. How long have you two been dating? What's the meet-cute story? Do you know each others' favorites?" She drums her fingers as she continues to spout off things me and Stone apparently need to talk about on the drive down to his hometown tomorrow.

His hometown.

I'm going to my boss's hometown tomorrow and will presumably meet his family as his pretend girlfriend while some pretty married woman, who gets him in a dark tizzy, will be watching us at his friend's wedding.

What in the romantic comedy novel is my life right now?

I should've said no.

Stood my ground.

But the romance author inside of me was a little too greedy to get her hands on this situation for "book research," the lonely girl inside me was chomping at the bit to escape for the weekend, and the dark woman inside of me was foaming at the mouth to experience a date with Stone Harper.

My brain packed up its bags and took a vacation during that interaction, much to its dismay now.

"Good thing we have six hours to discuss all the things," I jest with a roll of my eyes and another sip of my latte. "I need to quit my job after this."

"Why quit? You don't trust yourself to go back to professionalism after pretending to be his girlfriend for the weekend?" Emma Jane bats her eyelashes innocently.

"Correct." I decide to be honest with her since she's one of the few people I have in my life right now, and she's not directly connected with my other friends. "I might actually date him if I don't quit." *Or worse...* "This close proximity is slowly suffocating me. He's the devil, and I have no business dancing with him."

"You've danced with him once, I recall." She giggles and stands, mimicking parts of our dance from back in February with shocking grace. How does she remember that? I didn't even know her as well back then.

In fact, I still don't know her *that* well. We talk about me when we're together. I should change that.

Because I think Little Miss I'm Never Going to Get Married might be a closeted romantic. "The mistake of my lifetime."

"Well, if you do date him, then great. If not, that's great, too. I'm currently matchmaking an important person in my life, and I believe it's going well. I even smell a wedding on the horizon. If you and Mr. Desperately In Love With You don't work out for some reason, I can get you a new man."

Yep. She's a romantic. I should have known that by the nickname she gave Stone when I confessed to her about his insistent behavior a couple weeks ago.

"Matchmaking?"

She nods. "Mhmm. I'm quite good at it, too. I've only had this one success, but I used to mentally pair up couples in my head as a child. I've only now begun to act on it. I'm starting my own business. What do you think of my idea?"

Emma Jane is still dancing around tables on the wooden floors of the empty shop, her long skirt and apron billowing with her turns. She looks carefree and happy and graceful as the string lights create a warm ambience to the night. Books and Beans is technically closed, but she let me in and made me a cup of coffee anyways. I kind of adore this girl.

"I love that idea, E. J. What would your parents think?"

She stops spinning and sighs wistfully. "My father will be happy with anything I decide to do as long as I stick by his side."

I notice how she doesn't mention a mother, but I don't press her about it tonight. That can be a conversation for another time.

I glance out the window to the darkened skies. "I should get going."

"Text me details! I'm already on pins and needles wondering how this will unfold." She unties her apron and tosses it behind the counter. "I'll walk you out so that I can lock up."

"I'm sure it will be uneventful. Or full of stories of me embarrassing myself. Nothing sincere and romantic, though. That's a promise."

The bell jingles above our heads as we open the glass doors to leave. After she locks the door, she embraces me. "Regardless, I think there might be something there. Please, do protect your heart. But also don't be afraid to take risks and chances."

I think over her words my entire drive home, which is only five minutes, but still.

Stone would ruin me. I *know* that. It's not a risk or a chance I can take. My attraction to him is through the roof, but it's just that—attraction. There's nothing real between us. Just a bunch of heat and hormones and hellish thoughts.

Maybe this fake girlfriend thing will be good. I can get him out of my system without consequence. I can experience what it would be like to hold his hand and maybe even kiss his lips without forming attachment.

Then, when we come back to Juniper Grove, I can resume my workplace professionalism like none of it ever happened. I can find myself a man who I can trust and is good to his core and will be *my* prince.

Stone Harper will simply become an itch that I once scratched.

Though I'm an avid romance reader and pen novels myself, I'm not naïve. I know real life isn't like the books. Fake dating situations don't lead to more.

I'm safe.

Chapter 4

Stone

I knock on the door once more, but after another minute of waiting, there's still no sign of life. It's 6:08 in the morning, indicating I've been at this for eight minutes.

"Lucy May!" I shout, rapping my knuckles against the white door. "We've got to go!" Humidity mingled with heightened nerves is not boding well for me as sweat beads roll down the back of my neck.

And no, the nerves are not because I am about to be in a vehicle for six hours with Lucy. I can manage that. They aren't even because she's going to meet my family as my girlfriend. I fully trust in her capabilities of playing pretend with me.

I'm a bundle of nerves because the woman won't answer the door or her phone, and I'm halfway to the irrational conclusion that she's dead inside this building. I lazily swat at the wilted plant inside a terracotta pot by the door as I exhale a long breath. I don't have lockpicking skills, but surely it can't be too hard?

If that doesn't work, I might kick the door in, which neither of us will be happy about in the long run.

I try to call her again, but her phone goes straight to voicemail as if she has it turned off. *Something could seriously be wrong and no one would know because she lives in this little space all by herself. Does she have medical issues? I should know this as her boss!*

"Dang it, Lucy." I curse under my breath, running a hand through my still-wet hair. I pound on the door and holler her name. "Is everything okay? I'm barging in soon if you don't answer me."

I swiftly look around the building, but no one seems to have poked their head out of their door to check out the chaos on the second floor. After attempting to call again and jiggling the golden knob one last time (maybe I didn't turn it hard enough?), I take a couple steps back from the door. I'm leaning back against the metal railing that serves as a small balcony for the apartment, bouncing up and down and shaking out of my hands. "On the count of three, I'm kicking the door in, Lucy! One." I kick out my feet to flex my ankles. "Two." I dip into a little squat. "Three!" I extend my leg, and with as much force as I can muster, I kick the door.

Something cracks, but the door doesn't give way. I use the adrenaline pumping through my veins to catapult my body into the door, using my strong side—my right shoulder—as the primary contact point. The door flies open, splinters showering around me as I stumble into the darkened room, breaths labored and heavy.

An ear-splitting female scream pierces me as something hard hits my face. I collapse to my knees when I hear a crunch and a wave of nausea overtakes me, something darker than blackness covering my vision.

Soft fingers run through my hair, gently massaging my scalp. On my forearm, another set of gentle fingers caress my skin, leaving a heat trail as they roam. The touch feels like it's jolting my body, bringing back to life.

Because for some reason, I think I was dead.

Or a girl was dead.

I don't know.

I think someone was dead or dying.

My head is fuzzy and my face hurts, but my brain seems to think death was involved in some form or fashion. The warm smell of spicy vanilla encapsulates me, and I try to open my eyes to pinpoint the source of Lucy's signature scent.

But my eyes won't open.

I groan as I try again to no avail.

"Stone, oh thank God!" a worried, feminine voice speaks from somewhere above me, and I have the faintest recollection that the voice belongs with the electric fingers and dessert smell.

Lucy.

I try to say her name, but only another groan escapes my lips. Her fingers grip my hair and my forearm.

Open your eyes, Stone. At the insistent command, I blink, a bright light blinds me, and I immediately squeeze my eyes shut again. My head explodes in pain, and my stomach threatens to let breakfast make a reappearance.

"Lucy," I finally manage to say.

She releases her grip, her hands cupping my face now. "I'm here, Stone. I'm here. I'm—" A sob cuts off her words. I finally open my eyes and take in her frizzy red hair, smudged dark circles underneath her wide, worried eyes, and pinkened lines that seem to connect her freckles into a striped constellation across her puffy face.

"Lion," I choke on the word as I attempt to hold in a laugh. She's the human embodiment of the animal right now. Laughter breaks through, but I immediately cease because my nose scrunches and sends pain signals singing a malevolent tune through my system.

"Sh, I'm here. I've got you. I'm so sorry, Stone..." Tears fill her eyes, causing that hazel color to shine on the side of emerald green.

It registers that she is calling me by my first name instead of Mr. Harper, and I don't think I've ever loved the sound of my name as much as I do at this moment. I grin, even though the pain it causes in my face would put me on the ground if I wasn't there already. "Please never call me Mr. Harper again," I croak out in a hoarse voice. So much for being suave. I close my eyes and breath. "Unless we're role playing. I'm down for role play."

She slaps my arm but laughs through tears. "I guess I can officially not be worried anymore. You're obviously okay."

I open my eyes to find her relieved smile as she sits back on her legs. "But what exactly happened? My face feels like it was hit with a cast iron skillet, and I'm pretty sure my nose is broken based on my voice, the pain, the nausea, and the blood." I only just notice the blood on her hands as she folds them in her lap beside me.

"Your face *was* hit with a cast iron skillet, and it was *my* cast iron skillet, and I am deeply sorry for injuring your nose and ruining your pretty face. In my defense, I thought you were intending harm to me by bursting into my apartment. I used the smallest skillet. And I'm honestly not very strong, so there's that."

A meow comes from somewhere in the room like the cat is in agreement with Lucy. But honestly? I'm still stuck on "pretty face."

"You think my face is pretty?" I ask her, attempting a smirk but scowling in pain instead. Looks like my flirty facial expressions are on hold for the foreseeable future. That's going to make my pretend dating thing a smidge more difficult since I survive solely by flirty looks and body language.

Home. The wedding.

"We are supposed to be headed to Dasher Valley," I say, scrambling to get up. The moment I move, dizziness captures me, and I fall back into Lucy's waiting arms.

"Not until we get you checked out by a doctor."

I sigh, knowing there is no way around this. "You know, Lucy May, I think you might very well be the death of me at this rate. First the crabs and now this. I knocked, called, and yelled your name."

"The only thing I heard, which is what jolted me out of bed, was my door being kicked in. I had completely spaced that you were picking me up in that fearful moment."

That makes sense. She was some kind of dead, I guess. Dead asleep.

"I'm sorry," she whispers, and I have the sudden memory of her hands in my hair.

"Run your hands through my hair one more time," I say without thinking. I instantly regret the words because they make me seem needy and desperate, but the moment she obliges, I forget I should care. Instead, I let out a sound somewhere between a moan and a purr at the pure feeling of bliss that is numbing the pain in my head.

Her cat answers my call and licks my cheek.

"Okay, time to go."

The next couple of hours are somewhat of a blur (thankfully and miraculously, my nose wasn't broken), and before I know it, we are on the road headed to Dasher Valley.

Except this was not the scenario I had in mind.

In my head, I would drive Lucy to my hometown, stopping at a Cal's Diner, which is stationed around the halfway mark. We would share a shake, and I would quiz her on everything she'd need to know to keep our fake dating cover intact. We'd have so much fun talking, singing to random songs, and getting to know each other that the six hours would breeze by. Heck, by the end of the drive, she'd be in love with me and pretending wouldn't be so difficult for her. Where we went from there was a mystery because commitment is not for me, but I would sure have a good time figuring it out.

Instead, Lucy is driving at a snail's pace, which she constantly reminds me is not normal for her. She's only going slow because my motorcycle is in the back of the truck, I'm injured, and this is a new route for her.

I'm glad she's going slow. I won't lie and say I feel easy about her driving my truck, especially because my precious bike is on board.

Music plays softly in the background but not too loud because I'm still fighting off a headache from getting hit in the head with a cast iron skillet simply because I had worked myself up into a fuss thinking something was wrong with Lucy.

The reality?

She's apparently not a morning person, went to bed too late from writing, and forgot to charge her phone.

All very innocent.

Or not.

I'm the one with a bruised nose and newly developing raccoon eyes. She only has a weight of guilt and now has to drive us.

"We have about four more hours to go. Do you need to stop for a bathroom break or anything before we pass this next exit?" Her eyes flit from her GPS to the road as I lean against the passenger window, my head on a pillow and my gaze tuned into her.

"I'm good for now. There's a diner about an hour away if you want to stop there for food."

"That sounds nice," she responds quietly. Then she adds, "I truly am very sorry. I wish there was a better way to apologize."

"It's okay, Lucy. I've broken my nose before, which is worse than only having it injured and bruised. I'll survive. I understand you were frightened, and well, I'm glad you can defend yourself. That's a good thing."

She breathes out heavily and a smile pulls at the edges of her pink lips.

"But for heaven's sake, please charge your phone at night so something like this doesn't happen again."

"Right," she says with a sharp nod, her timid smile blossoming into something full and bright. I can't help the way I smile in return, though it seriously hurts.

The sound of soft country music fills the silence as I look Lucy over. She's wearing a flowy, long floral skirt that sits above her belly button, a peek of pale skin showing between the edge of the skirt and the start of her long-sleeved white, buttoned crop top. Her hair is thrown into a top-knot with only her cute bangs tamed. Flyaways and little hairs poke out around her head, but instead of looking messy, she looks wild and fierce. Like a lion.

The image of her hovering above me when I first opened my eyes reappears, and I fight off a snicker.

"So, my little lion, should we get our history straight?"

"Huh?" she says, knitting her eyebrows together as she focuses on the road. "What history?"

I'm surprised she didn't question my newly found nickname for her. It's honestly kind of a let down. I like when she gets heated and feisty. Like a little lion.

"Our dating history. Off the top of my head, I suggest we've been dating since April, I asked you out, and you're hopelessly in love with me."

She snorts, ripping her eyes from the road and turning the amused expression my way before she snaps her attention back to driving. She's laughing as she says, "April sounds good. Yes, you did ask me out... over and over again. Since February, actually. And I finally said yes in April to try and get you off my case. Turns out you weren't as bad as I had you pegged to be, and I fell for you. But just as I am hopelessly in love with you, you are smitten with me. So much so that you would destroy galaxies and wipe out civilizations in my honor."

The rumble of the road beneath the truck tires accompanies a soft and slow country love song. I blink, staring with amazement at Lucy, wondering about who she is down to the strands of DNA that make up her person.

"I'm sorry. That was too much. You are simply smitten with me," she says in a quiet voice, her demeanor becoming tight and rigid. I have the sudden urge to take her hand in mine and reassure her of... whatever she needs right now, but she's driving, and well, I don't think I've earned that privilege yet. I may be a tease and hopeless flirt, but I do respect physical boundaries.

At least while we are alone and not playing pretend for people.

"I like it," I beam. "It fits my character: bold, relentless, and sumptuous. Lucy May, while you are my fake girlfriend, I will be entirely smitten with you. So much so that I will go all Thanos on the universe if it so much as offends you."

I watch her stiffened shoulders relax an inch and her knuckles loosen on the steering wheel as she breaks out in a grin.

Narrowing my eyes as if to evaluate her, I ask, "Did you think I would be taken aback by you suggesting I become the morally gray hero of your story while we pretend to date?"

She chuckles nervously but then breathes a sigh of release. "A little, I guess. I got caught up in setting the tone of your epic love story that Romance Writer Brain took over. Don't worry. I know it's not realistic as I've been told before. And I do not expect you to avenge my honor. Instead, let's talk about how my younger man knows big words like sumptuous."

"It could be," I state plainly, ignoring her comment about my age and word usage so that unwanted memories don't resurface. I may look like an athletic meathead, but there's much more to me than that. Like the fact that I read often. She looks at me, a perplexed expression crossing her face. "To clarify, if some man so much as looks at you wrong while you are dating me, even if our relationship is pretend, he's got another thing coming for him. No one toys with a girl when she's with me. She's only mine to play with." I wink for good measure, but then the truck bounces, accompanied by a loud rumbling sound. My heart picks up as I realize she's running us off the road. Lucy yanks her attention (and the wheel) back onto the road. I let out a deep breath. "Eyes on the road, or there will be no play time for you, Little Lion."

She grits her teeth and murmurs an apology, her eyes once more glued to the two-lane highway.

After a few minutes, Lucy speaks up. "Okay, so we have the basics down. Will your parents ask us about our first date? How many details do we need to have up our sleeve? I'm great at thinking of things on the spot, but I do want to be as prepared as possible."

"My family won't pry too much. I think. At least they don't with me. My mom and sister tend to let me do my thing. They may question who I'm with and how things are going, but they don't seem to need too many details. They know it won't last long. Though, it has been a different experience with you since I said—"

I cut myself off, realizing I was on the verge of telling her my family already knows about her.

"Said what, Mr. Harper?" Lucy narrows her eyes suspiciously in my direction.

"It's funny," I say with a mirthless laugh. Might as well tell her. Hopefully she won't be too mad. "I may have actually told my mom and sister back in April that you were my girlfriend to get them off my back about committing and settling down..."

Moments pass before she bursts out in laughter. "Oh my gosh. You did not. No wonder you needed me for this trip specifically. Oh man. You're lucky I ruined lunch for us yesterday, or you never would have gotten me to agree to this sort of thing."

She shakes her head, and I find myself grinning ear to ear. I enjoy how easygoing she can be at times. "Oh, is that so? I can think of a few ways I could have gotten you to agree to a weekend rendezvous with me."

"You're a real lady-killer, aren't you?" she asks rhetorically, snickering and shaking her head.

"Are my charms working on you?"

"Not a chance, Pebbles."

"Pebbles?"

"Little, tiny stones." Her grin is victorious, and when I raise an eyebrow at her, she only laughs.

Shaking my head, I join in her laughter simply because I like the sound of it. But then she stops and sneaks a look at me. "You mentioned your mom and sister twice but not your dad."

My heart aches with a familiar twinge of loss that has somehow simultaneously dulled over the years and remained the same. "He passed away a long time ago. When I was only a boy."

"Hm," she says with a nod, her eyes fixed on the road. "So you had to be the man of the house growing up, huh?"

I'm shocked by her statement. I'm used to the "I'm sorry" or "That must suck" type of responses.

"Sorry. You don't have to answer that," she hurriedly says.

"No, it's fine. Just took me by surprise. Yes. That's exactly what I did. I tried to fill his shoes, though, to be fair, they were pretty large for a boy like me."

She laughs lightly at my weak joke, and I'm thankful. I continue. "My family consists of my mother, Marian, my older sister, Stella, and her husband, Lucas. You'll probably meet our family friends, Gracie and Jared, and, oh... Mom's new husband as of about a year ago, the pastor of Dasher Valley Baptist, Brother Johnny."

"Got it." Lucy nods her head affirmatively.

"And they are all really looking forward to meeting you. Especially my sister and Gracie. You might have to give details to those two if they pull you away from me, but I promise to try and prevent that from happening."

"It'll be okay. Like I said, I'm good at coming up with things on the spot. Part of my charm as a romance writer." She does this little side to side head tilt thing as she bounces her shoulders. The action is playful and cute and cheerful, like she's up to the task of creating some lovey-dovey backstory for us. "Oh, I love this song."

She turns up the volume and sings along with "Take Back Home Girl" by Chris Lane and Tori Kelly. As the words resonate, and I lose myself in Lucy's little driver-style dance moves, I can't help but wonder if I will ever meet a woman that I want to take home to Dasher Valley for real. So far, Lacey is the only one of my girlfriends to meet my family, and that was mostly because we were in high school together and dated for over a year. Lucy is only the second woman, but this is all a ruse, so it doesn't really count.

When the song comes to an end, Lucy catches me staring at her and apologizes for dancing and singing too loud.

I brush her off and tell her she can dance and sing as much as she wants as long as she keeps us on the road, but in the back of my mind, I wonder who ever told her to dull her shine.

BEAT THREE

A SEXY COMPLICATION // "GLITCH"

Chapter 5

Lucy

Six hours later, I pull the truck into a little gravel driveway that leads to a brick house with a lovely front porch. The house is two stories, and the wooden porch is seducing my attention. Hanging swings call to me; I'm dying to sit on one and write while the crickets sing and stars shine overhead. Maybe I'll do that tonight while Stone is away at the bachelor party. I don't want to impose too much on Stone's mama while he's not with me.

Speaking of...

"Are you sure I shouldn't run to a gas station and clean up more?" I ask Stone, who is biting his bottom lip as to not burst at the seams at my condition.

After we ate at a cute little diner in the middle of nowhere, I had the misfortune of running over a nail, resulting in a flat tire. Fortunately, he had a spare on hand, but unfortunately, I had hit the man in the face with a small cast iron skillet earlier in the day.

Which meant I had to assist in a tire change.

And now I am a certified grease monkey.

R.I.P. to my floral skirt and white top.

"This is Small Town, Mississippi, Lucy. This place is smaller than Juniper Grove. The only people who will see you this evening are my mom, Brother Johnny, and possibly my sister and her husband. But look around."

I do as he says, noting there is only a brown Tacoma in the driveway.

"See," he says. "That's Brother Johnny's truck, which means only he and Mom are home right now."

"But shouldn't I make a good impression on your mom?"

He laughs and opens the door of the truck. "The fact that you are here, my little lion, is enough to make the grandest impression of all."

My insides flip upside down at his new nickname for me. I can imagine it's stemming from my lion-like appearance this morning in my apartment, which is an every morning thing for me regardless if a man is breaking in or not. I could be upset by it, but something in the rich, smooth tone of voice he uses when he says it tells me it's an endearing term, not something he is using to mock me for my morning looks.

Stone closes the door, but I'm still clutching the steering wheel, feeling like I really should back out of this driveway and go attempt to better clean this grease off my skin and change my clothes. The wipes in the truck didn't cut it, and by the time we made it to a restroom stop, the stains had set and Stone wouldn't give me time to change due to the fact that we were already running so late.

The man is punctual; I'll give him that.

My door opens, and Stone holds out a hand for me to take as I quite literally drop out of his lifted truck.

Don't even get me started on how terrified I was driving this monstrosity all day long.

Once I'm solidly on my feet, I smooth down my skirt and grimace at the grease stains on my white shirt. I open the back door of the truck and dig inside my bag for my coat. Who cares that it's the middle of June in Mississippi? I HAVE to cover this dingy shirt.

Stone is laughing at me as I zip up my plain black cotton jacket. I ignore him and throw my backpack on my back and toss my duffle bag over one shoulder. Then I remember my purse in the front seat and grab it.

Stone grabs his things then bounds up the five wooden steps that lead from the ground to the porch, and within three giant steps, he's in front of the door and knocking. I rush up beside him as the screen door opens, revealing a short, older woman who has graying hair and wrinkles in her skin but whose eyes are bright regardless of their steel-gray color.

He must have his father's eyes, I think to myself.

Those steel gray eyes of hers widen to the size of softballs as she takes us in. "Did you two get in a wreck on your way here?"

Stone side-eyes me, and I stifle a laugh.

"More like I got beat up this morning, which resulted in Lucy here having to change our blown tire on the drive down," Stone says with a half-hearted wink in my direction, wincing at the action.

"Hi, Mrs.—" I glance at Stone, realizing he forgot to tell me her married name.

Thankfully, she speaks up. "Howell. But you can just call me Marian, honey."

I clear my throat. "Hi, Marian. I'm Lucy Spence." I hold my hand out to her, but she disregards it and takes a step out the door, wrapping me into the biggest hug I've ever experienced in my life.

On instinct, I hug her back as well as I can around my bags.

Because unlike my twin sister, who can't stand touch, I very much like warm hugs.

And this embrace feels like Mama's.

I miss Mama even though she only left a couple of weeks ago back on her cross-country road trip with Dad.

"Be careful with who you're hugging, Mom," Stone says, a tease in his voice. "She's the little gangster thug who beat me up this morning."

His mama laughs, a rich but aged sound. "Oh, come in and tell me that story, Lucy. I'm hoping you knocked some sense into that boy."

I follow the woman dressed in dark jeans and a t-shirt of a Shakespeare play company that reads "Saved by the Grace of Southern Charm" into the house. Immediately, I buzz with energy and life. The living room is cluttered but not in a messy way. There are pictures all over the walls, and I'm itching to get a closer look. The desire to see Stone throughout all the stages of life—from wee diapers to the cute single-digit years all the way up to the awkward middle school years and into his *homme fatale* high school years—is strong.

I knew about him in college well enough. He played football, and I was a cheerleader. He hit on me once at a party, but I don't think he remembers it. He was only a freshman at the time and had had a little too much to drink.

Instinctively, my eyes find him off to the side. He's standing with his arms crossed and feet spread while sporting a cocked eyebrow, which lets me know he knows exactly what I want—to view him in all his years-gone-by glory—and he's already vetoed the idea.

Ha, as if it were up to him. He's going to be gone in an hour, and I'll have free range to roam to my heart's content.

"Have a seat, Lucy, dear. Do you want some coffee, sweet tea, or water?"

"Water would be nice."

"I'll fix you up a glass." And with that, Marian hobbles off into the kitchen area off to the left of the living room. Stone still stands on the right-hand side in front of stairs that lead to the second floor.

"Your mother is a gem," I say. Sure, I just met her, but I can already tell I want to keep her.

"She's kind of the best," Stone agrees with love in his eyes, and the way he peers into the kitchen with gentle care while glasses clink and cabinets shut brings my melting point down to whatever the temperature is in this house currently.

I'll be a little gooey puddle on this hardwood floor if Stone turns that expression on me at any point.

"Here you go, Lucy," Marian says, handing me a glass of ice water. "Sit down, now, girl. Let's chat while I send Stone upstairs with your luggage."

"Really, Mom? I'm injured," Stone says.

"Oh, you've seen worse injuries than that, son." She waves a hand and sits next to me on the well-worn couch.

"Oh, it's okay!" I interject. "I'm the one who gave him a possible concussion." I side-eye the man standing in front of the stairs. "He wouldn't let the doctors test him, but that means I get to wake him up every two hours."

"What is with my children returning home to me injured with possible concussions?" She shakes her head and clicks her tongue.

"Did something happen to your sister?" I ask Stone with a curious glance.

He laughs. "You'll have to ask her about the Suitcase Incident."

Noted. I'm always on the hunt for real stories to include in my books.

"But, I do need to run upstairs and freshen up for the bachelor party tonight." Stone cuts his eyes from his mother to me. "You two ladies don't do anything I wouldn't do."

"That's a narrow list, Mr. Harper," I say with an edge to my voice, forgetting I can easily use his first name now that I am his pretend girlfriend. In fact, I should have used his first name. *Ugh. I'm already screwing this up.*

He saunters over to me like a panther on the prowl, hooks his finger underneath my chin, and kisses me on the forehead. He mumbles against my skin, "I like it when you call me Mr. Harper when we're not at work."

Though my temperature is rising and my face is burning—I might be on the verge of spontaneous combustion according to the way my body is humming—I distinctly remember him saying he liked it when I used his first name. He's saving my butt right now, and for that, I'm grateful. I should have known he wouldn't be shy of affection in front of his family.

And that's when I remember I forgot to do the most crucial task when embarking on a fake dating scheme...

"We should set some ground rules," I whisper to where only he can hear since his head is still level with mine.

He chuckles lightly, his smile crinkling the corner of his beautiful but blackened eyes.

"Later." He winks then winces at the action before snatching my luggage and ascending the creaky, wooden stairs.

"Whew, that was some heat straight from hell." I turn, slack-jawed, to face Stone's mother, who is busy fanning herself with her hand while sporting a wicked grin. It makes her look youthful and full of inappropriate mischievousness.

Now I see exactly where my playboy boss gets his personality from.

I laugh nervously, tucking a strand of hair behind my ear. "I should probably get cleaned up. I'm kind of a grease monkey right now."

"You just want to follow my son upstairs." The gleam in her gray eyes causes my face to flush. My immediate reaction is to object, but I am his girlfriend for the weekend, and I'm sure any woman of Stone's would want to follow him upstairs.

But I'm not just any woman, even if we are playing pretend.

"Nonsense." I swat my hand in front of my face, schooling my expression into a soft, loving smile. "That man chases after me, not the other way around."

Marian's smile widens, revealing a line of white teeth that adds to her youthfulness. "My, my. You just might be the one, then."

Her blatant admission leaves me speechless. *Me? The one for Stone Harper?* It's humorous, and I desperately want to laugh, but I strangle the outburst with a cord.

Instead of laughing at the impossible, I play coy.

With a slight tilt of my head, I ask, "You think so? We haven't talked about the future."

She chuckles but then presses her lips into a contemplative line. "You're the second girlfriend of his that I'm meeting. And the first one was years ago while the two of them were in high school, so it wasn't necessarily a meeting. I'd known her and her family for a while."

"I, uh... huh?" *Wow. Way to be literate, Little Miss Writer.*

Marian rests her hand on my knee in a loving way that only mothers seem to be capable of. "Don't let it scare you, darling girl. I just wanted you to know that this is a big deal for me. And for him, whether he realizes it or not. We've heard so much about you, and the way he talks about you... He's smitten. You've done something to my son."

It's all an act, though. He's been playing a part in a play that I had no inkling I was cast in. This is an episode of *Punk'd*, and I'm the unsuspecting star. I'm not scared. Not at the idea that Stone Harper sees forever when he looks at me, at least. That's an obvious, emphatic no. But I'm growing fearful by the second that I'm going to break this sweet woman's heart when Stone tells them we're over.

"Thank you for telling me," I finally respond.

A balding older man with kind eyes and a warm smile enters the room from somewhere behind the kitchen.

"Hi. You must be Lucy." He reaches out his hand, and I shake it while verifying his assessment. "I'm Johnny, but most people seem to think my first name is Brother. I'm this beautiful woman's doting husband."

I watch the way his brown eyes fall on Marian. There are oceans of love swimming in them, and I'd like to think that one day a man will look at me that way. I suddenly feel like I'm intruding on a life that doesn't belong to me, and the incommodious moment spurs me to action.

Standing up, I feign a yawn and stretch. "It's really nice to meet you. I better get upstairs and ask Stone to show me my room so I can get cleaned up and ready for bed. It was a long trip. I'm not sure how Stone is capable of going out tonight."

I do understand because I'm nowhere near tired, though I do yearn for hot water, strawberry-smelling soap, and a round of listening to *1989* by Taylor Swift.

We chat for a few more minutes before I go upstairs and turn down the small hallway with three doors, two on the left and one farther down on the right. There are pictures lining the wall, old school photos of Stone and what must be his older sister. As I pad across the wooden floor, smiling at the pictures of their childhood, the door at the end of the hallway opens, and a very shirtless, only-wearing-a-grey-towel version of Stone steps into my view. He's running a hand through his wet hair while his bicep flexes, and my eyes drop to his bare chest without my permission.

He has a smattering of light hair that disappears before reaching his abs. All eight of them. Leading to a prominent...

No, Lucy. Stop it!

My face heats as I snap my eyes back to Stone's bruised but handsome face only to find him frozen with his hand in his hair, eyes narrowed at me. Like a bird of prey who's zoned in on an unbeknownst victim.

And he looks ravenous.

Doing what I should have done in the first place, I avert my eyes and turn my back to him. "I'm sorry," I squeak out. "I didn't realize you would be... in the state that you are," I dumbly finish.

Somewhere behind me, a ghost of a laugh echoes off the walls. "No need to apologize. You *are* my girlfriend for the weekend."

Choosing to ignore the suggestion, mostly because I know he's toying with me and isn't serious, I blurt, "Which room is mine?"

I feel the heat from his body behind me before I hear his released breath. "First door by the stairs. It was my sister's room, so it should be to your liking. Would you like me to show you around it?"

Acting on impulse, I turn around and splay one hand across his chest, glaring into his eyes.

Big mistake.

That's one very nice chest.

A chest carved into a marbled Roman statue. A chest worthy of lines of lyrical prose. A chest only read about in romance novels. My eyes drop down his body and land on his massive tanned legs sticking out like tree trunks from the short towel. What would it feel like to have those wrapped around my waist...?

Snap out of it, Lucy!

"No." I bark out, then, remembering his mother and a PASTOR is downstairs, I lower my voice to a whispered hiss. "Stop flirting with me and trying to get us locked in a room together. I might fall in love with you." *There. That'll scare him.*

He blinks once, then twice, before a smile crawls slowly up his clean, handsome face. "I like it when you're bossy. Keep that up and I'll fall for you."

"Ugh!" I roll my eyes and turn back around, taking a few steps to reach the room I'll be staying in. *He might fall for me? Surely he was poking fun at me saying I could fall for him...*

After I enter and close the door, Stone speaks from the other side.

"I hear you, Lucy. I can't promise you I won't flirt with you because, let's be honest, it's who I am, but I do promise not to step over any line you draw with me. I will try. I don't want to intentionally play with your emotions." His voice is rough and serious, and I want to crack the door open to see if his light brows are pinched in deep thought. I'm curious to know if his lips are pressed into a line or if they are folded into his mouth. His voice, with the edge it carried, makes it sound like he's battling inside his brain, but the question is, what's he fighting? Attraction to me? The idea that though he says he doesn't play with a woman's emotions, he probably does? Actual feelings for me... so much so that he can't stop wickedly flirting with me when I'm around?

Ha, I snort. *That's a harebrained thought.*

I couldn't sleep, so I wandered downstairs and slipped out of the house.

Stone still hasn't come back.

No, don't focus on that. Focus on... the sounds around you.

The cicadas sing a harmonious tune with the crickets.

If I were describing the sound in a novel, I might paint it a soul-stirring sound that waxes and wanes to a tune of somber smiles. Or maybe that's my melancholic mind twisting a golden cheerful chirp into suffocating waves of blue.

Dew sticks to my bare arms; the baby hairs that usually fly around my face and neck are tamed by the dense water in the air. My thighs stick to the wooden swing beneath me.

I open my laptop and attempt to adjust my position. The moment I move my legs, it's as if a band-aid is ripping off my skin. Not a flimsy band-aid, but one of those heavy-duty waterproof ones. I wince, taking the pain like the southern woman I am, then cross my legs underneath me.

After pulling up my writing software, I open the story I've started to play around with in my head. I should apply the edits to my merman story, but something about this stoic, misunderstood vampire is beckoning my attention.

And by stoic, misunderstood vampire, I mean the centuries-old man who absolutely loves being a vampire and wouldn't trade it for the world.

Heh. Enter: odd but beautiful human woman who will restart his cold, dead heart. I laugh maniacally to myself and then remember I am not alone in my apartment and probably shouldn't cackle like a witch.

The thought is a bucket of cold water on the little fire of passion that was attempting to ignite within me. I've been sleeping in my space alone ever since Lorelei moved out mere weeks ago. The first night I cried myself to sleep and woke up way too late the next morning because Lorelei wasn't there to make little noises around the house alerting me to the rising sun. Thank goodness I had taken off work.

The following days and nights passed in what I refer back to as a Gaussian blur. Last night, I was up into the wee hours of the morning, writing to take my mind off Loneliness sitting in the dark corner of my room. I think I forgot to eat. Or maybe I snacked on chips at one point?

It's probably a huge red flag indicating I should seek some help, but I think it's only an adjustment period. I'll get over this hump. Change is hard whether it's good change or bad change, and overall, Lorelei moving and getting engaged is a good change. It's a good change that I am facing solitude after twenty-six years of having people in my sphere of living. I have to grow, and while I might not like these growing pains I'm faced with, I can acknowledge that, at some point, I will bloom from the dense, dark dirt I am entombed under.

"We are just fine," I whisper to myself as I wipe a single tear from my eye. "Now, what reason does a centuries-old vampire need to fake date a beautiful human woman?"

As I brainstorm the question I've been ruminating over for a couple of days, I find myself drifting off, thinking of Stone and this situation we've gotten ourselves into.

Excuse me.

That he has dragged me into.

Kicking and screaming.

And throwing cast iron skillets.

Okay, I said yes pretty easily, but I mean, who wouldn't? A taste of Stone Harper without the fear of attachment and then abandonment? Yes, please. But that's why our state of affairs is mussed. My attraction to him is off the charts and the feelings are reciprocated.

It's not an arguable point, however.

Attraction does not equal love, and I require love.

Love is something I don't think he is capable of giving me, especially now that I've gotten a glimpse of the man behind the curtain. He's been burned by Lacey. I once thought he might have been the one lighting the match, but upon further reflection of the encounter outside of Perry's Seafood, I think it was Lacey who struck it. She looked sad, but it wasn't a scorned lover's sadness. No, that's what Stone looked like. She looked like the one who lost a friend due to her own misgivings.

Is she the reason he's like this? Afraid to commit?

Stone says he doesn't intentionally seek to hurt women emotionally. I'd like to know more about that, but honestly, what's the point? He's not mine to explore and figure out, no matter how I adjust the picture and attempt to look at various angles.

I hear his motorcycle before I see the light coming down the driveway.

Stone.

His name in my inner thoughts is spoken like it's a breath of fresh air after spending the day in a city of smog. Like coming home after a long vacation.

No, ma'am. You stop that right now.

It's my nighttime companion, Loneliness, talking. It's the physical attraction manifesting in my head as something *more*.

You've battled this before. You know the signs of the beginning of war. Take up armor.

The light clicks off.

You're excusing away his playboy behavior with weak observations that you hope are true. We aren't supposed to justify behaviors anymore, remember?

The motorcycle shuts off. What would it be like to ride behind him on that thing?

You're attaching yourself to a possible idea of him you're piecing together in your mind.

He emerges under the porch light, walking down the pathway and up the stairs, his eyes zeroed in on me with an upward tug to his lips.

You're letting the attraction fester into lust because there is no way you love *this man.*

"Hi, Lucy May," he says with allurement in his tone. All my previous thoughts vanish in a wisp of smoke. He's wearing pale pink shorts that rest an inch above his knees and a tight white t-shirt under an open white button down. His effortlessly hot look is complete with a pair of white sneakers. "Like what you—" he says, but then stops, snapping his mouth closed.

I come to my senses. "What I what?"

He clicks his tongue and pops his mouth with his hand. "I was about to flirt with you, but I caught myself." Stone sits down next to me on the swing, causing it to sway back and forth, and I relish in the gentle breeze.

"Right. Thank you." *I almost regret telling him not to flirt with me. Since when has he listened to my requests, anyways?*

"What are you doing up?"

"Couldn't sleep. I sometimes struggle sleeping in new environments." I lean my head back and close my eyes as we move back and forth, the wind kissing my face and cooling off the misty summer heat of the night. Why did I admit that to him exactly?

"I see. Is there anything I can do to help?"

I jolt, my laptop wobbling on top of my thighs. I narrow my eyes at him when realization hits that he'd been staring at me. At my expression, he puffs out a little laugh.

"I didn't mean that in a flirty way." His gaze moves upward before he tilts his head and closes his eyes, a look of peace transfixing his bruised face. "Genuinely trying to help. What do you need? Warm milk? Melatonin? Tea?" He barely opens one blackened eye and peeks over at me. "A massage?"

I want to be mad and shove him, but I can't because I know he is honestly messing with me and not attempting to flirt. *Even if I wish he was…*

But for good measure, I do elbow him.

"Violent, Little Lion." He tsks and closes his eye.

"Only when necessary."

He laughs, and I join, kind of digging this side of him. Even though his eyes and nose are as bruised as a dropped apple, he looks tranquil sitting here in the middle of the night on his mother's front porch swing.

I have the urge to ask him about Lacey again—or for clarification about what he said regarding women's emotions—but I refrain with a bite of my lip. He's being what I presume to be his authentic self. He's not Mr. Harper right now. He's not a playboy trying to win all the ladies.

He's just Stone.

A young man who's home for a weekend surrounded by people who love him, cherish him, and support him.

As the swing starts dwindling down to a stop, I realize I haven't taken my eyes off him yet.

Worse yet, I'm authentically smiling. Teeth and all.

I fix my face before he opens his eyes, chastising myself as I hold my laptop to get up and go inside.

Stone grabs my wrist. "Wait, Lucy. You mentioned you wanted to set ground rules for our time here in Dasher Valley."

Right. Of course I did.

"What did you have in mind?" he continues. His touch doesn't let up, heating a branding ring around my wrist.

Maybe it's the time. *Nothing good happens after midnight, am I right?*

Maybe it's the innocent look of genuine care and concern in his eyes. *They sure do sparkle under the hanging outdoor porch lights.*

Maybe it's the loneliness I've been experiencing for quite some time, which has only gotten worse as everyone I know finally begins their own lives with husbands and kids.

Maybe it's the hot, countryside air filling up the space under a misty moonlight...

"One rule," I begin, swallowing a lump in my throat. I know the next words out of my mouth are a signature on a contract that I'll regret signing come morning light. "Whatever happens in Dasher Valley stays in Dasher Valley. Are we clear?"

Stone's lips twitch, a fraction of a smile forming. His eyes dance, two stormy blue pools of building desire. "That's one rule I'll willingly follow, Lucy May."

Without thinking, my gaze drops to his full lips.

He tugs my arm, and I fall against the swing, gripping my laptop so it doesn't crash onto the porch. He releases my wrist and takes the laptop from me, setting it onto the floor underneath the swing. When his eyes lock with mine again, something I had buried deep inside me awakens, clawing its way to the surface and begging to be set free.

I can't tell who gives the final stamp of permission to move. Is it when his gaze flicks to my mouth as he mindlessly licks his top lip? Is it when my hand moves on its own accord, coming to a rest on his upper thigh as if to stake my territory?

Before I can so much as blink, his lips connect with mine as one hand tangles in my hair, tugging me into him as if he can't get close enough. His other hand splays across my back, burning a hole through the thin fabric, and I tilt my head for a better angle. As he parts our lips, groaning into my mouth, sizzling electricity travels down to my toes. My head swims with his intoxicating taste, and if I could, I would crawl into his skin to know him fully and eternally.

I've never before been kissed like *this*.

Felt like this.

And I'd gamble to say it will never happen again.

Who would be so lucky as to experience getting their DNA re-written more than once in a lifetime?

Visions swim in my head, much like when I'm writing a story, as we give into months of building attraction.

Stone and I tangled in plaid sheets. A royal ball. Stone, in a tux, carrying me over the threshold of a doorstep while I wear a white gown. Me writing at a desk in an unknown house. Stone throwing a baseball with one boy while tossing a football with the other. Twin boys. A book I haven't written on the big screen.

Explosions.

I throw myself backwards, which forces the swing to move, flinging me off and onto my butt on the wooden planks of the porch. From my lowered position, I stare up at Stone, who's breathless and already standing, steadying the swing from its wild movements before it swings back to hit me. He reaches out his hand, and all I can think about is how moments ago he had it tangled in my hair, delivering the best kiss of my existence.

I knew he'd be good.

But not *that* good.

When I don't take his hand because my brain is still fuddled with his kiss, he sits down on the porch beside me. All of the twisting and swirling feelings inside me dance around, asking—no begging—for more of him, when he casually fingers the stray hairs that have fallen in front of my face. I release a deep breath in an attempt to regain composure, and he tucks the hair behind my ear, fingertips caressing the sensitive skin.

"Lucy..."

"Give me a moment." I hold up one finger, taking deep breaths in and releasing them slowly. What have I done?

I kissed my playboy boss.

On the front porch of his childhood home.

And... I KISSED MY BOSS.

We *work* together. I have to pretend he didn't resurrect my dead soul with the electricity in his lips come Monday.

"What happens in Dasher Valley stays in Dasher Valley, Lucy May. Remember? Don't think too much about what happens when we are back at work."

He grabs my hand I held up and kisses the tip of my pointed finger. I stare wide-eyed and a smidge hypnotized. Stone smirks, folds my finger down, then kisses my knuckles. "Are you still worrying about Monday?"

I shake my head, but then I say, "Well, I am now that you mention it."

"Hm." He pauses, moving to sit on his knees, and kisses the inside of my elbow. "And now?"

"If you keep reminding me, how will I stop thinking about it?" I ask, breathless and jittery with anticipation.

"Maybe I keep reminding you because I want an excuse to keep making you forget." He kisses the top of my shoulder, and I can't hold in my sigh. Somewhere, deep down, I know I'm going to regret every moment of this.

But right now is not that time.

Feeling emboldened by his free show of desire, I pucker my lips into a moue. "My lips miss your attention, Mr. Harper. Maybe if you appease their longing for you, I'll forget about Monday."

He raises an eyebrow. "You long for me?"

My face burns hotter than it already was. I open my mouth to protest, to tell him it was Romance Writer Brain's fault, but he captures my lips with his, effectively removing any semblance of embarrassment I felt.

Chapter 6

Stone

"Hold still," Lucy commands, her minty breath too close for comfort. It elicits memories from last night when I had the best kiss of my life, and that's saying something considering I've kissed a lot of women.

I suspected Lucy knew how to kiss, but I wasn't expecting to have my world turned upside down. And what was with those images of us getting married and moving into my house and having babies? The explosions, I understand. Her kiss was dynamite to my self-control. But the rest?

No way.

What happens in Dasher Valley stays in Dasher Valley.

"What are you thinking about, Pebbles?" I can hear the smirk in her voice. "Your face is getting pink."

"Pebbles? You're sticking with that?"

"You call me by my author name. And then you gave me the nickname 'Little Lion.' It's only fair you get one, too."

"You can't choose another variation of my name? Pebbles? Like I'm a caveman from *The Flintstones?*"

She snickers, patting me on top of my head. "Pebbles was the girl. You're thinking of BamBam."

"Great, so I'm a cave*woman*. Noted." I try to sound offended, but honestly, I'm enjoying this light, playful side to her. If she wants to call me Pebbles, so be it. As long as it makes her smile and not look like she's the blue emotion, Sadness, from *Inside Out*. Since we're talking cartoons and all right now.

Lucy's shallow breaths (I can tell she's trying to hold her breath as her face is near mine) once again reminds me of the twenty minutes we spent making out on the floor of the porch last night.

I want to open my eyes and see if desire swims in her hazel eyes as it pools in my gut, but right now, I'm forced to rely on my sense of touch as I sit on the toilet seat in the small bathroom I once shared with my older sister.

Lucy's finger brushes underneath my eyes as she rubs in arnica cream that she swears will assist in a quicker healing of my bruised eyes. She had given me a tub of it before we left her apartment yesterday, and I'd been applying it as she instructed. She took on the task right now, however, because she's going to apply makeup to my face to lessen the visibility of the bruising for the wedding. She apparently has this fancy concealer for covering tattoos that also works for bruises. When I asked her why she needed something strong enough to cover bruises, she laughed and said that it was due to job hazards. That's when I remembered she got a black eye a few months ago while at work.

I wince as she presses a little harder.

"I'm sorry," she says in a high-pitched voice. "I'm making sure the cream is soaked into your skin before I apply the concealer."

I don't reply because she once again brushes her finger under my eye, but she does so more gently this time as her palm cups my face. I hold as still as a living statue.

There is *nothing* like this feeling. I thought having her clean my face off after the crab incident was a feeling that couldn't be topped.

Nope.

Kissing her was a Fourth of July fireworks experience, but having her touch me while my eyes are closed, never knowing when the next touch is going to come, is deliciously excruciating. Lucy's touch brings a heat to my body like I'm once again on the football field in the middle of summer drills. At the same time, it grounds me like I'm an electrical current and she's the metal that absorbs my shock.

Too soon, her warmth is removed. Instead, something prickles my skin. I crinkle my nose and open my eyes.

Lucy is *right. there.*

She's focused, the red in her hair highlighting the green flecks in her eyes. The freckles across her nose provide a warm contrast to her cool skin as she tilts her head to get a better angle. She has some sort of brush in her hand, making gentle strokes right above my cheekbones.

"Does it hurt?" she asks, leaning back and grabbing something that looks like an artist's color palette. She mixes a brown powder into a liquid that resembles the color of vanilla ice cream.

"No. What are you mixing?"

"Just adding a dash of bronzer into the concealer. Where I could scare a ghost if I happened upon it, you are the color of a bronze trophy. Especially since you've been in the sun this summer. You were paler back in February."

My lips twitch upward. "You've been watching me that closely for that long, Little Lion?"

The brush she was circling slowly on the palette suddenly stops, but she keeps her eyes fixated on the color mixture, her shoulders raising just a hair. "I watch everything and everyone. Don't feel special. You're a person in my close sphere of living. Of course I watch you."

"I'm still going to feel special," I jest. "Being watched by you is simultaneously nerve-wracking and thrilling."

She snorts a laugh as she turns her attention back to me. "Just close your eyes and tilt your head up, will ya?" The brush circles within her mixture once more, then she holds it up in front of me while her eyebrow hitches as if to question why my eyes are still open.

And the answer to her unspoken accusation is that I *have* to see her reaction to my next words. I'm testing the waters since we haven't addressed what happened last night. We woke up, silently moved around the house like nothing happened, exchanged knowing glances across the breakfast table, and then I asked her if she knew of a way to cover the black around my eyes since she's the one who put it there.

"If you want to kiss me, Little Lion, at least allow me to stand so I can wrap one arm around your waist, stitch you to me, and run my fingers..."

The vile taste of concealer touches my tongue as she slides the coated brush across my mouth, a bewildered look painting her face. I spit into my hands and rub at my tongue, completely aware I look like a disgusting, uncouth pig-man right now, but hey... it's her fault.

"What was that for?"

She holds the brush, eyes wide as saucers. "I–I," she stutters, glancing from me to the brush in her hands, then she rambles. "I'm sorry! I don't know what came over me. You started talking about kissing me again and I got nervous and what happens on Monday when we're back at work? Will people know I kissed my boss?"

I wipe at my mouth once more as she continues spewing her worries aloud. I let her get it all out. If you're curious as to what concealer mixed with bronzer tastes like, it's something akin to what you'd taste if you licked the floor of a chemical factory. And the taste seems to be getting worse as I attempt to rid myself of it.

Lucy stops her anxious maunder then fishes around in her makeup box.

"Take this." She holds out a tissue, which I snatch, causing it to tear in half. She drops the half remaining in her hands onto my lap then walks out of the bathroom. I wipe my hands and face, not enjoying the taste of tissue either.

"Lucy May," I growl, jumping to my feet and walking out into the hallway. "This tastes disgusting, you know?" I stop a foot in front of her when she darts out of my sister's bedroom with a half-empty bottle of water.

"Here. Drink this."

"It's opened."

She shrugs. "I know. It's my midnight water. Now drink it or continue tasting my concoction."

"Do you even know what horrid taste you just shoved into my mouth? Water is not going to make it go away."

"No," she says, averting her eyes and crossing her arms after I take the bottle from her and take a swig. She's becoming defensive, and I can't help myself. She's hot when she's feisty.

She continues talking, a bite to her voice. "I tend to keep my makeup on my face. And you would have, too, if you wouldn't talk nonsense about kissing me. We've done it already. It wouldn't be smart to do it again when we have to go back to normal come Monday."

I drop the bottle and step closer to her, re-angling myself so that she's forced against the beige wall. Through my smirk, I whisper, "'It wouldn't be smart?' Who said anything about being smart? You said what happens here stays here. Besides, I think you should know what your makeup tastes like. For research. Who knows? Maybe you can write this scene into one of your books."

She glances at her feet then back to me, firmly setting her jaw. "You don't have the brush. You can't do anything." The trembling challenge dripping in her voice is something I can't back down from.

I laugh quietly and place my hands on either side of her head. *I want her desperately...*

Our foreheads touch, and she tilts her chin up ever so slightly. "The taste remains on my lips, Lucy May." I slide my tongue across my top lip. "On my tongue."

She whimpers, black-coated eyelashes fluttering closed while her pale pink lips part.

And in all transparency, I mutter a curse word.

"Lucy," I growl her name again as I ball my hands into fists against the wall. She might have been trying to be polite in saying no with her smart phrase earlier, so I have to know for sure before I let myself lose control. "Say the word and I'll stop."

She sighs, practically undoing me. "Don't stop."

I suck in a breath before closing my eyes and start removing her lipstick with my mouth. The moment her lips touch mine, I know last night wasn't a fluke. The woman tastes like she was tailor-made to my liking.

Her hands slide up my waist, across my chest, and then tangle in my hair as she tugs me closer. Or maybe she's pulling herself closer to me.

I can't tell.

All I know is that my hands have wandered on their own accord, and I hoist her against the wall. Her legs instantaneously wrap around my hips as I deepen the kiss. The minty taste of her cleanses away the chemical compound flavor with every passing second while also rewriting the code of my brain.

My control completely snaps.

I pull back from the kiss, groaning her name through another curse as I carry her the short distance to my childhood bedroom. I set her down on top of the unmade gray bed sheets, watching in building anticipation as her back hits the bed. I lean over her, holding my weight with one arm while my other hand runs up her bare leg. I thought seeing Lucy in athletic shorts and an oversized t-shirt was a treat earlier this morning since she's usually dolled up. Now I'm extra thankful for the attire.

She moans my name, and I never want to hear it said any other way again. Wrapping her arms around my neck, she drags my lips down to hers.

How can—

I mean—

That was—

Whoa.

Feelings. Massive feelings. Hit-with-a-baseball-in-the-eye type feelings. Tackled-by-a-250-pound-linebacker type feelings. Cast-iron-skillet-to-the-face type feelings. Feelings I can't even begin to dissect or name.

I continue to spin and reel as I put my t-shirt back on. How can a person do that to another person? Make someone feel like a detonated bomb? Sure, the books dramatize kisses and intimate moments with that sort of language, but what transpired between me and Lucy was not fiction.

That was very, *very* real.

And terrifying.

Who knows what would have happened had my mom not burst through the front door downstairs and announced her presence, sending Lucy darting from underneath me like a skittish little lion.

Oh, I know. I would have claimed her as my own right there on my childhood bed. Claimed her in more ways than I already had.

Mom and Brother Johnny put groceries away downstairs, and I feel an inkling of guilt creep in. We didn't go all the way, though, so I shove it down and head to check on Lucy.

Knocking on the bathroom door, I ask her if she can finish covering the bruises under my eyes. When she opens the door, I can't help but smile at her frazzled but pleased state. Her eyes shine with new light and the trace of sadness that had been as a rain cloud over her aura for a while has evaporated.

I did that to her.

"Is my hair okay?" she whispers.

I lean toward her and whisper back. "You're beautiful." I nibble her earlobe as she playfully swats my arm. "Now make me beautiful, please."

Lucy kneels down in front of me with the brush in her hand as I sit on the closed toilet seat. "Close your eyes," she whispers.

I do as she says.

The coolness of the brush seeps into my heated face as she works to conceal the bruises around my eyes. Within moments, though it feels like a lifetime of her fingers brushing across my skin, she says she is finished.

She's still knelt down in front of me with doe eyes and a satisfied smile, and I can't resist the longing racing through my veins at the new memories made only half an hour ago. I reach out and cup her face, drawing her lips to mine. She bends to my will easily, her mouth moving in tandem with me. The fiery passion from before is tamed this go around, but it's replaced with something sweet and enthralling.

"Stone," she says in between breaths. "What are we doing?"

"I believe we are making out. What would you call this, Miss Romance Writer?"

She spurts a laugh. "This is fake. It's all fake." She repeats the phrase a few more times as if to convince herself of its validity.

"We can say this was a practice round for when some drunk relative decides they'd like to see us kiss. Sound good? Nothing more attached to this moment."

Now I'm trying to convince myself that I didn't just have two of the most outstanding kisses of my life. Kisses that scientists would marvel at if they caught wind of the new discoveries I've made in the confines of my mom's house.

She nods her head, though she doesn't hide her frown.

Does she want this to be something? Surely not. She was adamant beforehand. And I—

"What happens in Dasher Valley stays in Dasher Valley, right?"

It's my turn to laugh even though I can't hide the traces of disgust at myself sinking in at the worry in her voice. "Again. We will call it practice. This will not happen again if you don't want it to, okay?" My stomach drops at the thought of her lips nevermore meeting mine, of never putting my hands on her body again, but I press on. "We practiced well. Very well. No one will doubt our relationship now because we will deliver upon the best PDA kiss the world has ever seen."

She laughs, her frown transitioning to a pleasant smile. I smile, too, hoping hers is genuine. So many emotions linger beneath the surface right now. I'm not sure I could tell which way is up and which way is down.

"Lucy, I do have one question before we put this behind us."

She swallows, pushing her bangs out of her eyes. "Yes?"

"All this time you've been adamant about not dating me when I've flirted with you at work. You've acted like I repulsed you, and you wanted nothing to do with me. Can you be honest with me? Do you like me?"

Her eyes cut down as she fiddles with a silver ring on her left thumb. "I've always found you attractive, yes. And I see so much good in you. But I know you cycle through women faster than I write stories, and it wouldn't be wise of me to even attempt to go there with you."

I nod in understanding, my heart faltering over the feeling of taking advantage of her physical attraction to me. I've got to be more in control of myself…

Closing my eyes and releasing a breath, I take a moment to steady myself. Then I open my eyes and say, "I can't commit, so you are wise to set that boundary. I'm sorry I kissed you… among other things."

"It's okay. Truly. At least I know what it's like to be kissed by you. Among other things…" she teases.

"And what's it like?"

Lucy laughs with a swift shake of her head. "For book research purposes, I'll just say it was explosive."

Holding my tongue from speaking of the strange visions from yesterday that involved explosions, I nod and flash her a flirty grin. "That it was." I'll work through all these weird feelings and guilt later while I'm in bed. Alone. Without her entrancing presence. "Let's finish getting ready for this wedding. Thanks for covering up my raccoon eyes."

Chapter 7

Stone

How does she have my heart constricted after six years? She's married, for crying out loud. I know I don't love her, so why do I still get myself in rut over Lacey Fraiser? Or Lacey *Hopper*, I should say. Why do I allow her to act like a dementor and suck my soul out of my body whenever I see her?

"Stone, your jealousy is showing. Better look at me before people think you're gunning after another man's wife." Lucy squeezes my arm with a little too much force, and I snap my attention to her. She flinches, and I take a breath, softening my features. No need to let my suddenly soulless existence impact her.

Enough with the dramatics, dude. You've read one too many of Lucy's romance books.

Lucy continues. "You know, it'd help me out a lot if you'd tell me what happened between you two. That way I can tweak my acting skills to better fit you and our fake relationship."

The idea of confessing to Lucy that I was once rejected while down on one knee for a woman is equivalent to crying during a sappy romance movie. Wholly emasculating. Plus, I know I need to get Lacey out of my head. It's not *her* that haunts me sometimes. It's her parting *words*.

I don't want to unintentionally hurt Lucy by giving another woman even an ounce of my attention. Not after I explored her body with my hands only hours ago.

I scan the reception crowd, my eyes flicking over the torch lights, pool, and white tables, before looking down at the woman still hanging on my arm, whose thumb I swear has roamed up and down a few times. She's glancing at me with an exquisite expression, waiting patiently for my answer.

Of course, I deflect. "You have every single person here convinced we are a real couple and that you are fully in love with me." I smirk, shifting my gaze to where her fingers mindlessly roam across my muscle. "Exhibit A. You're taking advantage of this situation, aren't you?"

Her entire face blushes, shades darker than her strawberry hair, which is styled half-up, half-down in big waves hanging loose down a long, baby blue dress with a half-open back. A silver belt cuts the dress at her waist, accentuating her curves. I move my hand to the showing skin of her back and gently run my fingers up and down it.

She shivers right as I imagine slipping my hand underneath that belt, tugging her closer to me, and picking up where we left off earlier.

"Pretty sure you were adamant about physical touch in front of everyone. I'm just honoring your wishes." Though her blush is running deep, her shoulders are back, and she's speaking in a sultry, albeit shaky, voice. The smile that crosses my face is as genuine as can be as I realize she's fully captured my attention away from Lacey.

Interesting.

"Use me all you want, Lucy May. I'm yours for the weekend. What happens in Dasher Valley stays in Dasher Valley. In fact, I think I'll give a hint to a drunk relative that they should want to see us kiss." I wink, and she squeezes my arm while turning her upper body away from me. Unless I was envisioning things, I'm fairly certain she licked her top lip as she hid her face from my sight.

Heaven help me...

My brain is definitely back in the bedroom, discovering her body and mapping the inside of her mouth.

Dude. Cut it out. I shake my head clear and attempt to focus my thoughts.

I can talk a big talk all day long about how I want to respect and honor Lucy's wishes. I can speak to the wind about how I desire to be upfront and clear with a woman that I'm not the committing type. But if the mesmerizing woman on my arm thinks she can get away with licking her lip like that in front of me after I give her permission to *use* me, she's got another thing coming.

Lucy Spence is a flirt. She had never turned her charm onto me, but I had seen it in action as she had dated different men and had brought them into the office. I was starting to think it was a good thing she has never flirted back with me. I mean, honestly, how could I have resisted her?

Now that she's started...

No. Control yourself, Stone.

Regardless of my attraction to her, my flirty personality, and the fact that she's pretending to be my girlfriend this weekend, Lucy is still my employee. She's still the woman I've seen crying in her office after a breakup, even if she didn't know I was stalker-ish in my watching. Even though I've flirted relentlessly with her, I always knew she'd block my advances. It was fun. A game.

But now...

She's flirting back.

We kissed. No, laid claim to each other is more accurate.

And I... I *like* it.

Too much for comfort.

Maybe she's right to worry. How do I go back to normal after this?

I clear my throat and gently remove her hand off my arm. "I'm going to chat with Jared and Lucas for a second. Why don't you go see what Gracie and my sister are up to? Don't let her ramble your ear off about her educational reform platform she's running for office on. I know she did it earlier today before the wedding."

She tilts her head and scrunches her nose, and I can see questions written all over her face, asking why I'm sending her off, but after a moment, she says, "Oh, okay," and walks through a small crowd of drunk, dancing people before reaching my sister. It's not until Stella meets my gaze from across the way that I realize I was watching Lucy to make sure she got over there safely and didn't get bumped into the pool by some chance.

Any gentleman would do that, right?

Tugging at my white collar (I lost the tie the moment the reception started), I undo one more button, bringing my total to three.

I walk around the opposite side of the pool to meet up with Lucas and Jared.

"'Sup, Stone?" my brother-in-law says, drawing me into a hug and clasping me on the back. "Want a beer?"

"Sure, short stuff."

He reaches into a cooler behind him and tosses me a can, fizzing it all up. I glare at him as he lifts a dark eyebrow, challenging me. Lucas is a tad shorter than I am, but he's still a muscular guy. I've recently taken to calling him "short stuff" just to mess with him.

"Just tease your curls out a bit. Then you'll reach my height." I crack open my drink while dodging Lucas's very physical counter attack as he lunges for my legs. The man's never been great with words, much like the lot of us boys from south Mississippi, but his physical prowess has improved. Probably due to continued boxing matches with Jared.

Speaking of which, the hulk of a man is standing by with his arms crossed, most likely placing a mental wager on who would win out of me and Lucas.

As if reading my thoughts, he laughs. "Money's on Lucas, Stone. I've been training him up well over the past year."

"Truce!" I call. "I take it back, Lucas. You are not short stuff. You are a reasonably tall stack of handsome." The brown-eyed man rolls his eyes.

"Where'd your girl go?" Jared asks, scratching the back of his faded hair. Since getting that haircut, he's looked less like a burly boxer and more like a man who stepped out of a military movie. Think John Cena.

It's intimidating, even to a tall, broad man such as myself.

"My woman," I say with a pointed look, "went to socialize with the girls so that I could see what you two menaces were up to."

Jared raises an eyebrow and bumps Lucas's arm. "You hear what I'm hearing? We are more interesting than his girl. You ever heard of that happening before?"

"I don't get to meet his ladies, much less determine how he acts around them. This is a first for us. Let's not scare the animal off, J."

I shake my head at my two so-called friends. To be honest, they are more like brothers to me. Lucas *is* my brother-in-law, but even before he married my sister two years ago, the man has always been in my life.

"Laugh it up, guys. Y'all are lucky I even brought her home to meet the clownish lot of you." *Lucky indeed*, I chide myself. Not wanting to expand the lie any further, I redirect. "So, Jared. How's it feel to have your little sister married off to that man?" I point to Tate, who is also like another brother to me and closer in age than the two guys standing with me. Tate is a school friend while these two are family-bound friends. "He's the one who was suspended for a week for reworking the art design of our mascot, Rudy the Reindeer, to include nudity and a mullet."

Naturally, I helped him. But I ran faster and was through the fence before the police made it to the scene of the crime—inside our school gymnasium.

Jared shrugs, taking a sip of his drink. "Her decision. She's her own person. Plus, he's matured. We all acted like heathen kids in high school at one point or another."

"Remember that time when…" Lucas begins to tell a story of a prank he and Jared pulled on the principal during their senior prank week. I was a freshman at the time, taking notes to go bigger and better my senior year.

I scan the crowd as they reminisce, my eyes locking with the pretty hazel-eyed, red headed woman who resembles a spring goddess in that open-back baby blue dress. That color looks stunning on her, and I recall her wearing a similar dress, though much less formal with more coverage, when she came into the center to ask about our job listing.

Her hair was up in a styled bun, and though she walked the floors with intentionality in every click of the white heels she was wearing, I could still tell she was nervous. She had one arm slung across her chest holding her other forearm, her fingers lightly tapping to some rhythm in her head, much like she's doing at this moment.

"Hold on, boys. Let me go check on Lucy." The words exit my mouth before I even comprehend they were knocking on the door and asking to leave. I turn my attention back to the guys. Lucas has a dropped jaw while Jared holds his can to his lips, frozen mid-sip.

A miffed laugh from somewhere deep in my throat emerges, and I have the sudden urge to defend myself against the action of *caring*. "Just to make sure my sister isn't harassing her about campaign stuff, that's all. No big deal."

Not that I truly care about Lucy in a romantic way or anything, but I have to act like I do. And any boyfriend worth his salt would look at his woman and know when she is anxious or worried or uncomfortable.

I do care about her as a human. And an employee. And as someone I kissed senseless and *touched* only a couple of hours ago.

Without another glance at my brother-in-law and Jared, I catch Lucy's attention again and begin walking toward her. She seemingly dismisses herself from the women and starts heading in my direction, a relieved smile playing at her lips.

Lucy is relieved at the sight of me...?

That's new, but I guess being in a crowd of unknown people while playing pretend will do that to a person.

When we are about ten feet apart, somebody decides to hit the slow motion button on life's video view.

Tate's grandmother is backing up, holding her phone in front of her as she positions a picture of Abram, Jared and Gracie's son, with Tate. Lucy is walking right into her path, but neither of them are aware of the other. On the other side of Lucy is the deep end of the pool.

I quicken my steps and hold up my hands in an attempt to get Lucy to stop, but she takes one more step forward with a confused expression on her face. Tate's grandma pushes into Lucy, and Lucy wobbles on her heels, arms flailing in circles as she tries to steady herself. Her wide, horrified eyes scream for help before she crashes into the pool with a decent-sized cannonball splash.

Right on time, I stop the older woman from tumbling in herself and steady her before whipping around to the undulating water.

Seconds pass as the pool calms; the gathering of people ceases all conversation. Sunlight reflects off the ever-smoothing surface, sparkling like a million diamonds.

Murmurs begin to fill the silence as kids laugh at the spectacle.

Lucy does not pop up with a head of drenched red curls looking like my little soaked, sad lion. She doesn't break the surface of the water laughing or crying or yelling.

Instead, she rests at the bottom of the pool.

Face up.

Eyes closed.

Chapter 8

Lucy

When I was five years old, Grandpa Neil brought me out to a lake to help him catch brim. The day was sweltering; I wore my swimsuit though I hadn't learned how to swim. Grandpa let me sit in the water on the bank so I could stay cool under the high July sun. He said if I caught a brim then I could also try holding a sparkler during Fourth of July celebrations that night. Determined, I cast out to the lake more times than I could count. On my last cast before we stopped for lunch, my hook got stuck on a mossy stump under the water right off the bank. Grandpa was busy transferring the fish he had caught from a line in the water to a bucket of water to transport back up the hill to his house. I didn't want to bother him, so I thought I would untangle the hook myself. I had done it before with his supervision, and the hook was stuck just paces away. I would still be able to stand.

I set my pole down and began my journey out. The warm water caressed my skin as I took one step, two steps, three…

Suddenly, the mushy ground was no longer beneath me. Before I could even let out a shout, I was submerged under the brown, stinky water. It rushed into my nose, and I gulped in the lake as I attempted to call for help. I flailed my arms and kicked my feet, all to no avail. At one point I broke the surface and screamed, but I sank back under. My head became foggy and I could no longer breathe. My throat screamed for air but it never came. My world shifted from the dark brown of the water to black, and when I woke up, I was in a white, bright hospital room.

My throat burns as I cough up salty water, my head foggy with little recollection as to why I'm in so much pain. I try to sit up to get the water out of me, but I end up flat on my back with jutted pebbles or stones sticking into my back.

Is this a nightmare?

Will someone wake me up?

"Lucy! Oh, thank God. She's breathing again," a voice shouts near my ear. I want to shush the loud man; his booming voice worsens the pain in my head.

I cough again and feel water dribble down my chin. I'm turned onto my side as someone pats my back. They aren't attempting to be gentle about it.

Can't they see I'm in pain? My chest feels like it's been crushed in.

"Open your eyes, Lucy May." Stone. His familiar voice. The only one outside my online sphere who uses my author name. I'm placed onto my back once more.

I swallow, or at least I try to. It's like sandpaper actively filing down the lining of my throat. Focusing all of my thoughts to my eyes, I command them silently to open as Stone asked me to. My lids begin to open as blazing bright light assaults my vision. Immediately, I revolt against his verbal command and my internal one.

If the sun seeks to ruin my sight if I open my eyes, I refuse.

The sun…

Stone.

The smell of a salty pool.

Water in my lungs…

I flutter my eyes open, and this time, I'm greeted with the silhouette of a human hovering over me, mercifully blocking out the intense rays.

Dripping wet dirty blond hair falls in front of anxious baby blue eyes as Stone's face forms in my line of sight. His sharp jawline is clenched as he focuses every ounce of attention he has to offer onto me.

If I were writing this moment into a novel, I might note how he shines brighter than the sun…

But I think I almost drowned, and that's why I'm coughing up salty pool water while lying on concrete, soaking wet at a wedding reception in Dasher Valley, Mississippi. The scene plays out before me: Stone was walking toward me, I was walking toward him, both of us wearing coy expressions. He shifted his eyes away from me for a millisecond, and when he looked back, he tried to tell me something as he held up an arm.

And then I was tumbling into the deep end of the saltwater pool, anxiety clenching me like a straightjacket, making it to where I could do nothing but succumb to the water filling my lungs.

Death almost felt like salvation, though. It was horridly easy to welcome it as a beloved friend to my lonely front doorstep.

"There you are," he says in a whispered sigh as his head falls back and eyes close. His shoulders relax as he exhales; he looks as if he will crumble on top of me from his position on his knees at any given moment.

I try to reply with "here I am" but it comes out as if I'm speaking through a mouthful of gravel. Feels like it, too.

That snaps Stone back to attention after his moment of reprieve. He hollers for someone to bring a cup of water then arches my back as if I'm not over a hundred pounds and sopping wet. He slides an arm underneath me while cradling my head with his other hand. The burly man lifts me into a sitting position, his large hand flexed across my upper back to keep me from falling backwards.

Which is a life-saving action because my head is fuzzy and lightly spinning.

"Can you sit up on your own?"

I don't attempt to answer verbally, opting instead to shake my head, which is a dumb move because now I feel like I'm a spinning top toy.

He adjusts himself into a seated position while still holding onto me. Stone spreads out his long legs and then tugs me backwards against him, letting me use his body as a solid place to land.

Though he's wet, he's warmed from the heat of the sun. And it dawns on me...

He must have pulled me from the pool.

Stone Harper, my playboy boss, saved my life.

His sister, Stella, kneels down in front of me, offering me a glass of water. I reach out my hand to take it and quickly realize I won't be able to hold it due to the ferocious shaking of my arm.

"Give it to me," Stone demands. Stella hands him the glass then backs away to give us space. His ear brushes against mine as he leans forward. He brings the glass of water to my lips and tilts it only a fraction. I suck in the fresh, cool water, my throat burning and chest aching with every gulp, but I can't stop. I'm like a woman withheld from water for days, and though it dribbles down my chin, Stone never pulls the cup away until I turn my head from the glass to indicate I'm finished.

"Better?" he asks in the most gentle, caring tone I've ever heard from him.

I take in a breath and prepare to try and speak again. "Yes," I reply in a clear but gruff tone. "Thank you."

"I'm just glad you're safe." Stone lifts the cup of water to my lips again, and I finish it off while Stella brings another glass to us. This time, I've regained enough control of myself to hold it. I think I could also sit up on my own now, but to be honest, I very much enjoy being pressed against this man.

The man who saved me.

Great. Now I'll have some damsel in distress complex when it comes to Stone Harper...

I roll my eyes and laugh to myself. The motion of laughter sends a pronounced wave of pain through my chest. "Did you... did you have to do CPR on me?"

Stone's voice is hard, and I imagine his full lips pressed into a line. "Yes. You weren't breathing. Thankfully, you spit the water out and came back to me after only seven compressions."

"How long was I in the water?"

"Not long. It was probably fifteen seconds before I realized you weren't coming back up. You didn't even attempt to swim, Lucy." He says that last statement like it personally offends him.

"I don't know how," I say, my voice cracking and throat scratching.

"Still. You could have tried to fight or something. You just... sank. Like the moment your body hit the water, you gave up."

His words attack me, touching something that's buried deep within me. I muster all the anger suddenly swirling within me and attempt to face him though my back is against his chest. "So what? I almost drowned, Stone! And you're sitting here telling me what I should have done in that situation? This has happened to me before, you know? Have you ever heard of something called a trauma response? 'Cause that's what happened. I couldn't fight." *I didn't want to fight,* I add, but only in my mind.

"Not here," he orders against my ear.

I bite my tongue to keep from saying something childish like "you started it" because he's right. I glance around at everyone staring at us and whispering. Some people wear concerned expressions while others look intrigued at our conversation. Those must be the small town gossipers of Dasher Valley. Every town has them.

"Can you take me home?" I ask, resigned and on the verge of crying.

"Like to Juniper Grove? I don't think it's wise to drive that far after you almost drowned." There's a touch of dark sarcasm in his voice, and that's a version of him I'm familiar with. His concern over me and his anger over me not fighting to stay above water are two unknown languages I'm not ready to think about decoding.

"I'm fine," I whine, but the fuzzy feeling that still remains in my head and the way my stomach is starting to churn speaks otherwise. "Okay, fine. Take me to your parent's house."

"I think I want to take you to the clinic."

Stella walks over, offering a hand to me. I take it willingly, ready to get free of Stone. Funny how a bit of anger will transform your desires in a second.

"You want to take her to see Dr. Marlee Gaines?" Stella says in a voice that sounds a bit disgusted as she tugs me up. "She'd be better off going to Hattiesburg to the hospital."

"Just because you and Marlee don't get along doesn't mean I should risk Lucy," Stone barks out, standing behind me with his hands on my waist as he helps his sister hoist me up. My dress is clinging to every inch of my curves, and I feel naked in front of all these people.

Stone must notice this too because he shouts over his shoulder. "Bring me my jacket!"

Lucas walks over holding Stone's black coat jacket and wraps it around me. I tell him thank you as Stone glares at his brother-in-law with disapproval.

"What? Isn't that what you wanted it for?" Lucas asks.

Stone grumbles something about how it's his job to place the jacket over me. Stella laughs and Lucas shrugs sheepishly as if the thought never crossed his mind. From the little conversation I've had with him, he seems like a good man who looks after those around him.

"Can we go now?" I whisper to Stone with a pleading look in my eyes. "Not to the doctor. Just take me back to Marian's for now, please."

He opens his mouth as if to protest, but he relents and places his large hands on my shoulders, guiding me through the whispering crowd of people. I wobble a little and contemplate taking my shoes off, but Stone stops us and picks me up bridal style. I immediately wrap my arms around his neck to keep steady while the once-whispering crowd erupts in applause as if we were the bride and groom of this shindig. My stomach flutters, but this time it's not from feeling sick. It's because the thought of me and my playboy boss tying the knot is as vivid an image as the visions that flickered across my thoughts when we first kissed last night. I itch to turn it all—the wedding night, the twin boys, the explosions and heat—into scenes within my stories.

They are visions I need to wash away in the shower when I get back to the house because they're causing feelings I don't want to have toward the man hauling me away from onlookers, tucked in his arms, the same way I imagine he emerged from the depths of the pool with me as he saved me.

He saved me.

The phrase repeats in my head as Stone opens the door of his truck while still holding onto me.

He saved me.

Stone sets me down in the seat and reaches over me to buckle me up. I smell the salt clinging to his drying hair.

He saved me.

After shutting the door, he walks around to the driver side and hops in, cranking the truck, which roars to life.

He saved me.

And for the first time in a while… I feel alive. Like maybe dying isn't such a good idea after all.

"We're going to the hospital."

Just kidding.

Chapter 9

Lucy

Upon waking to an aching, heaving chest, panting breaths, and a sticky sweat coating my... everywhere, I check the unnamed red flower app on my phone.

Ovulation week.

That's why I had that dream. There's absolutely no other reason that Stone starred in my dreams like a...

Like a...

I groan and smother my face with my pink pillow, resisting the urge to release a built-up scream of sexual frustration and immense guilt. Not to mention my chest is absolutely killing me from the apparent seven CPR compressions I had to be given yesterday. Stone forced me to go to the hospital, and I was checked and cleared with only bruising and no cracked ribs, but the way that man took care of me and watched me with his own two blackened eyes...

It did something to me.

Which is why I think I dreamed of him *doing* something to me...

Or it could have been my body wanting an extension of what we started yesterday morning.

You can't control your dreams, Lucy. It's okay. Give it to God.

Yes, that's what I have to do. What I *must* do. There's no other option right now.

I dig around for my journal, which I had shoved under the bed in case Stone came snooping around the room while I wasn't here. Frantically turning the pages until I'm on a blank one, I begin to jot down my feelings surrounding what happened yesterday and my dream from last night: guilt, pleasure, desire, frustration, anger, disgust... the list goes on and on. I let it all out and give it to the Lord, begging Him to strip away the heated urge to rectify the situation myself.

Or to bop myself right down the hallway where I know he's sleeping.

When I finish my entry, I throw the journal across the room and clench the bedsheets in my fists. Real life synthesizes with the dream, vivid in my head, making everything so. much. worse. Why is it always the dreams you want to forget that linger upon waking?

God, please!

Stone's hands running underneath my shirt yesterday...

No. Stop thinking about it!

His lips tracing my jaw, traveling down my neck and...

Jesus, please! Make it go away!

I kick my legs and jump to my feet, determined to find something to occupy my thoughts. *Anything.* Anything to distract me from the pain pooling in my stomach and the constant ache in my chest that reminds me he saved my life even when I wanted to die.

A gentle knock at my door startles me from the war raging within my head, and Stone's mother says she has breakfast prepared. I respond with a cheerful thank you and let her know I'll be down shortly.

I change into the floral maxi sundress I brought to attend Stone's home church and sit down on my bed, covering my face with my hands. Shame floods my entire being. Outside the guilt over yesterday that I've been locking away inside a vault, it's been months since I've had a dream like *that*. And the last one wasn't as vivid as this one. I didn't know the man who showed up in that dream.

Stone, I know. I learned more than I should have thanks to our slip up yesterday.

That fatal fantasy dream seemed to fill in the gaps of what I didn't learn.

And he's just down the hall...

Gah, stop it, Lucy! You made a mistake but you can't go there anymore.

Picking up my phone from the bedside table, I send a frantic, pleaful text to one woman I know without a doubt will understand me. She's been my confidant in the past when it has come to my slip ups.

> **Me:** I had a *dream* last night, Hads. A dirty one. And I haven't told you this, and I'm sorry for that, but I'm kinda dating the guy I dreamed about. And we totally made out and stuff yesterday morning. I think I would have gone all the way had his mom and stepdad not come into the house.

Bubbles pop up immediately, and I wait three grueling minutes for the text to come through.

> **Hads:** Can I call you? You don't have to talk. I just want to verbally say what I have to say. Text message isn't cutting it.

I click on her contact and bring the phone to my ear. She answers on the first ring.

"Okay, girlfriend. Listen up. First off, I love you. There is nothing inherently wrong with the dream you had. The desires you are feeling are natural. I know you understand this, but I just wanted to be sure I reminded you. You made out with him. Sounds like it went a little further than it should have, but that doesn't mean you are now hopeless and can't recover.

"Secondly, I am praying for you. You, Lorelei, and Braxton were so patient and good to me even when I dissed Christianity. Now, I get to return the favor and pray even more for you than I already have been. It's hard to believe He is there and working even in the midst of your dark thoughts and sins, but He is. Believe me, I know. I can look back and see His hand in my dark times. Especially that blackout summer of mine.

"Thirdly, if you mess up again or end up going all the way, you are still very much loved. The way the Lord loves you, the way I love you, the way your sister loves you, the way your parents love you... It's not diminished or taken away by a mistake. Do you understand me?"

I sniffle, trying to collect my bearings. Tears flow freely down my face as I clutch my free hand over my mouth to stifle my cries. Snot leaks out of my nose and onto my hand. I can't formulate words, nor do I want to try and respond appropriately on the premise someone hears me, so all I say is, "I understand. I love you, Hadley. So much."

I know she loves me. And my family and sister. I know God says He loves me, but honestly, I've doubted that lately. I try not to let the doubts win out, but it's hard when it's so loud and I feel so… *empty*. At least I finally felt alive again as Stone touched me.

"Ditto. Now dry yourself up, listen to some worship music, and steer clear of Taylor Swift for a while, okay? Oh! Or you can turn on some Dolly. That's what I would do. Will you be at church today?"

I laugh at her Taylor suggestion, but I can't deny it's true. "As much as you love Dolly Parton, I'll try the worship music. Actually, I'm in Dasher Valley with my boyfriend. I'll be going to church here today."

"Oh." I hear the shock in her voice. "So, who is this boyfriend of yours that you're all the way down in Dasher Valley?"

My insides twist like strings being pulled into knots over and over again. "Stone," I breathe out after a moment. There's no way I'm telling her this is fake and that I'm getting all hot and bothered over a pretend relationship. *That I let him touch me like that when it's all fake.*

"I see," is all she says. "Have you told Lorelei? Karoline?"

"Not yet." I sigh and plop onto the bed, wiping away excess tears. "Please don't tell my sister. I will eventually. I just need some time to figure things out first." *Time to go ahead and end it before I even need to tell them, that is.*

"'Kay. Well, I need to finish getting ready for church, but I love you and I'm here for you. Reach out if you need me, Luce Goose."

"Love you, Hads. Thanks." I hang up and toss the phone aside.

Finally feeling like I can breathe a little, I thank God for such a wonderful best friend. It's funny that I can actively thank Him or pray to Him when it's on someone else's behalf. I make a mental note to see her as soon as I get back to Juniper Grove and tell her everything. Even if I don't tell Lorelei I'm fake dating Stone, I can tell Hadley. She will understand me. I think.

She's got her life together, now, Lucy. She's not the troubled one in the friend group anymore. You are.

I dismiss the thoughts even as they continue to ring true and make perfect sense to me. Maybe I won't tell her it was a ruse, after all. Besides, it'll be over once we leave here. I can tell her I broke up with him because of the struggle I'm having. Yeah, that's believable.

Shaking my entire body as if it will free me from the tingling energy coursing through me, I blow out a breath of air and stare at my disheveled hair and fired-up, puffy eyes in the stand-up mirror across from the bed. My chest aches with each breath, a constant reminder of the kind of man Stone actually is—one that saves lives. And forces me to go to the hospital even when I don't want to. And takes care of me all evening long by turning on rom-coms and watching them with me, getting me food when I ask, and whipping up delicious hot chocolate simply because I spoke an off-hand thought stating I wanted it. "Okay. We are going to go to the bathroom and wash our face and put on our makeup and forget this dream—or yesterday—ever occurred, okay, Lucy girl? We've got this."

Not even remotely confident in my self-talk, I trudge out into the hallway, lifting a silent, unbelieving prayer that I do not run into Stone until I've had time to cool myself down. The Lord must be listening because I get through my makeup routine, brush my teeth, fix my hair, and make it back to the bedroom without even a peep from Stone or sounds of movement from within his room across from the bathroom.

I descend the stairs after putting on my jewelry and join Marian and Brother Johnny at the breakfast table. "Where's Stone?" I casually ask, willing my face not to heat.

"He's getting ready in our bathroom," Brother Johnny, who is dressed in a suit, says after he pours me a cup of black coffee. "Cream and sugar?"

"Yes, please." It's definitely a sweet coffee kind of day. I mix the cream and sugar into my coffee, watching as the blackness turns to a medium brown. It's soothing, and I begin to feel my shoulders relax.

Right on cue, I hear a door open down the way from the kitchen, and then Stone appears with perfectly styled-back hair wearing those ridiculously hot khaki slim-fit pants with a fitted purple polo tucked in. The lavender color matches my sundress, and we truly look like we are a couple doing the absolute most to sport our coupleness.

"You two have to let me take your picture," Marian pipes up, standing up from her chair and smoothing down her brown skirt with shaky hands. "Actually, Johnny. Can you take it for me? I don't want it to come out blurry."

"Sure can, sweetie. Hand me your phone."

Stone walks up to me wearing that stupid sensual smirk of his, and my body riots to be touched by him. He holds out his hand, which I have no choice but to take. *Ah, the awfulness...* The moment my skin touches his rough hands, the dream I've worked so hard all morning to repress comes back with a valiant roar. "You look beautiful, my little lion."

Flashes of him whispering that nickname into my ear as he nibbled on my lobe guts me.

How?!

How do I go to church when these awful, horrid thoughts that stem from my imagination blended with a morsel of real life keep popping into my head as a reminder of how shameful I can be?

Jesus, please.... Help me take these thoughts captive. I'm trying. Where are You?

"Lucy, hon. Are you okay? You look sick." Marian limps toward me, and I make a note to ask Stone about that later. I'm assuming it has to do with her rheumatoid arthritis. She places the back of her hand to my forehead. "Hm. You're a little warm. Let's take your temperature."

"Oh, I'm fine, Marian. Please don't worry yourself."

Skepticism etches across her face. "Are you sure?"

I nod, and she relents. "Well, get their picture, honey." She playfully elbows Brother Johnny as Stone casually slips his arm around my waist and tucks me into his side. As if the action is second nature, I wrap my arm around his back, turn into him, and bring my left hand to rest flat against his chest.

Brother Johnny takes a few pictures, and when he shows them to me, I'm speechless.

We look *good* together.

Like really good.

The perfect rom-com pairing type of good.

"Send those to me, will ya?" Stone says, patting Brother Johnny on his back. Then he sits down at the table, and we all have an innocent breakfast as if my thoughts don't keep bouncing between imagining pleasurable sins and guilty shame at how hard it is to control my thoughts. Though as the time wears on, I slowly gain control, thinking of everything else under the sun.

I assist Marian in cleaning up the dishes from the table while Stone quickly washes them. When everything is put away, Brother Johnny asks if me and Stone will be riding with him and Marian.

Stone replies that he has other transportation plans for us then takes my hand and leads us outside.

He opens the back door of his truck, and I walk around to hop in the passenger seat, ready to get out of the humid morning heat, but he stops me.

"We are taking the bike, Lucy May."

My jaw drops. "Do what? I don't have a—"

He cuts off my speech by holding up a pale pink leather jacket with a matching helmet. I don't know if I want to smack or kiss the stupid grin off his face. Of all the guys I've dated, none of them has had a bike, and I've always wanted to ride one.

"Are you serious? When did you get these?" I snatch the jacket from his hand and hold it out in front of me. It's genuine leather, the perfect pale pink color, has a golden zipper, and four pockets total.

I'm in love.

With the jacket. Not the man.

Stone chuckles, takes my new jacket from me, and then helps me put it on. "I bought it the evening after you agreed to come down here with me. I figured I'd take you riding at some point and wanted you to have appropriate gear. Though," he moves to stand in front of me and looks down at my sandaled feet, "I would prefer it if you slipped off the open-toed shoes."

"Say no more." I bound up the stairs and into the house, switching my white sandals for white sneakers. It's cool. I'll look like my sister rocking dresses and sneakers.

Dress.

"Shoot."

"Lucy," Stone shouts from outside. "Don't worry about the dress. It's long enough."

How in the world does that man read me when he can't even see me?

I meet him back outside beside the black motorcycle. "What do you mean it's long enough?"

"As you get onto the bike, tuck the insides of your dress into your thighs and sit on it. Your dress will ride up some, but it won't be inappropriate."

"You've driven many women in dresses on this bike, haven't you?" The tease in my voice is overshadowed by a trace of bitter jealousy.

Nope. Nope. Nope. He is not mine. This is fake. I'm not allowed to be jealous.

He shrugs and tucks my hair behind my ears. "None quite like you, Little Lion."

I stare into his eyes, which are brightly illuminated by the morning sun. He kisses my cheek, and I attempt to push him away but he pulls me into a hug. "Mom is walking out the door. Act like you love me, darlin'."

I wrap my leathered arms around him and lean my head against his chest. For the singular moment, I give myself permission to close my eyes and breathe him in.

Love.

My heartbeat quickens. No, I don't *love* Stone. That's impossible. It's just lust... Good old fashioned desire at play. Nothing more.

"Get to church, you two." Marian laughs then climbs into Brother Johnny's vehicle with his assistance.

"See y'all there," he says with a wave, and then he hops in and they drive off.

"You ready?" Stone asks, handing me the helmet. I smooth down my bangs, thankful I straightened them instead of wearing them curly like the rest of my hair. I'll have to pull my hair into a ponytail once we get to church, but I'm not giving up this opportunity. I place the helmet onto my head then Stone secures it into place for me. He knocks the top of it while grinning and commenting on how cute I look. I bask under the praise even though I know I should retort with a pushback or something. He slips on his jacket and secures his helmet before hopping onto the bike. I pause for a moment to admire the image, but then he turns around and offers his hand to help me on.

I oblige and do as he instructs once I'm on. It's not entirely comfortable, but I shouldn't flash anyone as we ride.

"Hold on to me tight, Lucy May," Stone says before cranking the motorcycle. It roars to life, and my entire body vibrates. I snake my arms around him and clutch my hands together, leaning into his body. I swear I hear him groan and say "there you go" before he revs and shifts, then off we go.

The air swishes around us as we drive down the gravel road and turn onto the highway. As he increases speed, the trees zip by us, and I've never felt more alive and free as I do at this moment. The wind feels as if it's hugging me, telling me I'll be okay. Like it's asking me to release all my troubles to it to be blown far, far away.

But then again, I think I'm only okay because of the man I'm clinging to. He's reignited a spark of joy within my life through his playfulness. He's sparked my heart back to life through his lips. And currently, his bergamot and cacao scent fuddles my brain as it infiltrates my screened helmet. I could go on smelling this for the rest of my existence and not tire of it...

We take a curve, our bodies leaning in tandem. My hands splay across his stomach as I hold on, and I find myself counting the abs I feel underneath his dress shirt. *One. Two. Three. Four. Five. Six. Seven...*

He slows down, pulling off to the side of the road, and stops the bike. He lifts the front of his face shield as he turns around, wearing a satisfied smirk. "Lucy May, are you feeling me up on our way to church?"

Heat blazes across my face, but I shake my head in denial and slight guilt. He only laughs, and as he lowers the shield, he says, "Keep it up. I don't mind. I'll flex for you, baby girl."

I slap my hands on his waist with a little more force than necessary as the nickname echoes around my brain. If he ends up giving me a "good girl" at some point, all resolve and restraint I'm clinging to may snap.

Yeah, I'm the girl who likes those types of nicknames and preens under praise. I personally do not feel infantilized or turned off by it like my twin.

Stone faces forward, chuckling to himself as he revs the bike and takes off. I wrap my arms tightly around him, willing them to stay put instead of exploring. He's not going as fast as before, and within moments, he takes to driving with one hand and places his other on top of my hands. When his pinky finger intertwines with mine, I once more wonder how in the world I'm supposed to pretend all of this did not happen come tomorrow morning.

The rest of the ride isn't long enough.

We arrive at the small, backwoods country church within a matter of minutes, and I already miss being pressed up against him, the wind caressing my neck, and the feeling of absolute freedom as we took the backroads.

Once we're parked and have our helmets off, Stone plays with my hair. "How was it?"

"Exhilarating," I breathe. "I should learn to drive it and get my own."

"Mm," Stone hums as he fingers my bangs. "I can totally see you in a black leather suit riding a pink bike. I support this new endeavor of yours."

"Stone!" I lightly tap his arm as he chuckles. "We are at church." *Not going to mention me copping a feel back there though...*

"Seems so," he says, all humor suddenly falling away.

I drop my arm to my side. "Do you want to talk about it?"

"About what?"

"Your change of demeanor just now."

He ruffles the top of my head, messing up whatever fixing he had done. "It's nothing, Little Lion. Let's go in, shall we?"

I nod, dropping the subject, and follow him into the little brick church.

The inside is as small as the outside. There is a rectangular foyer area with enough space for two elderly gentlemen to greet us.

"Stone! It's good to see you again." The balding gentleman shakes his hand and looks over at me. "Who's the pretty little lady with you?"

"My girlfriend, Lucy Spence." Stone's tone is flat even though he's smiling, and I suddenly feel out of place. Like I don't belong at his side bearing such a title. If I could shrink, I would.

I shake the older man's hand as he introduces himself as Ronnie, stating he used to hold Stone as a baby in the nursery. He then begins to go on a memory trail regarding hunting trips with Stone's father. Stone stiffens at my side, his hand finding mine. He laces our fingers together, clenching tightly as if my hand's the rail he's gripping onto for safety and stability.

Maybe he's not upset with me?

Gah, Lucy. Who cares? Quit overthinking things. This is fake. Just because we kissed and touched doesn't mean I'm his girlfriend. He said he doesn't commit right to your face. And that's why nothing more will happen regardless of your deadly mental imaginations in the depths of sleep.

"Well, Mr. Ronnie. It was good to see you. We better go find our seats." Stone drags me behind him as he bolts from the foyer and into the small sanctuary.

The walls are bare with stained glass windows for lighting. Wooden pews with beige cushions line either side of the sand-colored carpeted floor. The space is homey and comforting, or it would be comforting if I actually wanted to be here.

Wanting to be in church and needing to be in church are two diametrically opposed concepts within my mind.

Stone stops mid-way to the front of the room and whispers in my ear. "Mom would have us sit up front with her, but I'd much prefer it here. What do you want?"

I nod my head toward the back, and a slow smile creeps onto his face. He turns on his heel and then drags me toward the back. Once we sit in the last row tucked in the corner like two teenage lovers trying to hide the fact we'd like to hold hands during the service, he finally breathes deeply.

"Stone, what's going on? You've walled yourself up since I mentioned we were at church." I continue to grip his hand even when he flexes his fingers like he might pull away. "I'm not trying to help you, okay? You can feel however you want to feel. I just want to know."

He pegs me with a sharp stare, then giving in, he gestures around the building. "This. Being back here. I haven't been back to this church since two summers ago when I was home from college."

"Why does it bother you? Isn't it your home church?"

He shrugs, shifting his gaze to the white popcorn ceiling. "Maybe it's not just this church. Maybe it's church in general. I didn't go while in college, and I haven't been to one since settling down in Juniper Grove."

"What's keeping you away?"

"Lucy," Stone sighs, pinching the bridge of his nose. "Can we not talk about this right now?"

His tone is low, defeated, and a tinge frustrated like he's a bear preparing to swipe. I need to back down. "Of course. Thanks for sharing with me. I'm with you, okay?" Not to mention I've only been going to church because Hadley and Grandma Netty expect to see me there. I try to listen to the sermons, but lately, everything is lost on me.

Or maybe I just don't care to understand.

Brother Johnny stands behind the rectangular pulpit, greeting everyone and making morning announcements. I notice Gracie, with Abram on her hip and Jared by her side, arrives a little late, heading to the front to sit by Gracie's family. I remember them from the wedding yesterday. The service continues with old hymnals and then an offering. When the message begins, and Brother Johnny begins to speak on purity of heart and mind, my stomach suddenly begins to revolt against breakfast.

"I don't want to talk to you about purity culture today," the preacher says, looking over the small, gathered crowd. "Purity, at its core, runs deeper than whether or not you sleep with someone outside of the confines of the marriage bed. Purity is about your heart."

I swallow and rip my hand from Stone, conviction raining down on me like crashing waves over the dreamland grave I found myself in this morning.

Does Brother Johnny know? Did I make... *noises?* In my sleep?

Surely not. Lorelei has never told me I've talked in my sleep.

I know he wasn't in the house when Stone laid me down on his bed.

Oh, crap! Are there cameras?!

My breath comes in shorter, quicker spurts as Brother Johnny continues preaching. "God knows we make mistakes. It doesn't mean you are ruined or used or no longer welcomed in His court."

The words enter my head but they don't resonate within my heart.

So many people who call themselves Christian condemn girls like me. Why do you think I've had to hide it from my readers? They don't want to read closed-door romance books written by a tainted woman. I've seen firsthand what some readers do to Christian authors who dare to explore the nuances of lust and attraction within their closed-door novels. It's nasty.

If so many people who claim to love the Lord hold the opinion that women aren't allowed to make mistakes when it comes to sexuality, then how does God still welcome girls like me? Why would

He even want me when He has so many other perfect Christians to choose from?

"Lucy." Stone's lowered voice breaks my internal spiraling. I whip my head toward him, and I can see my own crazed disposition reflected in his glass eyes. "Do you want to get out of here?"

"Okay," I stammer, wishing I could disappear into the frigid air particles around me. He grabs my hand, and we duck out. I don't look back to see if Brother Johnny is watching. I follow Stone, willingly running away from this swarm of confusing condemnation.

BEAT FOUR

THE HOOK // "GUILTY AS SIN?"

A poem by Lucy May – July 13th

"BEDROOM GRAVE"
your hades touch
set my body aflame
night after night
as you screamed my name
if lovers of old
could awaken from eternal slumber
we'd be atop the pedestal
where they once were held in wonder
as we look down
from our elevated view

the skies darken and rain ceases the flames
it's not a pedestal we perch upon
but a graveside dug for two

Chapter 10

Stone

What happened in Dasher Valley didn't stay in Dasher Valley.

It followed me to Juniper Grove. Into my house. Tucked itself under the bedsheets with me. Invaded my dreams like the boogeyman.

For the past week, I've stared rapturously at Lucy while in staff meetings. I've had to seize my own hands when they've wanted to hold her as I've spoken alone with her in my office. I've bitten my tongue to refrain from flirting shamelessly with her.

Not to mention I've caught her checking me out time and time again. I've caught her licking her lips when we've made eye contact across the gym. Heck, we've even had Jeanie, my secretary, make vague comments about how me and Lucy can't keep our attention off of each other.

People are noticing.

And weirdly enough, they're shipping us.

Not accusing me of nepotism.

So yeah. I'm done tiptoeing around Lucy.

I have a plan to rectify the situation, but I will only go through with it if she agrees. I'll be forthcoming with her, and while I fully expect her to shoot this down, at least I can say I tried. Maybe after she tells me no, I can let these insufferable feelings go and go find another woman to play around with. One who's not my employee.

One I haven't grown to care about—at least in an I-enjoy-her-company-and-don't-want-to-see-her-sad type capacity. Because outside of the lingering stares and stolen moments across rooms, she still sports that same melancholic expression. Like the world has taken away her favorite toy and smashed it to pieces.

Maybe... *Just maybe...* This insane idea of mine will bring some joy back into her life.

I square my shoulders and knock on her door. She hollers at me to come in, so I do, immediately going to stand beside her desk.

"I've got an idea."

Lucy groans and rolls her eyes as she stops typing on her computer. While we've stifled our desires since we've been back—and I say ours because she's been as stealthy as a slow runner attempting to steal second base—when we are alone like this together, she keeps me at arms length, treating me like I'm her annoying male best friend.

Which I've acted like on all accounts to be honest.

I had so much fun with her back in Dasher Valley, and well, though our fake dating time ticked to an end, I wish it would have lasted a little longer. I didn't even get to kiss her in front of my family.

So naturally, I'm making it happen.

"What's your grand vision this time? Please don't adjust my Halloween Bash event plan again…"

I laugh at the worried tone in her voice. "I've only changed parts of it once. Don't be dramatic."

She mumbles under her breath as she turns her attention back to whatever she was working on. Her curly red hair is up in a messy bun, but the moment I focus on it, I imagine it floating around her pale face at the bottom of a pool.

I shake the recurring nightmare from my head and remind myself she's here in front of me, alive and breathing and fiery as ever.

"What if we started fake dating again?"

The typing sounds cease as she whips her head around to look at me. I'm leaning against her desk, the side of it uncomfortably jabbing into my backside, but I remain in this casual, laid-back pose with my arms crossed because, well, for the sake of sounding like a conceited meat-head, I know I look good like this.

"Huh?" Her wide eyes and raised brows attempt to draw a laugh from me. She's sort of adorable when she's taken with surprise.

"I have a meeting coming up in a few days with some investors, and I know they'll be bringing their wives along to the dinner. I thought it'd be nice to bring along my *girlfriend* to show them I can commit."

"But I'm not your girlfriend." She blinks a few times as if clearing away a daze. "And you can't commit for whatever reason you choose not to disclose to me."

"Duh. But you could continue to be my *fake* girlfriend. We could even set ground rules if you want since 'what happens in

Dasher Valley stays in Dasher Valley' isn't applicable to the foreseeable future."

"But why wouldn't we terminate it again after the meeting?" She tilts her head and brings a pen she'd picked up at some point to her lips and bites on it.

"The fourth of July will be coming up two days after that. Dasher Valley puts on a huge community event, and my family would like me to bring you back for it. My sister's birthday is in August. Then there's my birthday, Halloween, Thanksgiving, Christmas. Your sister's wedding and coronation. I want a date for my side of events. Don't you want a date for yours?"

She stares at me, pen between her teeth, as if I'm speaking a foreign language.

Finally, she removes the pen and speaks with caution in her voice. "You don't think I could find a real date to those events? And couldn't you...?"

"Of course we could. But I think we both had a lot of fun back in Dasher Valley, and to be honest, I don't want to settle down with anyone right now. You'd be a safe option for me."

"But then you're preventing me from finding a man who is ready to settle down. Isn't that a little selfish of you to ask?" She crosses her arms.

Oof. She's right. The thought never entered my mind as I was too consumed with thoughts of kissing her more. I relax my hands at my side and stand up straight. "You're right. I'm sorry. I didn't think about that."

"All is forgiven," she says. Then, she stands and faces me. "Fine. I'll do it. But only because I've had second thoughts about life after I almost drowned. And I owe you big time for saving me."

"Lucy," I groan and pinch the bridge of my nose as I close my eyes to collect myself. "I've told you time and time again that you do not owe me for pulling you out of that pool. You've brought me coffees, have organized my office, and continue to ask what else you can do to make up for it. Your life has no value attached to it. It's precious and invaluable. While I appreciate the things you've done, it isn't and never has been necessary."

"But still," she says in a lowered voice. We meet each other's eyes. Words go unspoken as I search hazel-green irises that are sparkling as if they're on the verge of releasing tears. She looks at me as if I'm her hero, and though, I guess, technically I am, the thought of her viewing me as such disturbs me.

Not because I don't want to be a hero to her but because I am certainly not a man worthy of a title like that.

I even dragged her out of church because I was uncomfortable with the sermon. That's not manly hero status. Granted, she looked as perturbed as I felt, but still. Who was I to take her away? God might not love me, but surely He loves Lucy.

"What will we do here at work? Are we faking it for everyone? If we start going out as a couple to town events and dinners and such, you know word will get around."

Something else I didn't think about, but to be honest, it's the least of my concerns. Everyone here seems to be cool with my interest in her. I like the idea. More public time equals more kissing and touching time. *And I love the way she feels beneath my fingertips...* "We will play pretend here, too."

"Aren't we a real couple at that point? The only time we won't be faking it is when we are off on our own."

I shrug and smirk. "More time to flirt with you openly."

"Incorrigible," Lucy huffs and shakes her head. But as she turns away, I see a smile spread across her freckled face.

"That was easier than I expected it to be," I mention. Though I can't seem to shake Lucy's hold on me right now, I know I will eventually. Playing pretend, keeping everything titled fake, will make it easier for the both of us to part ways when that wall demanding I let her go hits me. "I do enjoy spending time with you, Lucy. We can be friends. Good friends."

"With benefits?" she adds, arching an eyebrow.

I shrug. "I'll let you set the rules. Fair?"

She keeps her attention on her computer but tugs at the high-neck portion of her sleeveless lavender shirt. "But I'm a Christian, Stone. And so are you, right? Isn't friends-with-benefits kind of against the rules?"

Her point is valid, and it stirs penitence in my soul. But not enough to backtrack. "Like I said, we can set rules, though you know I despise rules."

"You live to break them," she mutters. Then louder, she adds, "Like I said, I've reevaluated things. Maybe I don't want to settle down right now, either. And I enjoy spending time with you, too."

"You? The romance author who writes happily-ever-afters time and time again? You don't want to settle down?"

"Mr. Harper, have you read my books?"

Her voice isn't shocked or embarrassed. She's intrigued.

"I've read a few," I admit. All eight of them, but she doesn't need to know that. "You're an outstanding author. And I've read enough to know I've got ample ammo to fire at you within the flirting range. You seem to like it when men do certain *things*."

This snaps her attention back on me. Her lips part slightly in a moment of shock. Or is it horror? Then she asks, "Like what?"

"For starters, shoving the heroine against a wall and claiming her as his own, which I effectively accomplished last week. I guess you'll be finding out the rest soon enough, *baby girl*."

She blushes but doesn't respond. Instead, she redirects. "Let's go ahead and set ground rules and boundaries."

"Boundaries like... I'm free to kiss and touch you? I'm very much a physical touch man, Lucy May. You know that." I step toward her and run a finger alongside her jawline, hovering just above her freckled skin. Heat radiates from the proximity.

"N-no," she stutters, her face flushing harder. "Only in front of people. To sell our relationship. No lips or hands in private. We can't have a repeat of Dasher Valley."

I pout my bottom lip. "But what about when we are back in Dasher Valley?"

"No," she says, but a hint of a smile appears. She quickly schools her expression and points to the chair across from her desk. "Sit down over there. I don't like you hovering over me."

I do as she says while she pulls a small notebook and pen from her rounded white purse that looks more like a mini backpack. "I'm going to write these down, so remember, if it goes on the list, it must be abided by."

She opens the phone-sized notebook as a smile plays at her lips with each flip of the page. Curiosity gets the best of me.

"What's the notebook for? Besides signing me to my ultimate doom by implementing," I feign a gag, "rules."

She shakes her head, unamused. "It's my Idea notebook. For when I get story ideas on the go."

"Can I see it?"

Lucy hugs the book to her chest with a shocked expression. "You never ask an author to see her ramblings. *Never.* It's a chaotic place and would make zero sense to you. It's Wonderland."

"My bad." I hold up my hands. "Was just thinking it would allow me insight into who you are. You know, to sell this fake relationship thing. Besides, I've told you once and I'll say it again: I can handle your rabbit hole of a brain."

She shakes her head, her unruly curls flying around with the motion. I might be a little obsessed with her hair in its natural state. I want to run my fingers through it just to get them stuck. Then, I would tug, tilting her chin up to me. Her lips would slightly part, and I'd...

Nope.

Keep your mind PG-13, dude. Lord knows you'll never manage PG.

"We will sell it well enough," she mumbles under her breath, setting the notebook back down and glancing away as she sips from her bottle of water.

"If you're talking about our chemistry, that is a correct assessment."

She raises her eyebrows and nods as she picks up her pen. Satisfied, I lean back in the chair and wait for her to continue listing her rules. She begins writing, and after a moment, she meets my eyes. "Okay. So number one, no touching or kissing in private. Only in front of people and only when necessary."

I grin, already planning for loads of time in front of people. "I agree."

"Number two. No getting involved with other people while we're together."

"I wouldn't dream of it, sweet cheeks." She must really think I'm a rake. I date a lot, sure, but I would never two-time a girl. Even if our relationship is for falsified purposes.

"Ack." She fakes a gag, pointing her finger to her opened mouth. "And that's number three. No gross couple names. If we adopt couple names, the other must approve of it."

She scribbles down the rules as I throw a list of names her way. "Honey bun? Snookums? Luce Goose?"

"That last one is reserved for my best friend, Hadley," she states with a pointed glare. "She'll hunt you down herself, pregnant and all, if you try to use it."

"Noted," I say. "Then how about sugar pie?"

She glares at me as I crack up.

"Fine, fine. I'll stick to Little Lion."

"Number four," she begins.

I release an exaggerated sigh, folding my arms across my chest. "This is getting pretty long."

"Number. Four," she repeats with emphasis, her eyes drawn to the movement of my arms. She tilts her head in consideration before blinking several times and looking back at her notebook. "When it's over, I broke up with you. Not the other way around."

"Now why you gotta be like that, Lucy May?"

She drops her shoulders while letting out a breath. "Because, Granite, if I break up with you, your family won't have a reason to hound you about marriage and dating. If you break up with me, then they'll be on your case again."

Hm. She has a point there, though it'll hurt the ego a bit. But also... "Granite? I like it. Better than Pebbles. It's approved. And you don't know my family. They'll hound me either way. It'll be my fault you broke up with me."

"That doesn't seem fair." She finishes writing rule four down before dropping the pen and focusing on me. "Have you given them a reason to believe you would be the cause of every failed relationship?"

"Depends on who you ask," I respond through a tightened smile. My mother and sister would be lenient on me, but they still say I'm the common denominator problem. The rest of Dasher Valley? Well, let's just say I have a certain reputation I haven't bothered to dismantle.

Lucy's tone softens as she says, "Well, I'll come up with a good reason that shifts all the blame onto me. Sound good?"

"You'd do that for me?" I... I don't know if I want to do that to her, but the simple fact that she'd be willing speaks volumes about her heart.

Also, it makes me wonder—as I did on the trip up here—who once decided she was the scapegoat? Or is she just *that* kind?

Though she's a kind woman, I don't think she'd take to being a doormat willingly...

She smiles. "I don't know why, but it seems I would. Maybe it's because you sign my paychecks. Maybe I feel a little bad for dumping crab all over you at lunch. Maybe I regret ruining your pretty face with a cast iron skillet." Her eyes search my face for faint lingering bruises.

I laugh, despite my growing concern for her. "So be it," I remark. I'll decide later if this is the best course of action or not.

Lucy stands and moves beside me, her white skirt swishing and tempting me with wild thoughts. "This is it for now. If I think of any more, I'll be sure to tell you." She sets the notebook down and holds out the pen to me. "But first, sign the list here. My sister is a lawyer and future queen of an entire country, after all."

I take the pen from her, brushing her fingers as I do. I narrow my eyes at her before signing my fun away.

"Will you sign your fun away, too?" I ask.

She rolls her eyes at me before signing below my name. "There. It's a gentlemen's agreement."

"Should we shake on it?" I stand up, offering her my hand. She looks as if it will attack her.

"Not a chance. You'll linger or tug me close to you or something weird."

I click my tongue. "How are you already catching on to my schemes, Lucy May?"

"Bro. What in the world are you reading?"

I lift my eyes from the words on the paper that were painting a scene of the male main character taking care of the female main character while she's sick with the flu. Lucy tends to write about men taking care of women a lot. Is that something she wishes would be done for her?

Yes, I'm taking notes.

However long this lasts between us, until the feelings I have dissipate, as they always do, I'm going to make it worthwhile for the both of us.

My best friend from college, Stanton Holloway, sits down across the table from me at Books and Beans. It's a small, square building with half of the space devoted to bookshelves and the other half a cafe. Lucy's books are somewhere in the stacks. I've asked Emma Jane, the full-time barista here, to restock them every time I notice she runs out.

I set the cartoon cover book down. "A how-to manual to fully win my girlfriend's heart."

Stanton's pretzel-colored eyes bulge. Speaking of pretzels, *when will my food be here?* "You have a girlfriend that you're actually calling your girlfriend *and* you're reading a romance novel to try and win her over?" He pauses and waves his hand in front of my eyes. "Who are you and what have you done with my roguish mate?"

Did I mention Stanton is British? He came here on foreign exchange, fell in love with a girl in college, and decided to plant roots. On their wedding day, I pulled his now-wife, Candace, aside and thanked her for keeping my friend here in Juniper Grove instead of running off to England with him like pretty much any other woman would have done. However, I told her I'd miss mine and Stanton's nickname from college (courtesy of the ladies): S&S, which stood for Sexy Stone and Smoldering Stanton. Candace, graciously, said we could keep it even though Mr. Smolder now has a wife that he could turn all his golden-eyed goodness onto.

I swat his hand away though the grin spreading across my face is one-hundred percent real. Should I continue letting him think I have a girlfriend or should I tell him the truth? Decisions, decisions...

He's my best mate, as he said, so I have to be honest. "The author," I point to the book in front of me, "is my fake girlfriend for all intents and purposes for the foreseeable future."

"That's the same woman who is your event coordinator?"

"And also my assistant director, yep." I pop the "p" and lean back, crossing my arms while gauging his reaction. He narrows his eyes and rolls his bottom lip into his mouth, contemplating the situation. He's going to tell me it's, and I quote, "a bloody ridiculous idea," but that's when I'll shrug and smirk and change the topic of conversation.

"Stone, this is a bloody brilliant idea." A wide smile stretches across Stanton's slim face as he steeples his hands and leans onto the table. At that time, Emma Jane sets down my turkey melt, but I can't stop staring at Stanton.

"I'm sorry, but what?"

"Look at you, mate." He gestures to my book. "You're reading her book in the middle of a coffee shop on your lunch break."

"I don't have lunch breaks," I interrupt, trying to change where I think this conversation is headed. "I'm my own boss."

"Be that as it may, you're reading your fake girlfriend's romance book. And this isn't the first one you've read, is it?" He gets a wicked gleam in his eyes as he leans forward further, placing his hands flat on the table.

"No," I mumble, looking at the big, pointy-leaf plant by the doorway instead of at my best friend who I can't lie to even if it would save my life. "I'm re-reading them because she hasn't published any more yet. Though it sounds like her new series will be fantasy, so that'll be a change."

Stanton lets out a long whistle as he sits back in the wooden chair and tosses his hands behind his head. "You're down bad, mate."

"I'm not down anything. Did you catch the word 'fake' before the word girlfriend? It's a dating-for-convenience type situation. It benefits both of us in our stage of life currently. Nothing more."

"Nothing more?" He raises one dark brown eyebrow.

"No. I mean, sure, she's stunning. And she's funny. She challenges me in ways no other woman has before. She likes me well enough, but it's only in the way that I like her. You know, lonely companionship and all." I pause and scratch my head. "But I don't want to hurt her, and I know she eventually wants to get married. I can't stop her from that. If she meets a guy along the way while we are faking it, I'll let her go. I'm not the marrying type. She knows that, which is why we set up ground rules. I think she just wants to have a little fun, too, you know? I want to give her a good time and make her smile."

Emma Jane arrives with Stanton's order, and I finally take a bite of my sandwich that has cooled.

Stanton's animated expression from earlier is replaced with a subdued, contemplative look. "If my advice is worth anything to you, which I think it is, you have two options: let Lucy go or make her yours. Really yours. Don't play with her heart, Stone. We aren't in college anymore." He grabs a spoon and stirs his soup while I chew over his words.

Is it really playing with her heart if she agreed? I'm attracted to her but I have no plans to settle down with her. I know these desirous feelings will go away one day. That goes to show she can be attracted to me with no plans to settle down with me, right? That she'll get tired of me eventually if I don't tire of her first.

"Everything will be okay. We are both grown, consenting adults. Like I said, if she finds someone, we will call everything off."

"What if it's too late by then?"

I look at him as if his accent changed the meaning of his words.

"What if you have fallen for her? Are you ready for another heartbreak like that?"

Stanton is the only person who knows what truly went down between me and Lacey back on graduation night. No, he doesn't know her nor was he there, but he's the only person I've confided in about the entire story.

"My heart is made of stone." I grin at my stupid joke and then chomp another bite out of my sandwich. Stanton stares blankly at me. "But for real. I haven't fallen for a woman in over five years. It's not going to start now. We are simply entertaining each other for a little while. It's not too different from other setups I've had.

Except I know Lucy, and I won't be doing much in the physical department outside of setting the world on fire with our kisses." *Anything else, that is...*

Lucy made a good point stating we are both Christians and shouldn't fool around. She's right, and I want to respect her wishes regardless of what my body wants.

"That's good," he remarks with a thoughtful nod. "You should really cut out the sex outside of marriage stuff anyway. Don't connect a woman's heart to you unless you plan to hold it carefully."

I shake my head, feeling a familiar tug of conviction. I know that the Lord says to save sex for marriage, but I don't think He fully understands how hard it is to wait when women throw themselves at you. Maybe He does. I guess I can't know for sure. Deep down, I know it's wrong. I know the Bible says to wait. Heck, science says to wait. Bonding hormones and all. I've tried to stop. The flesh is always winning, though. It's consensual, and I get tired of fighting it. It's not like God truly cares about me anyways.

I can't talk to anyone about it, either, because I'll just be judged. In fact, I've stopped going to church because it feels like every time I step into one, I'm silently judged for the actions they have no idea I've committed.

Like with that stupid sermon Brother Johnny preached last Sunday.

Which begs the statement, maybe people really do know. That's what a whispered voice in my head says.

Nothing is ever private business in a small town.

Chapter 11

Lucy

Who knew campaigning was such a gruesome task?

After spending most of the day going door-to-door with Stella and her insanely supportive husband—oh my gosh, the puppy dog energy rolling off Lucas Grady today—I'm beat.

And I'm now the proud owner of a new memorized spiel:

"Hi, I'm Lucy Spence, and I'm here on behalf of Stella Grady, Independent candidate for Mississippi's 4th Congressional District. I'd like to speak with you today regarding state educational reform and congressional term limits." Stella said the latter one would really get people talking, and that's when we could hit them with the former, her true passion, educational reform.

If I never have to say those words again, I'd die a happy woman. Though I have to admit, hanging out with Stella and seeing such a force of a woman at work was inspiring. Maybe I could write a book about her one day.

I take a gulp of water as sweat rolls down my back, and I frown, wishing for my air conditioned apartment and darkness and aloneness.

But that desire is obliterated in two seconds as I remind myself that this is *good*. It's *good* I'm in Dasher Valley for the Fourth of July. It's *good* I'm not alone, hulled up in my apartment numbing my brain by watching television dramas, listening to triste Taylor Swift songs, or losing myself in unrealistic happy-ever-after novels.

Because on the days that Stone and I aren't together for an event or random date—though there has only been one of those, and I suspect it's because he didn't want to go to the theater alone as a man to see a romantic comedy—that's what I do. I also write, and that is an analgesic, too, I guess. Building up fake worlds with fake people with fake conflicts and fake happiness that are forced by the powers that be to fall into love.

My phone buzzes in the back pocket of my mini jean skirt with white stars painted on, and I pull it out to find my sister calling me. I check the time and, while it's a little after noon here, it must be the wee hours of the morning in Korsa.

I hope she's okay...

I shuffle off of the front porch of Marian's house and weave through a few people standing around chatting until I'm far enough away to answer the phone without a ton of background noise. "Lorelei? You good?"

A yawn answers back. "Yeah, I'm good."

I stare at Stone, who is wearing stars and stripes Chubbies shorts that look exactly like they sound: one side stars with the other stripes. He laughs at something his newly married friend, Tate, says, and the way his blond hair bounces as he shakes his head in laughter, the sunlight creating a golden hue, mesmerizes me. The tanned man in a tight white t-shirt is a sight to behold. Anyone with a sense of vision would agree. Heck, even if a person was blind, they'd still be able to tell Stone Harper was the epitome of the predetermined Roman god by his heavenly, otherworldly scent. Maybe that's the writer in me running wild, but the man's scent—something akin to stardust and lightning and the rings spinning around Saturn—lingers in my mind after the long drive down from Juniper Grove yesterday evening after work.

Don't even get me started on the kisses and light touches he's given me since the moment we were in the presence of other people.

To keep up a dating contrivance, that's all.

"Uh, Lucy? Are you there?"

Oh, crap. "Oh, yeah. Hey, Lor. What's up? Why are you calling me when the sun isn't up for you?"

"Earth to Lucy. I just told you why."

I chuckle, my gaze still stamped on Stone. As if he heard me think his name, he glances my way and tilts his head. I wiggle my fingers in a wave to let him know all is well, and then he winks at me and blows me a kiss.

Even though I'm screaming internally at the cuteness, I don't catch the kiss. I let it fly right past me and into the woods on the side of the quaint home.

Because I'm here as his *fake* girlfriend.

Fake. Fake. Fake.

Remember that, Miss Falls Too Hard and Too Fast.

I turn my back to the nuisance. "Sorry. I was looking for a spot outside to talk with you away from people."

"Where are you?"

I rub my elbow with one hand as I grip the phone at my ear with the other. I haven't told my sister about this arrangement I have with Stone. Heck, I haven't told Hadley anything more about us after I told her I "called it off." She doesn't know we are "back together."

Nobody knows but me and him.

And apparently his best friend back in Juniper Grove, but that's all.

Even the player confides in his closest friend. And you can't even bring yourself to tell your twin. Tsk, tsk. What a mess you are...

I'm ashamed. It's as simple as that. I am Lucy May Spence. Voted Most Beautiful, homecoming queen, and prom queen of Juniper Grove High School. I was a cheerleader in college as I pursued my degree in creative writing with a minor in business. I cheered for Stone as he started on the football team his sophomore year when I was a senior.

I've dated. A lot. And I've never had to enlist a man to pretend to want me for the sake of having someone on my arm at functions and events.

Granted, they've pretended on their own in the past. As much as I've dated, I've experienced heartache for at least half the time because of lying, manipulative men.

But that's the thing. Stone hasn't lied to me. He's been completely upfront about his intentions and purposes...

And I went along with them.

I am *actively* going along with them as I stand on this green grass in his mother's yard trying to figure out what to tell my twin.

"I'm in Dasher Valley for a Fourth of July celebration." There. The truth. Most of it, anyway.

"All the way down there? With who? Did you go by yourself?" Lorelei's deep lilt indicates her suspicion. She sounds like she's put on her investigative hat. *Her and those stupid crime shows she loves so much...*

"No. I'm with my boss."

"Huh. Are you dating him now?"

I cough several times at her blunt response, but what else should I expect from her? She never holds back from speaking her observations. I love that about her even though it gets me in hot water sometimes. "Um, yeah. I guess I am..."

There. Still truth. Just leaving the embarrassing "fake" part out of it.

"Huh," she says again. "Hadley never told me that."

Something stirs in my gut. "Should she have told you? I mean, I haven't told anyone, really. It's fairly new. Besides, do you have Hadley watching me or something?" My tone is quipped, and I instantly feel regret. Sure, Hadley knew I was "dating him" at one point, but I'm glad she kept it to herself like I asked. Though it doesn't negate how small I feel when my sister casually insinuates she has our best friend watching me.

I mean, watching me for what? *I'm fine.* Does Lorelei think I'm going to do something stupid or crazy or unhinged simply because she's not around to maintain order? I can keep my own order, thank you—

"Not watching you," Lorelei says in her signature firm tone. "But I do ask her to check up on you for me. You're my twin. And you're missing from my life. We don't talk as much as we did those first two weeks after I moved. I worry about you. Not because you can't handle yourself but because you're literally my other half."

"I'm sorry I snapped at you." I bite my bottom lip as silence ensues on the other end. "I'm glad to have such an amazing older-by-one-minute sister like you."

"But Lucy. Are you okay?"

The hesitancy in her straightforward tone takes me back. Even from across the globe, she can still sense that something is up with me.

"I'm fine," I lie. Tears threaten to shove their way through, but I hold strong. I didn't tell my sister about the pool incident two weeks ago. I'm not telling her I'm fake dating my boss. I'm not telling her that dinner has begun to elude me or that I only vacate the apartment for work, "dates" with Stone, or necessary grocery shopping.

She doesn't need to worry about me. It's an adjusting phase. Everything will be fine, even if it's not fine right this very second. And when it comes to Stone, I'm just having fun. When he brought up the idea to fake date on a more permanent scale, I figured what the heck... I'm lonely. He's fun. I know where I stand with him so there's no confusion. And if I do happen to meet someone, I trust Stone will let me go. Furthermore, he's remained faithful to our agreement: we haven't kissed, touched, or done anything couple-y in private. That alone assuages some of the guilt I feel. Stone is a good guy despite his obvious commitment issues.

He lets me put my feet on the dash, sing in the car, and doesn't make me feel like I'm crazy or have too high expectations for men when I tell him my book ideas. He encourages my dreams to become a full-time author.

"I'm really okay," I say after she doesn't respond. "I see Hadley occasionally and chat with Karoline sometimes. Emma Jane is still at Books and Beans, so I pop in and see her every now and then. And I have Stone. He's—"

"Did he force you into anything? You know that's illegal, and I could—"

"No," I laugh mirthlessly. "He's done no such thing. I know I've said bad things about him in the past such as him being a player and all, but it turns out I misunderstood him. We've talked about it. He came onto me so many times, I just finally caved. He's actually a really good man."

He is. I told her that before she moved. I'll continue to stand by that assessment. And I'll also add "saves lives" to my list of reasons because...

He saved me.

That's not something I can easily forget.

I sneak a glance over my shoulder and find that he has positioned himself to where he's staring straight at me while he talks with Tate. He brings his thumb to his bottom lip and winks. I snap my head back around, a blush crawling up my face as I recall the way he traced his thumb over my bottom lip when he pulled me under the Ease-Up tent to set up lunch only thirty minutes ago.

"You've said that before, but I just want to make sure you're okay. If you say you are, then I'll believe you. But please check in with me more often than you have been. Don't make me have to call you every time we talk, okay?"

Guilt gnaws at my throat. "Okay. I'm sorry for worrying you."

"Don't apologize for such a thing, Lucy. I love you. Please... thrive."

More tears press against my lids, but I know they won't fall. I haven't cried in two weeks. "I am, Lor. Promise." *Lies, lies, lies...* "But I better get going. We are playing cornhole or something soon. Stone says I have to play at least one round."

At that, my twin laughs. "Good luck. I can't believe he's got you playing a yard game."

My mood rises at the upward vocalization in her voice. She's letting me be, and that's all I can ask for right now. "He's something, that's for sure. Love you, sis. I will call you soon, okay?"

"I'll be waiting. Love you, too."

After hanging up the phone and taking a few steadying breaths, I make my way toward my fake boyfriend, whose gaze never falters from my movement as every step brings me closer to him.

It's unbelievably hot.

The weather, I mean. July is a very hot month in Mississippi.

Oh, who am I kidding? The way that man watches me approach him is sizzling and popping hotter than the fireworks that'll go off tonight around the nation.

"Hey, Little Lion." Stone reaches for me, slides his arms around my waist, and pulls me flat against him. I look into his vibrant blue eyes while fastening my "good, real girlfriend" smile on. It's a sprinkling of sultry with a dash of coy and a heap of admiration.

I stand on my toes to kiss his cheek. He's clean shaven, and his skin tastes like an exploding galaxy. *Which is nothing compared to the black hole energy of his lips...* "Hey, Onyx."

He rolls his eyes at my nickname choice this time, but his beautiful, wide smile says he enjoys my antics. *Finally, a man who likes that I'm a little extra...*

"Ready to play cornhole? We will team up against Tate and Julia."

"Let me go find her real quick," Tate says, walking off toward the small two-story house.

Stone kisses my forehead before he releases me, and I struggle to stand on my own two legs from all that contact. Every time I form a physical connection point with that man, it's like I'm rediscovering what electricity is and just how potent it can be.

"Everything okay?" he asks, taking a small step away from me, leaving a noticeable shift in energy between the two of us. "You looked worried on the phone."

"My sister. All is well. She was just checking in."

"Ah, okay. Did you tell her about us?"

I shift away from him and look over at Lucas and Jared, who are busy grilling chicken and other meats. "I told her we were dating." I glance at him and smirk, attempting to bring lightness back to the air around us. "That I finally gave in to your incessant requests to take me out."

It works.

He flings an arm around me, and I once again learn that electricity is volatile and unrelenting. "They say only the annoyingly persistent ever win."

"Who says that?" I laugh and walk beside him. I slip my arm around his waist and learn that electricity can be applied at greater forces.

He gives me a big, toothy grin. "Me."

As we set up to play cornhole, banter back and forth, and fling bean bags at each other instead of the board, I realize that I'm a lot less lonely, a little less numb, and a smidge more happy when I'm with Stone Harper, my notorious playboy boss.

This is a dangerous game I'm playing...

Do you ever get the feeling someone is watching you?

Colors explode across the night sky, the sound vibrating my body as the fireworks pop one after another. Patriotic music blares in the background while the whole town of Dasher Valley plus some sit on the back of pickup trucks, in provided chairs, on metal bleachers, or lounge on outdoor blankets in the grassy field of the baseball diamonds. Earlier, there were live musical performances by local bands, a comedy performance, and then some evangelical guy preached. Stone and I ate dinner during that segment. We hung out with his friends and family for a while, and then we found our little spot to watch the show from. Presently, the fireworks have been going off for about thirty minutes.

He wasn't messing around when he said the private investors of the city put on a grand display.

His arm easily rests around my shoulders, tucking me into his side as we lie on a blanket on the tailgate of his truck. My feet are crossed under me while his dangle off the edge of the lifted vehicle.

My gaze is focused on the myriad of colorful sparks lighting the sky, but if I was to lift my head from his chest and tilt my chin up, I have an eerie feeling that he'd be looking at me.

And because I'm not good at not knowing things, I do just that.

Once again, my intuitions are correct.

His expression is stormy under the dark skies; pops of red, blue, and white reflect within the irises that are pointed at me. Stone doesn't smile. Instead, his lips part ever so slightly when I meet his stare. Naturally, I notice the movement of his lips like I'm a child tracking Santa, so he takes that as his needed cue to create our own fireworks in the bed of his truck.

The kiss is gentle and soft—there are families around us after all—but it still ignites my body all the same. After a few seconds, he pulls away with a satisfied grin and touches his head to mine as we continue to watch the fireworks above us. My heart aches with longing. Longing to have a deeper conversation with him that goes beyond our usual flirty banter and bickering. Longing to have him know me. Longing for all of this to be *real*.

Through the time I've spent with him, gleaning any piece of information about himself that he drops behind him as I follow on his heels, I've learned that he's not only considerate and kind to those around him, but he's also giving. Giving of his time, his money, and his attention. He makes any person that he speaks with feel like they have his undivided recognition.

And it just makes me wonder... What happened to this good man that he can't commit? What goes on within the depths of his brain that prevents him from giving all that he has to offer to a singular woman for the rest of his life?

The fireworks finally come to an end, and the mayor of the town takes the stage to ask people to help clean the recreational baseball fields and facilities we are currently using.

"Should we go help?" I ask Stone as we both sit up.

He nods his head, hops down from the tailgate, and then puts his hands on my waist to help me off. "We can do a lap around the outside of this field and then call it a night. What do you say?" He grabs a trash bag from his backseat.

"Sounds good." I follow him, picking up discarded water bottles and other cans. He picks up any plates or napkins that we happen upon, saying he doesn't want me getting my hands too dirty.

I mean, seriously... This man is doing the world a disservice by not allowing himself to love a woman.

"Is this something you and your family come to every year?" I ask as we continue our lap.

"Mostly, yes. Some years we forewent coming because of rain and such. I'm always amazed at the people who willingly sit out here after a rain shower. The mugginess is unbearable."

The heat and humidity as it is right now feels stifling and all encompassing. Like I'm walking around inside of a bathtub. A cold shower is in order when we get back to Marian's house.

"This is a really cool event. I wonder if Juniper Grove could do something like this one day."

Stone picks up a nacho container and tosses it into the bag I'm holding. "I've asked the mayor about it, and while he would like to, Juniper Grove is much bigger than Dasher Valley. Plus it's a college town. There are a lot of logistics to think about."

"Do you remember me from college?"

He stops and turns to me, wearing a crooked smile. "You were my favorite cheerleader to 'accidentally' bump into on the sideline."

I laugh, remembering several instances when he did just that. "Do you remember hitting on me at an athlete party your first year there?"

His smile falters, an uncertain look clouding his face. "I, uh—"

"It's okay if you don't. You were pretty gone that night."

"Yeah, my first year of college wasn't pretty. I got my crap together after because I wanted to continue playing football." He laughs sheepishly.

I place my hand on his arm and then remember I've been touching trash. "Oops, sorry." I pull my hand away.

"No, please. Hold onto me. I don't mind." We look at each other for a moment before he grabs my hand and places it back on his arm. We continue walking, only breaking contact to pick up more trash.

"We all have our moments in college," I say, trying to walk a tightrope, using my own stories as my balance pole. I don't want to frighten him off from opening up more, but I'm desperately craving emotional connection with him. "When I was a freshman, I got so tired of everyone confusing me with my sister that I chopped my hair off and dyed it blonde."

Stone stares at me incredulously. "I can't imagine you with any other hair color than this." He places his fingers near my hair but doesn't touch me. Regardless of whatever might be on his hands right now, I want his fingers knotted in my hair.

Another time, Lucy...

"I have pictures. I'll show you sometime." I chuckle at the memory. How ridiculous my short-lived identity crisis was. I cried and cried over the loss of my long hair. "It didn't last long. I dyed it as close to my natural color as I could get only one week later."

"Do you still find yourself getting upset sometimes? Over people confusing the two of you?"

I snicker. "Well, it certainly helps that she lives across the world now."

"You miss her."

I glance at Stone, who is going about his business searching for trash in the grass around the outskirts of the baseball field we parked behind. I was supposed to be digging into his brain, not the other way around.

"Of course I miss her. She's my other half. I've never known life without her until she left." I clear my throat, mentally swatting away the melancholy threatening to settle upon me. "I'm okay, though. Slowly adjusting. Do you miss your sister when you're away from her?'

Stone spurts a laugh. "When I'm away from Stella, I consider myself lucky. Because we are four years apart, she can easily slip into a mothering role over me." He pauses and worries his bottom lip. "When she left us for ten years, though, that stung. I was proud of her for pursuing her dream. I was happy she was happy. But I missed her a lot during those years. She was absent from my life my entire high school career. That was difficult for me."

My heart races as I search my head for what to say next. Any small acknowledgment that he's opening up to me may send him back into self-protective mode like the time I questioned him in church. So instead, I say nothing. I nod along as he continues to tell me about his sister's career as a campaign manager.

By the time we make it back to the truck, we've exchanged conversation about his time in college sports, my time as a cheerleader, and his dream to one day coach a little league football or baseball team. I may not know the ins and outs of Stone Harper yet, but tonight feels like a giant first step. A leap, if you will.

I place my feet on the dash, stretching out. When I catch him looking at me, I quickly move my feet. He hasn't said anything before, but maybe now is the time he's finally going to ask me to stop. "So sorry. It's a habit."

He gives me a perplexed expression. "I don't mind, Lucy. Has someone in your past told you not to place your feet on the dash, sing loudly in the vehicle, or not to talk about your books and stories? Because you seem to get skittish when you think you might be annoying me."

Not knowing what else to say, I turn and look away, whispering, "Yes."

"Lucy May Spence." When I don't look at him, he reaches across the truck, taking my chin and turning my face toward him. "I want you to let all of that go, okay? You are vibrant, fun, and more than welcome to sing, put your feet on my dash, and tell me all about your stories. It's not bothersome nor annoying."

Tears threaten my eyes, but I push them back. No guy has ever been this invested in my passions or has liked me more than the stupid dash of his truck. Stone is—I curse inside my head. Stone is everything...

He cranks the truck, and as we drive back to Marian's, we both sing loudly to "God Bless the U.S.A." by Lee Greenwood.

When we get back to the house, we take turns washing up, telling Marian and Brother Johnny about the fireworks display since they opted to stay in, and then we both head upstairs for bed.

"Goodnight, Lucy May," Stone says with a slight rasp to his voice. Something burns behind his eyes, and I know he wants a goodnight kiss as badly as I do. But we made that stupid contract that says no kissing or touching while we are alone. And we've done such a great job adhering to it while in Juniper Grove.

But we are back in Dasher Valley...

I take a step toward Stone as we stand in the middle of the small hallway between our rooms. "What happens in Dasher Valley..."

I don't have time to finish my sentence because he pushes me against the wall, pressing his body against mine and claiming my lips. Stone kisses me with a passion that feels sweeter and deeper than the first time he kissed me out on the front porch. Maybe it's because we've shared personal details about our lives tonight? Maybe it's the romance of fireworks on the Fourth of July.

Or maybe it's just *him*.

My heart threatens to exit my chest as his hand slips underneath my sleep shirt, his fingers setting the skin of my hips on fire. A siren sounds off faintly, but I push it out of my mind, focusing on the feel of his touch on my skin. When I moan, he whispers breathlessly against my ear, "Baby girl, there are people downstairs. Shh."

I nod, closing my eyes and biting my tongue as his lips trail down my throat. He pulls away for a brief second, so I open my eyes to see what he's doing. Wickedness glints in his eyes as he tilts his head and smirks. "Good girl."

His whispered words of praise seep into my bones, and I become putty in his hands to do whatever he wants with. He takes my hand and leads me to his bedroom.

And mercy, it feels so good to be desired like this.

Someone *wants* me.

I'm *not alone* anymore.

Stone Harper is *mine*. And I'm not letting him leave me like everyone else has done. Whatever it takes.

After he lays me down on his gray sheets, I whisper in the darkness. "I don't want to pretend anymore, Stone."

His hand stiffens across my stomach, and he lets out a curse. "I don't want to, either, Lucy May. But I don't know how to commit. I don't want to hurt you."

"Honesty is the first step," I say, playing with his hair between my fingers. "You're honest in your struggle to commit. Whatever comes next, we can face it and get through it together, okay?"

Silence echoes around the room.

"Okay?" I repeat with a little more force.

His body presses against mine, and in a small, broken voice against my ear, he says, "I haven't wanted someone like this in such a long time." He kisses beneath my ear. "I don't want to hurt you, Lucy. What if I'm not enough? What if these feelings fade?"

"I understand your struggle, Stone. I see it. But, let me ask you this: What if the feelings don't? What if they grow?"

His kisses move down my neck. "That may just terrify me more."

I moan again, my mind glitching. "Tell me now. Are you willing to try with me? If we go down in flames, so be it. I'm a big girl. I can handle another heartache." *No, really, I can. I promise...*

"For you, Lucy May, I will try. I'll try to overcome my issues."

Then his lips continue their exploration in the dark terrain of this jungle I find myself in, and I say a silent plea to whoever is listening: *Please let it be so...*

Chapter 12

Stone

She's going to murder me for this one...

I splay my hand, take two steps toward Lucy, and smack her lightly on the butt.

She whirls around at tornado speed, her hand up and flying toward my face. She stops mere inches away before dropping a balled fist to her side. "Pebbles, babe. You scared me. Don't sneak up on me like that."

She uses one of the many nicknames she has for me, but I've learned this particular one is used when she's upset with me. A few of the older employees snicker and laugh at our antics. It's not uncommon for the two of us to try and embarrass the other in front of everyone at the community center since we've announced our dating relationship.

And yes, an official one.

Who would have thought?

After that night in Dasher Valley over a month ago when I took her to bed with me, I knew that whatever was happening in Dasher Valley was not staying there.

I still don't know what I'm doing when it comes to an honest relationship, but I'm trying. For her, I'm trying.

Embarrassing each other at work has become a game of sorts, and with that nice little love tap, I think I've tipped the score in my favor.

Her eyes blaze with heat, promising retribution in the future, but she can't say a word right now because it would blow our make-people-want-to-puke-at-how-cute-we-are relationship personas.

Who knew I had it in me?

"Sorry, Lucy May. I just can't help myself sometimes."

"Ain't that the truth," she mumbles under her breath before fixing a smile back on her face.

"You two are the cutest," my secretary, Jeanie, says as she pats me on the back before giving me a chilling, stern look only a mother could manage. "You better keep this one. I'm glad you finally came to your senses and asked the girl out."

"I try my best every day." That's not a lie. We ripped up the rules we created two days after we got back from Dasher Valley, and now, with every day that passes, I've taken to actively begging God to not let me screw this one up. I have no clue what's going to happen between me and Lucy because fear still grips me when I think too long about the fact we are together in an official capacity. Some days we are good and have the time of our lives together while other days she seems dazed and lost.

And I don't know what to do about it.

I just want her to be happy.

"Okay, guys. We have to focus. Kids will be showing up for the Back to School Bash at any time. Jeanie, will you sign people in at the door? I'm going to make my rounds to make sure everything and everyone is ready." Lucy doesn't give me time to respond before she jets off, her heels clicking down the tiled hallway of offices. I watch her walk away, admiring the sway of her white, flowy skirt and wishing I could take her back to my place right now.

Jeanie pats me on the back once more before departing to heed Lucy's instructions.

My phone buzzes in my back pocket.

Keaton Welch.

I invited my potential investor to today's event so he could see firsthand how the center is beneficial to those in the community. He's down from New York with his business partner who is visiting family in our neighboring town of Hartfield.

Putting my phone away after reading the message saying he arrived, I go to meet him at the front doors.

The lobby is bustling with people. The plants by the doors undulate each time the wind is let in accompanied by a wave of mid-August heat. Jeanie sits behind a white fold-out table with her tablet, checking people in alongside a parent volunteer. A man who looks to be in his thirties and is wearing a suit, sticking out like a sore thumb among all the adults in shorts and t-shirts, casually leans against the white brick walls by the water fountain.

"Mr. Welch." I wave my hand and offer a smile as his attention lands on me. He smiles and waves back before meeting me in the center of the room under fluorescent lights. I stretch out my hand. "Glad you could make it."

"This looks to be quite the facility you have here." He shakes my hand.

"How about a tour before things kick off?"

He gestures outward with one hand while shoving the other in his pant pocket. "Lead the way."

I take Mr. Welch through the office rooms, telling him about the seven full-time staff members I have on board. Next, we head toward the open gym where volunteers are setting up for various games and activities. We pause in the middle of the court. "Volunteers pull most of the weight around here. This place wouldn't continue to exist without the many volunteers that come through. Parents, siblings, grandparents, college kids, you name it... We have a variety of people in this community ready and willing to help. It's one of the many reasons I love the area."

"Juniper Grove is a nice little town. Seems to be full of people who look after one another, so it does make me wonder where the need for a center like this came from if everyone is so kind and helpful." Mr. Welch stares off in the distance, and I follow his gaze.

Lucy is holding her tablet and writing something down in the far corner by a "toss the bean bag into the trash can" carnival-type game. She pauses for a moment and taps the pen against her temple while she examines the game. Her hair is in a curled ponytail, her bangs straightened, and I can't get over how doll-like she looks today.

I shift my eyes back to Mr. Welch. Apparently he can't either...

Something churns inside me, and I clench my jaw. Guess I'll be walking him over there next so he can meet *my* girlfriend.

"Walk with me," I start. "As you already know, the Juniper Grove Community Center is a product of my capstone class in college. It was a little risky to choose such a project, but where is the fun in choosing the safe option?"

He laughs and nods in agreement.

I continue as we walk toward Lucy. "While we do have many supportive people here, it's not like they can take in kids who aren't thriving in a functional family. Believe me, there are many kids who fly under the radar. Kids you would never know experience abuse and are bullied and neglected. The center gives those kids a place to escape to, and it also gives people who wish to be of more assistance a place to gather and, well, assist the kids."

Mr. Welch hums in thought as we approach Lucy. I sneak a glance at him, and his eyes are locked and loaded on my woman.

"Mr. Welch, I'd like you to meet my assistant director," I slip an arm around Lucy's waist as she locks her tablet and sets it on the table next to her, "and girlfriend, Lucy Spence. She was with me last month when I met with some local investors, so I wanted to make sure you got a chance to meet my lovely woman as well."

Am I going overboard on laying my claim? Probably. But she's mine.

His dark brown eyes flit between us, but his smile never falters. He offers his hand, and Lucy grabs it as she says it's nice to meet him. Does anyone else hear the slight tremble in her voice? After a light shake, he brings her hand up to his—

I clear my throat and clench my fist at my side to keep from doing something I'd regret like bloodying those lips he's placing on my woman's knuckles.

Lucy nudges me, and I slowly drag my eyes from staring daggers into Keaton Welch's skull to Lucy, who looks up at me with a pained expression. It's then I realize my hand is molded around her hip, squeezing a little too hard.

I relax my grip but don't dare drop my hand.

"You have a beautiful girlfriend, Mr. Harper," he says, dropping her hand. *Finally.*

Flashing my teeth as I smile, I cock my head and answer in a low-pitched tone, "Don't I know it. I sure am one lucky guy."

I soften my smile and direct it at Lucy, but she's locked in wide-eyed with the man in front of us.

"Why don't we continue our tour, Mr. Welch?" I suggest, wanting to get him and his leering eyes away from her. I'm not too sure I want his investment money now, but I have to think of the needs of the center and not my own personal vendettas.

"I'll see you later, Miss Spence," he says with a slight bow and a faux tip of an invisible hat. Who even is this man? Acting like a remade regency side character in a Jane Austen novel or something... Jeez.

"Please, call me Lucy," she says through a tight grin and a nervous laugh. Is he mistaking her nervous energy for cuteness?

"Lucy," he says in what sounds like a seductive whisper. At least to my ears.

Enough of this. I stand straight and square my shoulders. "With all due respect, Mr. Welch, but would you please refrain from flirting with my girlfriend?"

His brown eyes cut to me, and his slender frame straightens to match me. "With all due respect, Mr. Harper, I was simply exchanging pleasantries with your girlfriend. Please do not mistake my kindness and gentlemanly mannerisms for flirting." Before I can respond, he smooths the side of his styled brown hair and flicks his amused eyes to Lucy. "However, how she reacts to me is out of my control."

Nope. Not on my watch. Not toward my girl and not in my beloved community center.

Right as I open my mouth to lay into this tool of a man, Lucy steps in front of me. "With all due respect, Mr. Welch, do not mistake my friendliness and ability to make those around me feel welcomed and seen as romantic interest in a knavish man such as yourself. I wasn't aware you were throwing your hat into the investment ring, or I would have told my boyfriend," she grabs my hand and looks up at me with purpose and passion in her eyes, "that you are as corrupt as they come in Wall Street." She turns her attention back to him. "Do you know Emma Jane Williams?"

I snap my attention to him and watch as his eyes widen in horror.

Lucy hums. "That's what I thought. You see, she's a good friend of mine, and she's told me all about how you and your partner, Mr. Frank Weston, have returned to this area in an attempt to pawn off your debts onto his father. It seems she forgot to send you off when she sent Frank Weston off."

If I was holding a microphone right now, I'd drop and applaud the beautiful and intelligent Lucy May. How in the world did she know about his financial woes and I didn't?

"Right," Mr. Welch stutters out. He checks his watch before hurriedly stating, "I better be on my way. I have another appointment to attend to."

He half-jogs out of the gym, and once he's out of the double doors, I embrace Lucy. "That was brilliant. You are brilliant."

She wiggles out of my arms and tightens her ponytail. She averts her eyes downward, a shy smile forming. "It was nothing. Once I heard his name, I remembered Emma Jane ranting and raging last week over coffee about how Frank Weston almost got away with pawning his debt onto her friend Halle, who is married to Weston's father. I was going to tell you in private after he left, but with that ridiculous, unwarranted comment of his, I couldn't stand to not take his sorry butt down a notch or two."

I chuckle and cross my arms, giving her a sideways grin. "More like a hundred notches. That was impressive. I was about to take up for you, but the way you handled him was so much more than what I could have said and done."

She shrugs then picks up her tablet from the table. "We don't want investors like that."

"No, we don't," I echo, secretly liking the way she said "we" as if this place belongs to the both of us. As if her name is signed right alongside mine...

Hair rises on my arms at that thought, and my mood immediately shifts. Scratching at my arm, I scan the gym for something to do. Somewhere to go. "I better go check on things. Make sure he found his way out."

Lucy smiles at me before giving me a quick kiss on the cheek and turning her attention to her tablet. "Of course. I'll see you around. I need to check on the outdoor activities."

She walks away, and as I watch her go, I wonder how in the world I can go from possessive boyfriend to acting like a skittish cat at the thought of something permanent such as owning a building with her. Trust issues run deep.

Maybe I should consider Stanton's advice from a few days ago when I told him I was trying something real with Lucy. He told me to see a therapist.

Men don't need no therapy, my brain says in a deep, old-western voice.

Right. I can get through this on my own. And even if I don't and I end up losing Lucy, I'll stay single after that for good. What I have with Lucy is fun, playful, passionate, and new. I'm terrified there will come a day when I am bored with her and will want to end things. I truly do not want to hurt her, which is why I suggested a fake relationship in the first place. No strings. No commitment.

But the woman has flirted and sassed her way right into my soul, so when she whispered she wanted something real with me within the confines of my childhood bedroom, I couldn't resist. I shoved the fear deep down and jumped into the wind with her.

I only hope I can be the man she needs so I don't crash and burn us.

"Are you certain you don't want a plate of crabs?" I ask Lucy with mock concern in my voice as she tells the waiter at Perry's Seafood for the third time that she'll take the fried shrimp meal.

Her hazel eyes darken as she glares at me, and I chuckle. After ordering a shrimp po-boy, I hand our menus to the older gentleman and feign an innocent expression at the woman sitting across from me.

"Are you trying to get on my bad side tonight?" I scoff.

"You have a *good* side?" She tosses a piece of bread at me then smiles as she looks away.

Over the past few days since our Back to School Bash at the center, she's seemed to slip into one of her little down-and-out moods. It's rare to get a genuine smile out of her, and even when I do, it's not a full one. Something is plaguing her, but I don't know how to ask.

"There's that smile I enjoy," I casually mention. She turns her attention back on me, but apparently that was not the right thing to say because she frowns. I clear my throat. I just need to man up and go for it. What's it going to hurt if she doesn't tell me? At least I did the proper boyfriend thing and checked in.

After taking a sip of sweet tea, I ask, "Lucy, is everything okay? You've looked a little down and out over the past few days."

Her eyes glaze over as she picks at the piece of bread in her hands. "Yeah, I'm good. Just tired. Not sleeping well."

It's a start...

"What's causing your lack of sleep?" And because I can't help myself, I tack on with a wink, "Besides me."

Silence stretches on as she looks anywhere but at me, her face reddened.

"Ha, ha," she mocks. "Just busy with writing. I get sucked into my stories easily."

"Hm. Are you sure that's it?"

"Positive," she says through a wavering smile.

It looks so fragile, her smile. I lean in and set my elbows on the table, resting my chin on top of my fists. "Lucy, you can talk to me, okay? I was kind of hoping we had some measure of trust between us."

Her eyes narrow, an incredulous expression contorting her freckled face. "Trust? Is that why you still haven't told me about what really happened between you and Lacey?"

My immediate reaction is to play defense, so I do. "How does she have anything to do with this? She's in the past; I've told you this. I told you yesterday when you tried to ask about her in your little covert way by casually mentioning how she kept staring at me at Tate's wedding."

She leans onto the table, dropping her bread and matching my pose. Challenge dances in her eyes. "One, it was true. It happened. Two, I want to know why she looked at you as if you had ripped her heart out even though she's a married woman. As your *girlfriend*, I have the right to know."

"The past should stay in the past," I dismiss, sitting back and fixing my attention on the taxidermied hammerhead shark hanging above the entrance of the small seafood restaurant. I wish I could die and stuff myself right now to get out of this conversation.

Silence stretches on between us, only the chatter of the few families in the seating area around us.

"Stone, if you want me to trust you enough to let you into my private life, then you have to trust me to let me into yours. Trust goes both ways. And don't worry. I know you didn't hurt her. I'm sorry for saying that. I know she hurt you, and I'd like to know what happened simply so that I can understand you better."

In the middle of her monologue, my eyes betrayed me and shifted back to her. In fact, my entire body straightened and tuned into her.

Has a woman ever mentioned that she'd like to *understand* me?

Not one that I can remember...

I search her expression, and it's genuine. There's no trace of feigned interest in me just to get me to do whatever she wants. There's no sign of her pretending to want to know the real me just so she can turn around and use it against me.

Just... authentic curiosity and concern.

Am I ready to take that leap?

No, not a leap. It's a small step. A toe across the safeguard line I've worked on keeping in place for years. If I want something real with Lucy, then I have to let her in. At least a peek inside. A therapist doesn't have to tell me that much...

"I proposed to Lacey the night of graduation. And she said no." I evaluate Lucy's expression, but her face doesn't so much as twitch. "It's the way she told me that hurts the most."

The memory comes back in full force: my clammy hands reaching into my jacket pocket to pull out my class ring. I was going to take her to the ring shop to pick out her own ring the very next day if she would have let me. The humid air and pent-up nerves made it difficult to breathe as I took Lacey's hand and slid down onto one knee. When my eyes met hers, I knew something was off. But I was already kneeling, and the wet grass was already soaking through my pants, dampening my knee.

"After I laid my heart bare to her, she looked at me with something worse than an expression of sadness. She pitied me. Asked me to stand up. Placed her hand on my arm and looked me in the eyes as she told me she was glad she had spent the last couple of years with me but it was time for us both to grow up and move on. Said she wanted to go off to college as a free woman and live her life. Maybe meet an older man." A familiar ache settles in my chest, but to my surprise, it's not as forceful as it once was. Not even as forceful as the time Lacey stopped us outside the restaurant. As I lift my gaze from my twiddling fingers to Lucy, I realize she's the reason why. Her openness, honesty, realness, and boldness captivate me. She's quite the woman, and I think I—

I think I want to continue trying this relationship with her. Maybe if it's Lucy, it'll be easier for me. I guess it's a waiting game.

"For what it's worth," Lucy says in a soft tone as she tucks her hands under the table, "She's missing out on a kind, honest, smart, and stupidly flirty man."

I laugh at her last statement, and that seems to break the built up tension. Our food arrives, and we dig in, eating in comfortable silence.

About halfway through the meal, I take another shot at figuring out what's going on with my date. Which means another moment of vulnerability for me tonight. "In baseball, we have this term called beaning, or throwing a beanball. It basically means that the pitcher throws the ball at the batter with the intention to hurt him."

Lucy stares at me with a scrunched nose and narrowed eyes, most likely wondering where I'm going with this. I release a breath, thinking over my next words.

"One of the reasons I hide my scars is because I'm scared that someone will use them against me. They will bean me with them, so to say. Especially a woman who is remotely older than me." I give Lucy a pointed look before continuing. "After Lacey rejected my proposal, I went home and cried for the second time that I could remember, the first time being when my father passed away. I couldn't sleep, so I texted her and told her that I didn't buy into her reasoning. I demanded to know the truth from her. It didn't make sense to me, you know, why she would reject me after we had dated for so long. After all the plans we had made."

I pause to take a sip of tea and collect my thoughts so as not to ramble on. Lucy casually continues eating, not pressing me to hurry. She's letting me go at my pace.

Who knew actually talking about it with someone who isn't interrupting or trying to offer sympathy would be... therapeutic? Is that the right word?

See? I don't need a therapist. I just need to talk to Lucy.

Why didn't I do this sooner?

"She agreed to meet me, and we went up into this old treehouse behind the house that my sister and her ex-boyfriend—who is her husband now, as you know—would sneak off to sometimes. I remember the ladder cracking under my weight as I climbed, but it didn't break. Lacey was already there, waiting for me. She had this blank expression on her face, and I could only see it because of the sliver of moonlight shining through the open windows. I wish I hadn't.

"I asked her once again to give me the truth, and she said words that still haunt me sometimes. She said, 'I can't marry a man who is younger than I am, even if it's only by a few months, and can't present me with a diamond ring. That's not a real man. I don't think I ever truly loved you, Stone. You're not enough for me.' Then she left after throwing that huge beanball at me. I never bothered to tell her that I saved up enough money to buy her a diamond ring by working jobs around the neighborhood on top of my full-time school and sports schedules."

Lucy and I stare at each other for a solid minute. She slowly chews on a french fry, and I attempt to work out the "why" behind not feeling shameful and emasculated as I often felt when I recalled that moment of my life.

Suddenly, Lucy grins and tosses the darkened end of the french fry onto her plate. "Please tell me you went and spent the money on some flashy watch for yourself or maybe put it toward a new vehicle or motorcycle. And tell me you flaunted it in front of her."

Laughter overtakes me and all the uneasiness I felt at sharing this story with her vanishes. I bite my bottom lip before admitting to what I used the money for. "Lucy May, I pocketed that money and it became the foundation of the start-up funds for the Juniper Grove Community Center."

This gets a reaction out of her.

Her lips part and eyes widen as her cup halts midair, her straw inches from her face.

I reach across the table and guide her drink to her mouth. She swats me away with a sound of disbelief. "Really? You kept it that long. You didn't even try to get even with her or show her what a mistake she made?"

I smirk. "I think she might have had an inkling that she made a mistake when she saw the pretty redhead on my arm over a couple of months ago. And again when I brought her home. What do you think?"

The compliment seems to go over her as she hums. "Yeah, probably so. Her reaction to you makes so much sense now. And how she watched you at the wedding. Watched us. It all makes sense." She takes a sip of her water with lemon. "And I'm sorry I joked about our two-year age gap. I swear it was all in good fun. That truly doesn't matter to me."

I wave her off, knowing good and well she didn't mean any harm by it. I know her to be above that kind of nonsense.

But I still want to know more about her...

"All right, Little Lion. I've told you about my past and scars. It's your turn. I promise not to beanball you with the information you tell me tonight."

Her shoulders raise just a hair, and she presses her lips together as if in thought. "I'm not too worried you will use it against me. I'm more worried you'll throw me in the psych ward."

"Baby girl, if I put you in the psych ward, I'll be rooming with you." She laughs and rolls her eyes at my words. "Go on. Tell me what's worrying your pretty little head."

Lucy takes a sip of her drink before clearing her throat. "It's stupid, really. Ever since Hadley went and got married, Karoline got married and moved, and now my sister moved and is about to tie the knot in December, I feel left behind. Rejected. Burdensome." She pauses, but by her contemplative expression, I know she's not finished. After a few seconds, she huffs and meets my eyes. "Lonely. I'm very lonely. Not to mention Hadley is now pregnant. It's like everyone's life is moving forward except mine."

For the sake of not knowing what to do with her admission or what to do with the emptiness in her eyes, I feign being stabbed in the heart. "Oof, Lucy May. You're lonely even while dating me?" Maybe I was too preemptive. I thought she might be upset over something not working out with her writing career or friend drama. I didn't think it would be this deep. And not going to lie, it kind of stings that she's lonely even while dating me.

Lucy adjusts the light beige shirt she's wearing, then places one arm across her chest, holding on to the elbow of her other arm. She looks down, not bothering to laugh at my joke. I can't blame her. After what she confessed to me, that definitely wasn't the appropriate response.

But I don't know what is, so... humor attempts it is.

"Actually, the loneliness hasn't been so bad since we started *this*." She gestures between us with a small grin that still doesn't quite meet her eyes. "So thank you for your wacky suggestion to be each other's designated date. It's led to something I never expected with you. Never allowed myself to hope for."

Her words warm me to my core, but they also terrify me. What if I mess it all up? The feelings I have for her only seem to be growing stronger, and what if I can't be enough?

Shaking the thoughts off, I lean back in my chair and place my hands behind my head, making sure I flex. She had a male character do this in a book, and now it's time to see if it works in real life.

It does.

Her eyes immediately land on my arm before shifting to look at the other. She blushes but then stifles a giggle, covering her mouth with one hand.

"What is it, Lucy May?" I ask in a deep, flirty tone.

She stares me right in the eyes as she smirks and says, "Nice pit stains you've got going on there."

I drop my arms, hitting the edge of the wooden seat with one hand when I do. I hold back from making a pained noise, but when her giggle gives way to a full-blown laugh, I decide I'll sport pit stains every single day if it means she'll smile like that.

Full white teeth. Crinkles in the corners of her eyes. A boisterous sound emerging from somewhere within the depths of her belly.

I may not be able to emotionally meet her right now because I need time to process the depth of what she told me, but if I can at least make her smile and laugh when she's feeling so low, then I'll take the win.

We continue eating, talking, and cracking jokes at each other's expense. She drove herself to the restaurant tonight because she needed to spend tonight alone (and we all know I would have followed her inside whichever place we ended up at if we would have ridden together), so when it's time to go, I hold her outside her car for a little bit longer than I normally do. The seafood smell of the restaurant lingers in her hair, and while it isn't a pleasant scent, I can still pick up the undertones of her spicy vanilla perfume. She's warm in my arms, and I wish I had comforting words for her before she drives back to her apartment where she'll spend another night alone, lost in her dark thoughts.

"Are you sure you don't want me to come over and stay with you tonight?" I play with her hair as she sighs deeply, her chest rising and falling against me.

"I don't know, Stone." She pulls back, her hands sliding from my back to my stomach. "I'm just... sad. I don't want to bring you into my mournful midnight."

Her eyes are round and pleading, begging for me to see something. To say something. But I don't know what she needs. Does she even know what she needs?

After a moment, she sighs deeply again, turning away from me and getting into her car.

Maybe I should go over anyway. Just to be sure she's okay...

Is that what she truly wants? I don't know. She said she wants to be alone, but it sounds like the aloneness is self-induced because she doesn't want her sadness rubbing off on me.

Frustrated that I don't know how to make this better and I want to respect her wishes to be alone tonight, I get into my truck and slam the door, beginning the short drive to my house.

From the small bit she's told me tonight and the little comments she makes in a humorous manner though the content is black,

Lucy was right that one day when she told me that I might run screaming if I knew what went on inside her head.

Key word: might.

Because instead of scaring me off, I think she's creating a black hole around me that's continually sucking me in deeper and deeper.

Chapter 13

Lucy

I lock eyes with Stella as we circle each other in lithe squats with our arms at the ready. Her husband pulled me aside earlier and informed me that her tell was when she slightly rocked back onto her heels, so I break eye contact occasionally to sneak a glance at her feet.

It may be her birthday, but I'll be danged if I don't fight to the finish to beat her in this wrestling match. My competitive streak knows no boundaries.

She rocks back, and I prepare to shift to the left side like Stone taught me when he told me Stella's birthday celebration would most likely end up in a wrestling match. Fresh memories of us rolling across the center's matted floors as Stone taught me to wrestle days ago superimpose with the lingering remnants of wicked memories of what happened *after*, gluing me in place and allowing Stella to pounce and easily swipe my feet out from under me. I fall onto the black mats of the makeshift rink in their house. "Oof."

I go ahead and tap out, knowing it's a lost cause with the NR movie starring me and Stone playing in my head right now. Looks like my competitive streak's boundary is a mere memory of a breathless and sweaty Stone Harper rolling on the floor with me.

The small crowd consisting of Stone's family and a few close friends erupts in applause for the birthday girl. I bow out gracefully, meet Stone's heated gaze, and feel my soul tremble when he licks his lips.

Lord, help me...

"Excuse me. I'm going to sneak off to the restroom," I mention to Stella after I give her a victory hug. She has quickly become a good friend, and whenever Stone decides he's had enough of me, I think she might be as heartbroken as I will be.

The Harper family holds a special place in my heart.

Would I really have to lose them?

My heart whispers yes.

Fear over Stone leaving me grows louder every day. Even in the dead of night when he brings my body to life and makes me forget I was ever dead inside, I'm scared he'll leave when the morning comes. It's like I'm preparing for his eventual departure while simultaneously clawing at the walls inside my glass cage to keep his attention on me.

Walking through Stella and Lucas's house, I make my way to the guest bathroom and am met with a certified wild woman staring back at me in the mirror. My hair, which was up in a high ponytail, now frizzes and sticks out in every direction. Black smudges coat the underneath of my eyes and the sage green halter top I'm wearing looks boxy and baggy on me now instead of fitted like it was at the start of this day.

How could I have been thinking of Stone like *that* when I'm looking like *this?*

As if he's having any thoughts of me. *Pft.* That heated gaze from earlier is my brain short-circuiting, thinking I'm starring in my own rom-com. It was probably an examinatorial look that meant, *huh, maybe I should call things off with her. She's a mess.*

I sit down on the lid of the toilet and pull out my phone to distract myself from thinking. At least thinking about my oh so attractive and hot and flirty-but-kind boyfriend that I fear is on a countdown to letting me go.

We've been dating *for real* for almost two months. I think his longest fling lasted right at three months. I feel like a ticking time bomb is stationed above my head.

Opening social media, I check messages from readers and then click on a post I was tagged in. My heart rate quickens when I notice it's a review for the last rom-com release I published to close out my second series. A smile spreads across my face, however, as I read the caption. Pride swells as I bask in the glowing, positive review. The reader said I was now an auto-buy author for her, complimented my author's voice, and mentioned how she loved that I wrote clean romance from a Christian perspective.

But think of those dirty, dirty thoughts you were having moments ago. Think of those dreams that keep happening. Think of all those nights you've tangled up with Stone...

"Gah!" I shout as I rocket to my feet, clenching my phone in one hand and slapping the tiled bathroom wall with my other. In a breathless whisper, I bite, "What a hypocritical phony I am."

My readers think of me as this pristine, polished, put-together Christian girl who writes squeaky clean romance that their upper-teen could read without issue. Attraction fully exists in my stories, but it's not the soul of my stories. The emotional bonding is. Attraction is countered with characters who try to capture their thoughts. The author persona I've carefully curated with each book published, each post shared, each email sent, each video created, and each interaction with my readers is who I wish I was.

I wish I was the girl who waited until marriage like my characters do.

I wish I was the confident lady who didn't cave to desires, who could easily put a stop to things before they went too far. Who didn't freely let her thoughts wander sometimes because it felt good to do so.

I wish I didn't feel like pie with all the gooey middle filling removed only to have a crusty shell remaining.

And I can't share this struggle with anyone. Sure, maybe Hadley, but I can't admit to her that I haven't beaten this yet. When she asks how I'm managing, I tell her I'm fine and thank her for checking before changing the subject. Church burn is real, and I've been scorched way too many times by Christian women who shut me down and tell me to try harder to be better when I attempted to confide in them over my sexual inclinations as a teenager. We as women aren't allowed to talk about our sexual temptations because it's a "man's struggle."

I set my phone down on the marbled counter and lean back against the white wall, closing my eyes and taking deep breaths. Being with Stone—touching him, kissing him, catching little glimpses behind the man who is scared of commitment but is trying, learning his heart—has done a number on me.

And the fun of our encounters has begun to wear off. Don't get me wrong, we bring the chemistry. The heat. The passion. The spice. I'm completely lost to him when it's happening. But after, as he falls asleep with his hand on my hip and leg swung over my body, guilt drowns me much like when I was five.

Like when I was knocked into the pool at the wedding.

Except this time there's no one around to save me.

The one who once saved me is becoming the rock tied to my feet as I sink further and further into the dark depths of the ocean.

After smoothing down my hair, wiping underneath my eyes, and making the most out of my frazzled appearance, I exit the restroom with my head tucked down and run straight into a man's very firm chest.

"Easy there, Little Lion," Stone says, hooking his finger under my chin and tilting my head up. All thoughts of him leaving me soon or my guilty premonitions vanish into thin smoke as he moves his hand to cup my cheek and presses his lips softly against mine. He controls the kiss, gently pushing my mouth open and pulling it closed as he slowly coaxes us deeper into each other. It's a dance I know all the steps to but still surprises me as I move.

He tastes like the sweetness of the vanilla cake we consumed earlier. My brain short circuits as my hands roam up his chest until I eventually snake my arms around his neck and tug him closer. He moves his hand from my cheek and works his fingers into my hair, completely messing up what I had just fixed. A sigh escapes my lips, and that signals him to push me back through the bathroom door and up against the cool, tiled wall.

I'm a goner to him in this small, darkened space.

My thoughts are repeating his name over and over. He's a broken record loop, and I never want to fix it.

Stone frees his hands from my hair, opting to travel down my neck, shoulders, sides, and landing on my hips. He grips me like he's never letting go, and I think I might die if he did. In fact, I do die a little when his lips rip from mine.

"You are a—" *curse* "—forbidden sin to me, Lucy May." Stone's voice is husky as his lips travel down my neck.

Warning bells sound in the back of my head, but they're muffled by fabric layers of Want and boxed in by Need.

I don't know how much time passes by as we get lost in one another against that bathroom wall, every touch and taste reminding me I have a reason to live.

A knock sounds at the door, causing both of us to jump in surprise. His presence departs from me, and as I'm trying to catch my breath, the lights flick on.

Stone stares at me, crazed and hungry.

I turn my gaze to the mirror as he cracks open the door, and I notice my expression mimics his.

And then a tsunami of guilt and sadness floods my demeanor as I take in my messy hair, swollen lips, and red splotches on my neck. With trembling hands, I rip the ponytail holder from my hair, not bothering to wince at the pain as hairs are yanked from my head.

I deserve the pain.

I watch as I visibly shrink into the smallest woman who has ever lived. Someone is talking, and then I hear Stone, but I've tuned it out. All I can feel is overwhelming shame.

It's too much to stand under.

So I reach for a little string in my brain labeled "numb" and pull it, forcing myself to stop *feeling*.

"Lucy? Everything okay?"

Stone's grip on my upper arm drags me back to the here and now.

I paste a plastic smile on my face. "Oh, um. Yeah, I'm good."

He smirks, and I realize he probably thinks my silence and fearful expression is because someone interrupted.

Good. Let him go on thinking that. He doesn't need to know the truth.

"That was—" He blows out air and runs a hand through his disheveled blond hair, his beautiful blue eyes alight with passion.

"Something," I finish for him. Because he isn't wrong. I follow him out the door, thankful he sent off whoever it was. I don't think I can face any of his family members or friends after that. "But why did you do that? Your family is around." *Not that that has stopped us before, but...*

His expression dims as he clenches his jaw. "You're right, and please forgive me. But as for the reasoning, which by no means justify my actions," his eyes darken, "your post-wrestling messy appearance made you one of the most tempting creatures I've ever seen."

Here I was, thinking he was disgusted and thinking of ending things with me...

Silly, silly girl.

"Huh," is all that comes out. I fiddle with my hair, hoping that it will cover my neck while still maintaining some semblance of style, but I know it's no use. The frizzy mess is unfixable.

Stone removes my hands from my hair and holds them. "I truly am sorry, Lucy. I know I can get a one-track mind when it comes to you sometimes."

"I know," I whisper, then add, "me too. I could have stopped you. To be honest, I wanted—"

"You should never have to be in charge of stopping me. That's not your job."

Something inside me awakens, pushing against the numbness.

No, not *that*. I've put the Beast to bed right now through my process of numbing out.

Stone's the first man to ever tell me I'm not in charge of stopping things. I vividly remember one of my college boyfriends telling me it was my fault he kept having sex with me. He said I should do a better job at stopping him before things went too far. I tried to explain to him that my drive wasn't like other girls, but he said it didn't matter.

He said it was my job to metaphorically pump the brakes, not his.

"Thank you for saying that." I squeeze his hands before letting go. We walk in silence a short distance into the kitchen. He motions for me to sit, which I do, using the opportunity to try and relax my body. After a moment, he returns with drinks.

He hands me a glass of water before telling me to take my time calming down. Then he's off to rejoin the group. I don't have time to even begin to think over why I'm suddenly feeling so guilty before Stella walks in and joins me at the kitchen table.

"Do I need to fight my brother for you?"

Her question catches me off guard. "Why?"

"You look sad. Like really sad."

I contemplate how I should answer for a moment, but she interrupts and moves to sit beside me instead of in front of me. "Let me be blunt for a moment. I know he's my brother, but I also know he has a not-so-pretty streak in him when it comes to commitment. Trust me, we were all shocked when we found out about you. And to be honest, I'm surprised he's still with you, so that's saying something."

"Oh, that?" I laugh nervously. "Yeah, I know about his past. But he's been nothing but committed to me. I'm not sad because of him. It's... personal."

She tucks a strand of loose brown wavy hair behind her ear. When I meet her eyes, the steel-gray color acts as a knife slicing through to my inner core. I feel cut open and laid upon her husband's biology classroom dissecting table. (Yes, he showed us today while we were galivanting around town).

I quickly avert my gaze.

"I understand," she finally says. "But please know I'm here if you need me. I've thoroughly enjoyed having a sister—even one who lives six hours away—over these past couple of months. For the record, I'm cheering you on. I'm praying the two of you are end-game."

Stella leans forward and wraps me in a surprise hug, and after a moment of pause, I hug her back. Normally, I would cry over a moment like this, but the string labeled "numb" is still pulled taut, and I have no idea when I'll release it this time.

After she leaves, I remain in the kitchen long enough to finish my water. Once I rejoin the group, who have moved outside to a campfire, I fake smiles, answer questions when asked, and clutch Stone's hand for dear life for the remainder of the night.

He doesn't kiss me goodnight once we are back to his mom's house. He allows me to hole myself up in Stella's old room, not bothering me with intrusive questions I don't have answers to.

My soul is numb. My brain is tired. My body is growing fragile.

So I take out my computer and I go to a place where happily-ever-afters always come, communication is always good, and the leading females are virgins and strong in their Christian walk.

Chapter 14

Stone

The crushing weight stinging throughout my arms and into my chest feels like due punishment.

"Push it, mate!" Stanton claps his hands, creating a loud environment for me to get swept into. Using the adrenaline from the workout, from the reasoning for this late night session, and from his encouragement, I shove the barbell upwards and rack it with a loud clanging sound.

"Atta, boy. Is that a new max?" he questions while I catch my breath. He moves to stand in front of me as I straddle the workout bench I was just laying on.

"Sure is."

He playfully punches my shoulder, but I don't feel it because my entire body has become absent of nerves. We've been in the gym for over an hour, and while Stanton has worked out about half that time, I've been going.

And going.

And *going*.

I dropped Lucy off at her apartment after a bowling date with Stanton and his wife earlier tonight, and well, I asked Lucy if I could come inside for a while and she turned me down.

I'm disappointed not because she turned me down but because I shouldn't have asked.

After we returned from Dasher Valley earlier in the month, she confided in me about how she felt convicted over us having sex and wanted to try and stop. Not going to lie, it upset me, though I didn't let her see it. The guilt is there for me, too, but I've shoved it down for years; it's barely an inkling of a feeling at times. I've tried to be better for her since I can see she's struggling with guilt and I don't want to add to it, but it's so hard when I already know what she's capable of in bed...

The images I play over and over in my head aren't fantasies.

So alas, I found myself wide awake and high on thoughts of her after going home, and when midnight rolled around, I couldn't stand it anymore.

"Okay, mate. Now tell me why you dragged me away from my wife in the middle of the night." Stanton yanks me up from the bench, and I follow him to the lockers to retrieve our belongings. No one else is in the facility, so I can freely talk.

"To be honest? I couldn't seem to get Lucy off my mind, if you catch my drift." He raises his eyebrows, but I continue. "Look, you're the one who said I should stop the whole sex before marriage stuff. This is me trying, dude. Midnight gym sessions." *Trying for her more than for myself, but he doesn't need to know that.*

Stanton laughs and wipes sweat off his forehead with a rag. "That's hunky-dory, but have you considered taking your inclinations to the Lord?"

"Of course I do," I half-way lie. He catches it in my tone instantly and shoves me. "Okay, okay. I try. I do pray occasionally. I ask Him to help me. But it seems to be a dead end. It's not working. The only thing that is semi-working is actively doing something to distract myself." Occasionally meaning like once a week because every time I try it feels absolutely useless and only heightens my desire for Lucy because I start to think about the very things I'm attempting to give up for her.

He nods thoughtfully as we walk out of the gym. "As you should. That is a productive, healthy way to redirect." He pauses for a second before continuing. "In my experience, God doesn't remove things to make our paths easier, but He is there for us to turn to when the blockage feels too intense—too enormous—to maneuver around. You know, to show us and remind us that we need Him."

I don't respond as I chew on his words. We arrive at our vehicles, and Stanton waits for me to reply as I open my driver door and throw my gym bag into the passenger seat. I envision Lucy there with her feet on the dash singing to Morgan Wallen as we drove to the bowling alley earlier.

It's then I speak words I've only thought in the recesses of my brain, words that I haven't allowed myself to vocalize on the account of causing my father to roll over in his grave. "If He brought Lucy into my path as an obstacle, I'm not so sure I want to continue attempting to follow Him. Lucy has helped me heal in so many ways. Yes, she's as big of a temptation as ever. I mean, look at her. But not only that, she's kind, intelligent, sensitive, funny, and... And she honestly cares about *me*. My past scars, my life growing up, and my dreams moving forward." I pause, my breaths coming heavier as my voice rises. "Why would God put a woman like her, someone I could so easily break because I'm weak when it comes to sexual desire, in my path as an obstacle to overcome?"

I meet Stanton's brown eyes. He presses his lips into a line and gives his head a small shake. "I don't have the answers, Stone, but I'm here for you. Even if you feel like doubting God. I will stand by your side until you come out on the other end of it. Because you *will* come out on the other side. You need to evaluate *why* you're weak when it comes to sexual temptation."

He says nothing else as he gets in his car and drives away, leaving me standing under a parking lot light with a million questions that have zero answers.

Lucy

Nights are the hardest.

It's in the dark abyss of my bedroom when the feeling sinks in.

The loneliness that stalks me all day finally catches me. Even the monster that hides under the bed flees at the sight of this particular killer.

I'm alone. My only companionship comes from the rectangular digital device I hold in my hand where my online friends and community I've built through publishing interact with me. And while I supremely enjoy their company, they are locked away behind tempered glass, inaccessible to warm hugs and kind smiles and loud laughs.

As I scroll, feelings of imposter syndrome begin to creep in. My post about how God is good no matter what is receiving a lot of "likes" and "amens," but why did I even post it? I'm finding I don't quite believe it to be true these days.

If He's so good, then why am I strangled with sexual temptation that seems to be squeezing me harder at every spiraling curve? It's like no matter how much I beg and plead with God to take it away, He doesn't. And for the life of me, I can't figure out why. Hadley has asked me how I'm doing a couple of times over the past week since I finally confided in her and told her I had slipped up with Stone—many, *many* times—and all I can tell her is that I'm still struggling and don't know why. I don't know what happened other than I have a hot man in my life who knows how to please my body. But even before, with the past few boyfriends I've had prior to Stone who looked as if they could please me, I've remained clean. Why I'm struggling like this now, I have no idea. I was clean from sex for a few years...

It's mid-September now, and it's only getting worse and worse every time I'm with him. Last week, I confessed I was torn up over the fact we kept sleeping together. And I've seen a real effort out of him to not pull me into temptation. But it's been a week since we last did it, and when he asked to come inside after dropping me off from a bowling night with friends, I almost said yes. I don't know how I stopped, but I did.

I fear my resolve is unraveling, however. That's what I told my journal tonight, at least.

If losing Stone is the only way off this winding road, then I'm not so sure I want to take the exit. What has God done for me anyways since I've stopped? Given me more dreams? Made my stomach ache with desire? Increased the area of this dark cloud of depression hovering over my head?

I don't even know why I'm refraining at this point. Why do I need to wait until I'm married to have sex? What's the big deal?

This is the big deal, something inside me whispers. *You are looking to him to save you from your sadness instead of Me.*

I hit the ignore button.

Dating Stone over the past few months has been the most fun I've ever had. When I'm with him, I forget about the haunting loneliness. Yes, my body and brain seem to be living in a constant state of depression to where I'm somehow not allowed to experience full bliss and joy no matter how much I want to, but I'm still determined to shake it off. Being with Stone helps. It takes the edge off. He makes me *happy.* Even if I'm an even bigger ball of anxiety than I was a few weeks ago and still scared he's going to for sure leave me now that I've asked to refrain from sex.

Why am I doing that again? What's the point?

I don't want to lose him.

I don't want this to ever end.

It's more than the obvious chemical and hormonal bonding of sex. Yes, that's definitely had its effect. It sucks in a way because I think a lot of my anxiety stems from being bonded to him in that way when I don't have a ring on my finger signaling a permanent commitment. Why do I need a ring to have sex with him anyway? In my heart, I—

The thought hits me upside the head like I once knocked Stone unconscious with a cast iron skillet.

Stone is everything I want.

He's been open and honest with me about his past. He checks on me in his own little ways. While he doesn't attempt to fix my overarching sadness, he does crack jokes and gives me random gifts like Ferrero Rochers, my favorite chocolate, or shows up randomly to take me out somewhere when it registers with him that I'm sad.

It's unbelievably sweet. He's not who I pegged him to be. His flirt game is as strong as ever, but he's also considerate and listens to me. He helps me with my writing and listens to me drone on and on over story ideas. He never tries to tell me to stop singing in the car, to get my feet off his dash, or that I'm expecting too much by waiting in the passenger seat for him to open my door.

Because he does open it.

Every. Single. Time.

And I love that man.

I think, in my heart, I'm already married to him...

And shouldn't that mean more than a lousy ring?

Part of me says of course while another part says there's something more. That there's a reason I'm supposed to wait even if I can't see it or understand it right now.

God, if You even care. If You even exist. If I refrain from sex with him, will You allow me to keep him forever?

BEAT FIVE

SWIVEL // "STAY STAY STAY"

A poem by Lucy May – October 8th

"PAN'S SHADOW"
lurking, creeping, stalking
like a calculated killer
cloaking in darkness
a shadow so familiar
under my bed
around the corner
further in line
outside my door
nowhere and everywhere
consuming my existence

suffocating my presence
Loneliness: a predatory sentience

Chapter 15

Lucy

"Seriously, Karoline! Help me out, girl. I have no idea what to get this man, and I'm usually great at gifts. All I can think about is writing him a love letter, but I can't do that because—" I cut myself off because there's no way I can tell him I love him, but she doesn't need to know that. She doesn't need to know me and Stone are a few weeks past his typical three-month period. She doesn't need to know I have refrained from sex with him for the past month on a stupid bargain with the God I'm not sure cares but I'm too entrenched in religion to give up in case He does. She doesn't need to know I feel splintered because I want to tell him I love him, but I'm terrified that would be the nail in the coffin to this relationship I have with him.

"You want him to say it first, I get that," Karoline finishes over the phone. "Is there anything he has been hinting at or outright saying he wants or needs?"

I groan. "Ugh, no. And anytime I ask, he says he has everything he needs with me. His birthday is tonight, and he said we're celebrating after our final business meeting with the investors."

"Aww, how cute. I love that he says that to you."

"Vroom, are you ready?" I hear Karoline's husband, Mason Kane, a famous country singer, shout.

Karoline must have muffled the phone because I hardly hear her when she shouts back, "Almost."

"Okay, Lucy, I've gotta run now. We're heading to Nashville, but I'll text you some ideas."

"Bye, Kar. Have fun and eat delicious food for me at that Turkish restaurant."

"Ah, I know. I'm so excited!" I can hear pure joy in her voice, and for a moment, I wish I had that. A solid life. A husband who adored me and loved me. The idea of a family on the horizon. "Love you, bye."

"Love you," I say with as much bravado I can, then I hang up and toss my phone onto my pink quilted bedspread.

"Well, shoot." I whisper to myself as I stand in front of the mirror smoothing down my black peplum dress. "What does one gift her boyfriend who she's terrified is going to break up with her at any moment because we've reached the limit?"

At this point, I'm going to have to tell him that what I ordered him is running late and that he'll get his present as soon as it comes in.

Whatever it is I finally decide on…

A meow pulls me from my thoughts, and I look down at my feet to find my cat, Frannie, who has been my sole companion during the dark nights as of late.

"At least you stayed." Her green eyes seem to be on the verge of spilling tears at any given moment, and I can't say that I blame her.

I glance over to the chocolate brown couch where Lorelei and I used to lay together watching movies or just chatting about life. Frannie and Frizzle, Lorelei's cat and Frannie's twin, would often jump on us, and it would be a little redheaded twin girl pile.

Those memories are a double-edged sword. Making me smile and want to scream at the same time.

"I know, Frannie. I miss them, too."

I check the time and realize Stone will be here to pick me up in thirty minutes, and my makeup still isn't done. I set to work while listening to worship songs instead of Taylor Swift as Hadley once instructed me to do. Though, if I'm being honest, it's doing nothing for me. In fact, it's making me angry.

Why am I still suffering and struggling? Even when I've prayed, asked for forgiveness, and continued going to church? I stopped having sex with Stone. Shouldn't God be making things better now?

I'm still left wondering what the point in all of this is...

I cut off the music as I finish applying my makeup.

Later, a knock at the door sounds, so I exit the cluttered bathroom and hunt under a pile of dirty clothes in my bedroom for my black shoes.

As I'm digging, a pair of pink glittery pumps catches my attention.

Surely I shouldn't wear those to a business dinner, right?

But it's Stone's birthday, and he will like them. He always says pink brings out the happiness in my soul. And he isn't wrong. I adore the color.

I snatch the heels and carry them to the door with me. I slip them on and grab my pink purse from the stand by the doorway, and I briefly feel a twinge of sadness over the dead Bird of Paradise. I forgot to water it one too many times, and I fear it can't be brought back from the dead.

Huh. There's a metaphor in that somewhere...

I open the door with a soft smile on my face. I no longer try to hide my innate sadness from Stone, but I also try to at least look like I'm surviving.

Which is barely.

Heck, even Emma Jane has noticed and told me that I should look into trying therapy.

But they're wrong. I'm not depressed like that. It's just a readjustment phase, as I've said before. A long one, but that's okay. I'm not sad all the time anymore. Stone has helped with that. And my writing brings me happiness. In fact, I'm almost ready to publish my first urban fantasy, which is exciting.

"You look... wow," Stone says. His crystal blue eyes, which sparkle in the evening daylight, appraise me. "I'm one lucky man."

I laugh, but then tack on in a flirty, "Hm. I think I'm the lucky one."

His expression changes subtly. One wouldn't notice it unless, like me, they have cataloged every movement of this man's face. It's a look that is contemplative and confusing.

I swear, if he breaks up with me on his birthday...

Changing the subject, I peruse him, openly admiring the way that black suit fits him in all the right places. "You look dashing in that suit, Mr. Harper. Are you ready to go sign the final deal with the investors? You'll be opening up the Dasher Valley Community Center in no time."

He grins and holds out his hand to me. I slip my fingers between his, locking down thoughts of breakups, as he leads us down the stairs from the second floor apartments.

"Do you want to come in?" The question hangs in the air as I search Stone's eyes, a stormy gray illuminated under the light of the porch, for his intentions. The business meeting went wonderfully. He signed contracts with all three investors. We all had a glass of wine with our steak meals to celebrate. I asked the waitress to bring out a cake to sing "Happy Birthday" and all was well. He said we were going back to his place for a movie tonight.

But when we got in his car, he didn't hold my hand as he usually does. In fact, he looked angry. I tried to ask him what's wrong, but he flashed a fake smile at me and said nothing. I asked if he's upset that his present was running late, but he exhaled a quipped laugh and shook his head. Was he lying about the movie? Is he about to...?

Fear is settling in my stomach because it feels like the exit ramp is near, and I am determined not to take it.

Stone will not remove himself from me. I can't allow my little slice of happiness—my distraction from the constantly stalking Loneliness—to leave.

I love him, and I might just have to risk telling him that tonight.

Angels are rolling their eyes at me right now, but that's okay. I'm going to roll the dice.

You can do this.

"Yes. I'd love to."

Stone doesn't smile, nor does the storm swirling in his eyes clear away, but instead, he releases a breath as he runs a hand through his blond hair while unlocking the front door with the other.

The door clicks, and my heart picks up triple time.

He turns the knob and pushes the black wooden door open, then he steps to the side and motions for me to enter.

My gaze darts from his tumultuous eyes to the threshold.

If I take that step, I'm vowing to pursue Stone until he recognizes and reciprocates these unpropitious feelings entrenched in my very soul. I refuse to let him end things. Our relationship may be at his timeline's end, but the way I covet forever with Stone Harper is as strong as the tingling nerves underneath my skin.

I catch his eyes again, and he tilts his head as if asking "what's the hold up?" So I move.

The tip of my glittery pink shoe connects with the floor on the other side of the door, and I close my eyes as I enter the darkened house. Stone moves silently behind me, and it's not until I hear the click of the door that I feel his chest against my back. The smell I've grown accustomed to over the past months envelops me in a sage, cacao, and bergamot cloud of heaven. I fight the desire to lean against him and release a sigh.

But I don't have to lean back. He presses further in, our bodies becoming seemingly one.

"Close your eyes. I'm going to turn the light on," he whispers against my ear as his hand wraps around my forearm.

"I already—okay." I don't tell him I've been living by my other senses alone since stepping through the door.

"Open," he commands in a way that shouldn't send a wave of shivers racing down my spine and goosebumps rippling up my arms, but it does.

When my eyes flutter open, I'm broken from the hypnotic circumstances of the dark. We are standing in his entryway, which is only big enough to host a shoe rack bench on the gray oak floor.

His hand drops from my forearm, and he creates space between us so he can slip his dress shoes off. I follow suit, sliding out of my heels. Then he steps around me and walks into the living room. I trail behind him, examining the living space I've spent countless time in.

The cleanliness and tidiness confounds me as I inspect the living room that's typically a little messy. A black leather couch, a matching recliner, and a glass-topped, low-rising coffee table sit upon a deep maroon area rug. A widescreen television is hung on the wall above a stone fireplace; pictures of him and his family don the mantle in an inward position with a beeswax sandalwood candle tucked in the middle of the homey array. After examining the pictures since I haven't been in this house in a month, I glance back at Stone. He was the cutest kid who turned into the cutest teenager who is now the devilishly handsome man across the way in the kitchen pouring drinks.

It's as if my thoughts beckoned him. When he calls my name, I snap my attention to him. "Hm?"

"Would you like a drink? I have water, tea, coffee, and," he pauses before cocking his head and nailing me with one of his infamous flirty smirks, "bourbon."

I don't have to think twice, though in retrospect, I should have...

"Bring out the bourbon, Onyx. It is your birthday." I wink, but he probably can't see that from across the open floor. I turn my attention back to the pictures on his mantel. "Speaking of, are your friends coming over to celebrate with us?"

"No. It's just me and you tonight, *Little Lion*."

I freeze in place, my mind spinning.

Maybe he's not ending it with me?

But what if he is...?

I told myself if I crossed that threshold tonight I was making a vow to myself to make Stone fall for me the way I have fallen for him. Yes, I definitely need the bourbon over water or coffee. Bourbon will make things a little easier on me. Just one glass. Nothing more. That will be enough to loosen all these nerves twisting and tangling and tingling everytime I so much as think of telling him I'm in love with him. Then I can confess my true feelings and go on some spiel about how I refuse to let him walk away from me.

Clingy? *Probably.*

A little toxic? *Aren't we all?*

But when I say I've fallen for this man...

"Do you want to watch a movie?"

I jump at the nearness of Stone's voice. When I spin around, I'm met with his dazzling smile as he holds two whiskey glasses not even a quarter of the way full. He stretches a glass out to me, and I take it with both hands, careful not to spill it on his pretty rug.

"A movie? Are you trying to get me to *chill* with you, Mr. Harper?" I'm teasing, but the bobble in his throat and the sudden fire in my veins at the idea of watching a movie in a darkened room alone with Stone has me taking a sip to cool the heat. He mimics my actions. It's been so long for the two of us...

"I, uh—" I breathe an awkward laugh and shake my head. "I didn't mean that. Sorry."

He chuckles, and the storm in his eyes evaporates, leaving sparkling droplets in its place. Against my better judgment, I let my eyes wander lazily over him. His white button-up collared dress shirt is still tucked into his black slim fit dress pants. The top three buttons of his shirt are undone, and he's already lost the black tie he was wearing.

"Don't be sorry. I am your man, after all." He laughs, and I snap my gaze back to his face. But that doesn't help, either. Because his tanned skin brightens his blond, tousled hair. His long, black eyelashes brush his cheek as he blinks, and then I'm invigorated again at his round eyes, which are transitioning to a softer baby blue with every passing second.

When Stone is happy and amused, his eyes lighten.

When he is sad or angry, they dull in color but still retain a blue hue.

When they're stormy, he's in a *mood*. A sexy mood...

"So, a movie? With *no chill?*" He picks up the remote from the coffee table then sits on the couch and splays out.

"Only if I can pick the movie." I ignore the chill comment because my face is flushed enough as it is from ogling him. As always.

I'm tired of blushing. Can someone tell the author of my story that?

Stone tosses me the remote. I take it and turn on the television. "Okay, Granite. Let's see..."

I sit down on the couch, but I'm sure to leave adequate space so that my Grandma Netty could fit between us. She's been pestering me to bring him to church, but the few times I've asked Stone to go with me, he's been busy. Or so he said. I know he doesn't go to church unless we happen to be in Dasher Valley on a Sunday morning.

Heck, the only reason I think I go these days is to appease Grandma Netty and Hadley. And to keep up an image.

I search for a rom-com because I know Stone loves them. He even helps me with my books when I'm struggling.

Of course I can't let a man like that walk away from me!

When that genre section pops up on the screen, Stone jokingly groans to keep his manhood intact, and I throw a bright smile his way. After a quick browsing session, I settle on *Just Go With It* simply because I love Jennifer Aniston and Adam Sandler together. But as the movie begins, I remember this story has a fake dating plot involving an employee and her boss...

I hope Stone doesn't pay too close attention to the movie.

But my hopes are severed when after the first ten minutes, Stone is laughing and commenting on the hilarity of Adam Sandler. He actually makes me pause the movie while he goes and pops popcorn for us.

When he returns, he sits next to me.

Right next to me.

My shoulder is brushing against his bicep, my thigh squished against his.

All points of contact are molten lava from the volcanic eruption of my heart. His spicy scent wraps around me, mingling with buttery popcorn and a hint of bourbon.

I throw back the rest of my drink, the burn reminding me I need to rip the band-aid off and tell this man how I feel before I burst with all the love-struck feelings I'm harboring. I set the empty glass on the coffee table a little too hard.

"Easy there, Little Lion. You good?" Stone asks. When I glance up at him, his eyes are still sparkling, and as I stare into his very soul, I watch the sparkles fade, replaced with that stormy gray color from the doorway. I am so in love with this man, and that love is going to end up hurting me deeper than any other heartbreak I've ever experienced. Stone may struggle with commitment, and while I know that logically and understand the reason behind his hesitancy, my heart seems to think I could be the one woman who could tie him down. He's tried for me.

Now I have to take a gamble.

What a hopeless pursuit.

"I think I love you," I blurt. Then I will myself to be bold. "No. I know I love you."

Since the movie is paused, the silence that surrounds us is deafening. But right as I am about to retract my stupid confession, Stone turns his body and takes my face between his hands, dragging my lips to his. Electricity courses its way through every molecule of being. I'm a livewire and Stone's lips are the metal initiating the shock. My eyes flutter closed.

He is not gentle.

His mouth moves against mine in a fury of desire. I feel him move closer against me, and then I hear the bowl of popcorn that was resting on his lap tumble to the ground. As he moves his hands from my face and wraps one arm around my waist with the other around my neck, hoisting me to my knees, popcorn crumbles beneath me and I groan into his mouth.

All sensible thoughts are kissed out of my brain. The only word present is his name.

Stone. Stone. Stone...

I love him, and he is kissing me like he loves me. The man terrified of commitment, who has been *trying* for me, kissed me when I said I loved him. That means the world to me, but I need to know...

Breaking free from his soft lips, I ask him through pants, "Stone. What does this mean?"

Searching his stormy eyes, I know Stone has desired me from the moment he closed that passenger door and left the restaurant.

"You frustrate me, Lucy. In the most delicious way. It's been a living hell staying away from you." He draws closer with each word that comes next. "You. Are. Irresistible." Stone claims my lips again, and the thrill I was experiencing earlier is now ten-fold.

He thinks I'm irresistible. His eyes are saying everything I need to know. His touch is gentle yet strong. His lips are devouring yet intentional. We fit together like I've never fit against anyone in my existence. And I don't want anyone else ever again. He is it for me. This is it for me. I have no reservations now. Forget rings and bargains with God.

My body is vibrating, and only one thing, one *person*, can satiate this hypnotic desire...

Stone Harper.

"Happy birthday," I whisper into his ear after giving it a little bite, tearing and burning every red flag attempting to raise itself.

I'm *tired* of holding back...

So. Freaking. Tired.

I love him.

"Best present ever," he growls.

Chapter 16

Stone

"What in the—" *curse* "—did I do?"

I slam my palms against the bathroom sink as I stare at my reflection with insurmountable disgust. My hair is sticking up in every direction, long, red marks trailing down my chest, an outward expression of the guilt clawing my insides.

Images of Lucy running her hands through my hair, gripping my arms, among many, *many* other things race through my head, acting as a driving force, demanding I return to my bedroom where she's snuggled up in a plaid blanket cocoon, sleeping as if she's in perfect harmony with the world.

Peace settled upon me, too, last night, when she said she loved me. Except that peace was a falsified monster and now I want to run out of my own house in a desperate escape to flee the conversation I'm going to have to have with her when she wakes up. Those three words bounce around my brain, tightening my chest and pressing a heavy weight upon my shoulders.

The least I can do is make her breakfast and coffee, right?

After smoothing my hair down and tiptoeing into the room (purposefully avoiding letting my eyes wander to the woman in my bed) to swipe a t-shirt and jogging pants, I make my way into the living room.

Popcorn litters the couch and floor, and I set to work cleaning it as best as I can without breaking out the vacuum. Once I'm finished, I get a pot of coffee brewing and begin to start on breakfast, opting to cook bacon, eggs, and toast. Simple but nutritious.

As I'm cooking, a mindless task for me, I try to come up with the right words to say to Lucy. I could immediately apologize for slipping up and tempting her and say it won't happen again, but I'm not so sure that's the truth. If she still wants to stick around after this...

I could tell her that it was the bourbon's fault, but I think we both know I handle my liquor well by now. She'd see right through that.

I could be completely honest and tell her I enjoy her company more than I enjoy breathing, and I adore the way her real smiles tend to come out when we're alone together. I could say that her kisses and touches bring me to my knees. I could say that she has me wrapped around her finger.

But none of that would matter because regardless of those things, I cannot fully give her my heart. This freak out I'm having this morning is proof of that. I'm not ready. I've given her my time, my money, my history, and my body... But my heart? The idea of loving her absolutely terrifies me. What if I was to propose to her and she walked away from me? What if she wakes up one morning and realizes I'm not enough for her?

Those walls will stay up. Admittedly, the walls are growing shorter and shorter with every personal, non-judgmental conversation we have together, but they remain as strong as ever, nonetheless.

Whatever I decide to tell her, or whatever stupid excuse bolts from my mouth the moment she questions me about our relationship status, I have to keep better control of myself if she sticks around.

I didn't realize the importance of doing that until I woke up with a pit in my stomach over the thought that she told me she loved me last night and then I took her to bed.

I slept with her after she told me she loved me.

And that right there is the reason I am not in a space to love her in return. The lust is too strong, and I have the slimmest of control. Lucy deserves so much better than who I am and what I can give her. Heck, even if I did allow myself to love her and could commit to her fully, I still wouldn't be worthy.

Excuses, excuses, my inner thoughts taunt, but I kick them out for the moment. I have to focus and see what I can salvage between me and Lucy. Especially because we work together.

That thought punches me square in the jaw, and I groan. *How in the world are we going to navigate work?*

"Oh, this smells divine," a feminine voice that's registering on the sleepy end yanks me from my thoughts. *I'm not ready...*

But I spin around to face her anyway.

Lucy's strawberry curls are scooped up into a messy bun on top of her head, and she wears one of my oversized dress shirts.

And that seems to be it.

I swallow, fighting to keep my gaze from traveling down her bare legs. She smirks as if she notices the restraint I'm attempting to hold. "It's okay," she whispers, walking toward me in a sultry manner. "You can look."

Not needing any more permission than that, I freely take her in, admiring the sheer beauty of the woman in front of me. Why, *why* can't I just let myself love her genuinely and without restraint? Why can't I control my desire for her and respect her by not bonding her to me without a lifetime commitment?

I snap my gaze back up to her face as she laughs. The sound is carefree and buoyant, and I can't remember a time where she sounded this happy.

Joyful.

She finally sounds like she's living life instead of barely surviving.

Guilt eats at me as I try to form words. I tell her she looks amazing in my shirt, which is God's honest truth. I ask her how she slept. I make her eggs scrambled and her coffee with sugar and cream, just as she likes it.

Because regardless of my fear of commitment, and regardless that I'm scared as a cat in water to get down on one knee for a woman again, I know Lucy.

I know her so well. And now she openly loves me.

Why did I sleep with her last night when I can't bring myself to say those words back to her?

It's not like I haven't slept with women before, but none of those women confessed they loved me prior to it. None of them had been spending days upon days working alongside me during the day and then going on dates with me at night. None of them revealed feeling like a burden to other people or like they couldn't escape loneliness or like they were rejected in life.

But Lucy May Spence did.

I—I care about her. Deeply. And that has to be why this guilt is crushing me like a loaded barbell. For the first time in a long time, I genuinely don't want to even *mistakenly* do wrong by a woman.

But I did. Oh, I did...

"Lucy, I'm so sorry," I blurt. Tears push against my eyes, but I know better than to let them out. *Men don't cry.* Not in south Mississippi.

"Sorry for what? You have nothing to be sorry for, Stone." She gets up from the kitchen table where she was scrolling on her phone and stands beside me, placing one hand on my arm. "If it's about last night, don't apologize. I'm a big girl. I made my choice. And now I feel happier than I have in a month. I feel free. All thanks to you." She stands on her tiptoes and kisses my cheek. "Are you well?"

I nod my head and attempt a smile, silencing all the emotions for the time being. She looks as happy as she claims to be, and I am not going to take that from her. Not today.

Today, and for today only, I'm going to play pretend one more time and treat her like the gem of a woman she is.

Then I'll let her go so she can one day find someone worthy of her. Someone who won't sleep with her when she says she loves him even though he can't figure out his own emotions and thoughts. Someone with better control of himself.

I turn with two prepared plates in my hand and kiss her forehead. "Ready to eat, Little Lion?"

"I'm starved," she says, bouncing on her toes as she navigates back to the kitchen table.

After we eat, exchanging small talk and bantering back and forth, I take Lucy home and immediately begin the long drive to Dasher Valley.

I send Lucy a text a little while after leaving her saying there is an emergency back at home, and I am going to spend the rest of the weekend there. I tell her I won't be back until Tuesday and ask her to hold down the center for me on Monday. Finally, I send a message to Jeanie saying I will be out and Lucy will stand in for me.

Having my ducks in a row, I run away to seek solace at home like the broken and scarred twenty-five-year-old man that I am. This is my breaking point. *Something's gotta give.*

Lucas lets out a long whistle as Jared stares at me like I'm the biggest idiot in existence.

He's right, of course, but it still doesn't feel great to have a hulkish man like him look at you that way. I take a swig of sweet tea, looking out from the bleachers at the soccer field we are currently having a work day on. We came out here after our post-church family lunch because I told Lucas I needed to talk to him about Lucy. He sighed, shook his head, and said if I was going to make stupid choices and run to him about them then the least I could do was to help him do some field work. Football season ended about a week ago, and now he's getting the field prepped for soccer season to begin. Though he is the athletic director at Dasher Valley High, he wanted to maintain coaching soccer and teaching. At least until he has kids of his own, he says.

Eventually, Lucas speaks. "Why don't you just let yourself love her, Stone? I don't get it. You talk about her like she hung the moon and stars. You might be obsessed with her, to be honest. Why not give her the chance to open your heart back up and bring some healing into your life?"

He's not a man of many words, so I'm shocked at his open evaluation. I finally told the two of them the full story behind Lacey so they *would* understand why I'm resistant, but apparently that didn't matter. "I told you. I don't feel worthy. She'll see that and will toss me to the side."

"Isn't that what you've been doing with women?" Jared retorts, lifting his brows.

"It's not the same," I defend. "All the women I've been with or have dated short-term knew that's what I was doing. Lucy knew this was all fake. It's what we agreed upon. And then when it became real, I tried. I opened up some to her. I really tried. But then she went and fell in love with me, and I'm just not ready."

"No, you are. You fell in love with her. You just won't admit it," Lucas adds sardonically.

I glare at him with a look that would set fire to the field right now.

"I am not in love with her. I care about her and respect her, but I don't love her." How can I possibly love her if I have sex with her after she tells me she loves me when I know I can't say it back?

Jared clicks his tongue and then knocks me on the back of the head. I shoot to my feet, prepared to hit him back, but as he stands, I remember he's a walking one-man army and opt to sneer at him instead.

"You're a fool, Stone. Caring about a woman and respecting her are the primary ways we men show love. You've watched me and your brother fall in love with our wives. You know what it looks like. And if you care for and respect her so much, why didn't you keep it in your pants?"

And with that comment—the very thing I currently hate myself for—I do swing at him, but he catches my fist and twists my arm until I tap out.

"Chill out, dude. Let's be real, okay? You've already told us everything, so now it's time you listen to what we have to say without getting angry or offended. We care about you and want to see you happy," Jared yells before he releases my fist. I shake out my arm while rubbing my wrists as Lucas begins to speak, both men now flanking my sides as we stand on the bleachers.

"You should really listen to Jared. He smacked sense into me when it came to your sister. There's a wise man underneath that muscle."

Jared scoffs and folds his arms, which hopefully means there will be no more smacking.

After a minute of silence passes, I realize they are both waiting for me to say something. "I know I shouldn't have slept with her after she told me she loved me. Guilt has been eating me alive since it happened, and I know I need to tell her that we can't be together, but she just looked so happy the next morning. I hadn't seen her look that light in such a long time. How can I take that from her?"

"Bingo," Jared says at the same time Lucas replies with, "You love her."

Right as I open my mouth to protest, Lucas cuts me off. "You love her at least in some capacity. While I can't tell you that it's in a 'you want to marry her' type of way, though I'd venture to say it is, what you feel for her as shown by your stupid actions and thoughts is love. The fact you don't feel worthy of her and you want her to be happy is love. Now the question remains: Are you going to do what it takes and put in the work to be worthy of her or not?"

Chewing on his words while picking at my fingernails, I can't deny what he's saying. I care about her. I respect her, even if I didn't show it by hopping into bed with her after she confessed. The guilt that clawed at my throat was like none other. I'm usually only a smidge guilty when I sleep with a woman. With Lucy... how could I do that to her? She's precious and kind and understanding and patient, and I—

Do I—

Do I love her?

"I'll think about what you've both said. But for now, I think I need time to process in quiet. Let's resume some field work."

They both agree, and I head to the fieldhouse to work on moving soccer equipment in and the football equipment out.

When we finish for the day, I realize I had left my phone in Lucas's truck, so I start checking messages, most of which seem to be from Lucy.

> **Little Lion:** Good morning :)

> **Little Lion:** Hope you have a productive day. I'm going to take this time to get some work done on the business side of authoring.

Three hours later...

> **Little Lion:** Afternoon! Hope all is well and hope to hear from you soon.

An hour later...

Missed call from Little Lion.

> **Little Lion:** Stone? You good? I'm kind of worried about you.

Forty-five minutes later...

> **Little Lion:** Are you upset with me? Did I do something wrong?

> **Little Lion:** Please don't tell me you're bailing out on me after I told you I loved you...

> **Little Lion:** Don't do this to me, Stone...

Two hours later...

> **Little Lion:** You're probably just busy and I'm acting like a deranged girlfriend. I'm sorry. But do please message me to set the record straight when you see this.

Releasing a long breath, I begin to type a reply.

> **Me:** Hey, I'm sorry. I haven't really been on my phone all day between church, a family lunch, and then doing some field work with Lucas and Jared. Everything is fine, and we are good. You haven't done anything wrong, I just haven't been around my phone. I'm sorry.

I know deep down that the message doesn't justify anything. Any person in their right mind would feel jaded and dismissed after going all day without so much as a "hey" from the person they care about. I have so much to process and work through. The last thing I want to do is hurt her.

You're going to hurt her, anyway, Pebbles. I roll my eyes. Great. Now my own consciousness is using the same nickname she does when she's perturbed with me.

Even *I'm* apprehensive of myself.

My phone vibrates in my hand as we pull up to Lucas's house where I left my bike.

> **Little Lion:** I'm glad you're okay! And all is well. Thank you for letting me know. I appreciate it. Did your field work go well?

I'm not in the right headspace to speak with her right now due to all the up-in-the-air thoughts racing through my brain, so I ignore her and tell myself I'll message her back when I'm back at Mom's and in bed.

Except when I drift off into a fitful sleep, I remember I never messaged back.

And while it rips me apart that I can't seem to do it, I push the feelings down and fade into blackness.

Chapter 17

Lucy

I stare at my phone while my computer boots up as I sit in my office chair at work.

> **Me:** I'm glad you're okay! And all is well. Thank you for letting me know. I appreciate it. Did your field work go well?

It's been opened. Read. I wonder if he even realizes he has his read receipts on?

He never responded, and while I wanted to cry over it to release the whirlwind of negative emotions consuming me throughout the night, I couldn't bring myself to shed a single tear. Instead, I screamed in the shower. I screamed at God for allowing Friday night to happen. I screamed at myself for being so blindly stupid that I let Stone's flattering words impact me.

He never said he loved me back.

That was the big red stop sign that should have ended everything.

But instead, I gaslit myself into believing that 'you frustrate me' phrase meant the same thing.

It obviously didn't.

If I was the heroine of a rom-com right now, he would be bursting into this office with flowers and chocolates, telling me he's sorry for running away after Friday night.

But as time ticks by and my message remains unanswered, I'm positive I've been mistakenly placed in a women's fiction novel without an HEA.

A message pops up on my phone, and my heartbeat quickens, but my shoulders slump when I realize it's just my sister. She's asking me if I'm bringing Stone to the wedding and coronation in a couple of months, and right now, I have no idea.

So I text back saying that I don't know. We will see how things work out.

The desire to text Stone torments me. To try and call him. To call a news media site and tell them to report I'm going to jump off the water tower to see if that will get him to message me back. I'm a lunatic, but this feeling to get his attention, to make him see me, is a force to be reckoned with and a second by second fight not to act upon it.

My phone rings, and it's Grandma Netty calling.

Guess I'm popular with everyone this morning except for my boyfriend who ran away from me under the excuse of a family emergency. Yeah, I know that was a lie. I text with his sister, after all.

So is he really even my boyfriend now?

I would think so after the way he claimed my body the other night.

Men are different, though. They can have sex with a woman, and it does not mean a thing.

I know that.

Logically.

Emotionally, I want to die.

"Hello," I say with as much of a mellow tone as I can manage.

"Lucy girl, it's Grandma Netty. What are your dinner plans?"

I chuckle at her introduction despite my sour mood. She forgets caller ID is a thing now, and just hearing her voice brings a small light into the cave of darkness. "I was just going to heat up leftovers at the apartment and write. Why?" It's a lie. I was most likely going to obsessively watch my phone and attempt to distract myself with writing all the while starving myself because I'm way too anxious to eat.

"Take yourself a break and come have dinner with me, will ya? I'm lonely and I miss my grandgirl."

Beats anxiously sulking around my apartment. I can go anxiously pretend that I'm not actually anxious and shovel down a good meal at Grandma's.

"Of course. Thanks for the invite. What time should I be over?"

She gives me the details and then we click off the phone. The rest of the work day passes torturously slow. I check my phone every few seconds, so much so that it's become habitual.

He never texts.

And I pray it's because he's dead. Because if he's not...

He'll wish he was when I'm through with him.

If I've learned one thing in the past—through being used by men for their sexual gratification—it's that I won't let the same mistake happen twice with the same man. Stone doesn't get to touch me anymore if he can't commit to me. If he can't tell me he loves me.

No matter how desperately I crave his hands all over me...

Thank goodness he isn't at work today to see what a mess I am.

With a newfound determination, I set to work applying the finishing touches to the Halloween Bash happening next week, checking the list of volunteers, and doing some other administration work.

Mind. Numbing. Business.

Which is disastrous because my newfound determination wavers as quickly as it settled in with all of the excessive thinking time.

What if he's cheating on me right now?

Then you walk away.

What if he tells me he doesn't love me like I love him?

Then you walk away.

What if he continuously ghosts me?

Then you walk away.

What if...

Oh, for heaven's sake, Lucy! Walk away and write a freaking book about it to get all your pain out, okay?!

Why can't I be like Taylor Swift and infuse all my heartbreak into songs instead of crafting full-length novels? My poetry is my escape from pain, but I can't sing, and I don't think my audience would like my anguished poems.

My readers want *happy*. They want perfect communication. They want clean characters. They want unrealistic, eternal joy...

"Gah!" I scream aloud as I throw the pen I was holding at the door, which I didn't realize was opening until it was too late.

The pen hits Stone in the forehead, and for one derisory second, my lips twitch as I bask in the teensy karma-filled moment gifted to me.

But then I control my expression because I'm at work and he's technically my boss.

And he has a bouquet of...

Ferrero Rochers?

"Well, Lucy May. I guess I deserved that one." He rubs his forehead and closes the door to my office. He picks up the pen and walks over to my desk, setting it down in front of me alongside the wrapped chocolates on fake flower stems. His arm is fully in my line of vision, and I get a wild hair to bite it. Whether it's to deliver pain or pleasure, I don't yet know.

"Are you here to talk to me as my boss, or..." I don't say the word boyfriend, because regardless of my twisted thinking on Friday night and the following morning, I don't know where we stand. *He never said he loved me...*

But he brought my favorite chocolates...

He sighs and leans his backside against my desk. I don't bother to spin my chair to address him, but I can smell his cologne—an intoxicating blend of cedarwood, sage, and cocoa. He wears Bad Boy by Carolina Herrera. I snooped through his bathroom while I was over at his house and sprayed my shirt with it before I left.

How fitting that he chose that brand.

"I'm sorry I haven't responded. No, I won't use the excuse I was busy. I could have texted back, but I—" He pauses, and I side-eye him. He has his head hung and hands folded. "I'm processing everything. I'm sorry I'm a slow processor, but Lucy, I don't want to hurt you. I've had so much fun with you over the past four months, and I like the friendship we've built. I care about you, and I respect you. I shouldn't have let my desires get the best of me on my birthday after you told me you felt guilty over *us*. After you said you loved me. You deserve so much better than that."

My mind reels over his words, glitching over his honesty. I fully expected some lame excuse such as being too busy or saying his phone died.

"Uh, I—" I shake my head and finally turn to meet him, my words breathy. "It's okay. Thank you for your honesty." *But if he says he's too good for you, you're supposed to believe him...*

He looks down at me, and by the puffiness of his cheeks and the red tinting the whites of his eyes, I swear he's been crying.

I stand, and against my better judgment, I throw my arms around his neck and pull him tight. If this is the last time I'm going to get to hug him, I'm making it count.

One hand plays with his hair while my other slides down his chest. I risk a glance at him, and those blue-gray storm clouds have once again formed in his eyes.

My body tingles, and it's as if I've forgotten all of my anxieties and worries. He's here. In my arms. Looking at me as if he wants me. And he brought me apology chocolates...

"It's okay, Quartz." I stand on my tiptoes and kiss his lips. It's just a small peck, but I aim to reassure him that I'm fine.

Even if I know deep down that I'm not.

I can fake it 'til I make it.

He finally slides his arms around my waist and tugs me closer to him.

"I understand commitment is hard for you. I understand you may not be ready. But can I ask you, once again, to try?" *Please, please don't leave me alone...*

His Adam's apple bobbles as he swallows. I can practically feel the nervous energy radiating off him. He releases his hold and moves his hands to grip my hips. "I don't know, Lucy. I'm really trying to work it all out in my head. I'm trying to overcome my fear. I don't understand why it's so hard for me, but it is. My head feels like a hurricane and typhoon are clashing together."

I nod, biting my bottom lip to stop myself from blurting practical ways he could work on those issues. This is clearly something he needs to work through himself, even if every moment that passes rips me to shreds, taking the stitches he had once sewn into me out one by one.

Hello, Numb String. Welcome back, Old Friend. Time to double-down.

"Can we continue seeing each other through the Halloween Bash and then reconvene? Is that enough time for you to process? We can press pause on this conversation until then."

Stone sighs, closes his eyes, but he nods all the same before kissing my forehead. "What are you doing tonight? Want to come over and watch a movie?"

I think of Grandma Netty. I should have dinner with her, but my heart yearns for Stone. Maybe if I can just spend a little more time with him, it will convince him that I'm a woman worth settling down with. *Am I, though?* "I'd love to."

He smiles, plants a chaste kiss on my lips, then leaves.

My thoughts range from guilt over canceling with my grandma, excitement over watching a movie with Stone, anger at myself for even suggesting that we continue on until the Halloween Bash, and revulsion over clinging to Stone Harper like he's the broken plank Rose held onto for dear life, despite all my big talk that I won't ever let another man use me or pull me around.

Because if I lose him for good, what's the point of even existing anymore? I might as well go down into the icy water like Jack.

I'm twenty-six.

Unmarried.

He's my only prospect in sight.

He's the only prospect I want.

I love him.

Like I've never loved before...

BEAT SIX

THE DARK MOMENT // "HOW DID IT END?"

A poem by Lucy May – November 3rd

"GOOD RIDDANCE"
the wind thrashing my hair
matched the wild coloring your soul
gravel beneath the tires
final destination: unknown
Unknown became a diseased reality
when the wind slapped our faces
gravel under my heels
as I rejected the complacent
you said you'd come back
but a fool's word is a lie.

complacency is an altar
where good girls go to die.

Chapter 18

Stone

"I swear you'll be the death of me, Lucy May. Who gave you permission to look this ravishing at a community event?" Within the privacy of my office, I tug my literal little lion close and kiss a trail from her jaw to her collarbone, careful to avoid her carefully crafted lioness makeup.

"Marble, stop it." She laughs and pushes me away. "You'll ruin my face."

I purr playfully, pulling her back to me and kissing down the other side of her neck. "Don't tempt me."

Lucy moans softly, and I feel my body react to her. Better stop now so I don't lock that door and lay her down on my desk. A man can only hold out for so long.

Over the past two weeks, we haven't hung out as much as we were prior to my birthday night and her confession. We haven't slept together, though admittedly, we've come close a few times. She has given me space when I need it, which I constantly tell her I appreciate because I can see how hard it is on her. I see it when she's secretly crying at work. I see it when she posts on social media in the middle of the night. I see it in how her clothes seem to be getting looser. I see haunted ghosts in her eyes, and it absolutely kills me that I'm the reason.

But tonight, everything changes.

I've tried my best to be good to Lucy over this past week. She deserves a good, Godly man to lead her and love her. That's the conclusion. How I become that man is still up in the air. And how she heals from this... I don't know. I see how anxious I've made her, and her sadness is overwhelming sometimes. I don't know how to help her through it anymore. My jokes don't work and I don't have answers for her. I'm starting to think she needs space, whether she realizes it or not, to work through her own stuff. I think... I think I'm hindering her.

"You seriously did an amazing job, Lucy," I step away, my eyes traveling from her curly, teased hair down her sharp and dangerous makeup meant to give her the face of a lion. She wears a golden beige knee-length dress with fringe hanging off the sleeves and at the bottom hem. Typical Lucy, she's running around in black-heeled boots.

How her feet don't fall off at the end of every day, I'll never know.

"Thank you," she says with a happy smile and little twirl. "Makeup is my second love after writing."

Even the mention of the word love tightens my chest, but I breathe through it, fighting the feeling.

"Ready to go entertain kids for the night?"

She smiles and takes my hand in hers. I will relish the feeling of her skin touching mine for the rest of my existence. Even if I never get to experience it again outside of my dreams at night.

"You could have dressed up, you know?" She squeezes my hand.

I shrug. "I am dressed up. Don't I look great in my boss outfit?"

She laughs as we walk into the gym of the community center, and I'm once again taken aback at Lucy's eye for details. Halloween has thrown up in here, and I'm thankful it came without horrors.

Because Lucy is scared easily and didn't want to terrify kids with our Halloween Bash, she's put together the most epic fall festival this town has ever seen.

There's the basic bobbing for apples, throw the football through the hanging tire, and our town's favorite game even in the midst of Halloween—Ring Pacey the Panther—where people toss hula-hoops around Juniper Grove High School's mascot.

I wonder what poor, unfortunate soul got stuck in the suit tonight.

But aside from the classic games, Lucy has a live game of chess happening in the middle of the room, reminiscent of the scene from *Harry Potter*. There's a section devoted to giant games such as UNO and Jenga. Children wrapping their parents in toilet paper like mummies and pumpkin tic-tac-toe is going on. Plus so much more.

"Wow, Lucy May. This is incredible." I tuck her into my side, kissing her lightly on the top of her head.

She scoffs. "You're acting like I haven't shown you the game plan a million times."

I shake my head. "But still. It's nothing compared to the reality of what you've done here tonight." I glance at her, and she's positively beaming with pride.

I thought I knew exactly what I needed to do tonight, but now I'm not so sure.

How could I let a woman like this slip through my arms simply because I don't feel like I'm enough?

I just need to do it.

Be enough.

For *her*.

"Oh, look! There's Emma Jane, and is that…" She bounces on her toes. "The mayor is here tonight. Let's go say hello to Mr. Knightley Austen." She drags me behind her, and I paste a smile on my face, forcing all other thoughts from my head.

We approach the red-headed older man who just dropped out from the mayoral race a couple of days ago. "Mayor, I'm glad you could come out tonight." I shake his hand, and he gives me a warm smile. I had invited him over email and reminded him about this event a week ago at the town's Sweet Tea Festival.

"Thank Emma Jane. She forced me out of my office."

I glance between the two of them, smiling like fools at one another. They sure aren't letting the media tongue lashing get them down.

Emma Jane is twenty-three. He's thirty-six. The people of this area have not been kind to the announcement that they are a couple. To be honest, it kind of weirds me out.

Not your place to judge, Stone. Age isn't that important once both parties are out of college. You had to get over your woman being older than you...

"Thanks, EJ," Lucy says, embracing her friend in a hug. "I like your female knight costume. I wonder what inspired that..." The two women link arms and walk away. Knightley and I exchange glances, and by the way his red undertone skin deepens, I wonder if he thinks I'm going to say something about their relationship.

I'm not. It's not my place to pry nor is it my story to infringe upon. I can't even keep my own relationship from falling to fragments.

"How's the law firm doing? Lucy says Lorelei occasionally mentions missing it."

"The firm misses her, that's for sure. It's not the same without her organization and attention to detail." He shoves his hands in his khaki pants, and I'm glad I'm not the only one who didn't feel the holiday spirit. "I like what you're doing with this place, Mr. Harper. Each event you host seems to get bigger and better. I know it's had a wonderful impact on the community."

Pride swells within me at his praise. "Thank you, Mayor Austen. That means a lot to me. I'm glad I can help and provide for this community in this small capacity. Though you should thank Lucy for the events. She's the best of the best when it comes to planning. That mind of hers is fascinating."

He smirks at me and shakes his head. "Women. Once we fall in love, there's nothing we wouldn't do or praises we wouldn't sing for them, am I right?"

I laugh nervously, my chest constricting. "Right. Well, I better go make sure everyone is safe and having a good time. Thanks again for coming."

We shake hands to say goodbye then I dart away, heading for the men's restroom in our office quarters.

With every human I dodge in my path, my vision grows fuzzier. The various masks—ghosts, Freddie Kruger, Scream, etc.—are somehow enlarged within my sight, haunting and taunting and torturing me.

Love. Love. Love.

I do love her. But...

I *can't* love Lucy.

She's too precious.

I'm too broken.

I burst into the bathroom and cling to the edge of the sink, taking quickened breaths. After a few moments, and I've slowed my heart rate down a little, I splash water on my face and scowl at the man in the mirror.

Just who have I become?

"What an amazing night! I can't believe we pulled that off so well." Lucy rubs circles on my thigh with her thumb as we drive to my place. I smile softly at her, but I know she can tell something's up.

It's the deadline, after all.

And she's tried her hardest to be the strongest soldier for me tonight. She has smiled hollow smiles, laughed ghostly laughs, and eyed me when she thought I wasn't looking as if she has a sadness disease that she must keep hidden from me.

It's no use.

I know the truth of it. I see through her Happy Mask.

I'm the reason she even has to don one.

She needs someone who can say he loves her. A man who will lead her in Christ. I am not him. I can't even lead myself to Christ. I don't even know if I believe anymore, but I know I have to figure it out. Everything inside me screams that that is the most important thing at the moment.

We pull into my driveway, and I watch Lucy eye her car with a sense of hopelessness.

I open her door for her, grasp her hand, and walk her toward the door. She follows me inside but doesn't leave the entryway.

"Would you like something to drink?" I ask, walking toward the kitchen.

"I'm okay, thanks." Her voice sounds like it's on the verge of shattering, and I feel like the smallest man who has ever lived for unintentionally stringing her along because I wasn't brave enough to call it off earlier.

Heck, I still don't know if I'm brave enough.

Part of me hopes that maybe I could heal alongside her, but another part of me says that it's no use.

I don't know which is the angel or which is the devil.

Not to mention she is utterly depressed, and it's time she works through that without me dragging her deeper and deeper into the darkness.

Sipping the glass of water I just poured, I walk toward Lucy.

I set the glass down on the table, take four steps toward the doorway, and wrap her in the tightest hug I think I've ever given anyone. Her vanilla scent burns in mind, branding itself on me to terrorize me later tonight. My brain continuously flickers between keeping her and letting her go.

I hold on tighter.

Finally, she slips her arms around my waist and matches my tug.

After what feels like a millenia, she pushes me away, moving her hands from my back to my chest. "Stone..."

My name is a desperate plea on her lips.

"Lucy..."

Her name is a glass heart in my hands.

"Don't do this," she whispers in a broken, anguished prayer.

"I—" I can't even finish my sentence before her mouth is on mine, kissing me with fervor and passion. I relish the strawberry taste and lose myself to the frantic kiss, switch our positions so I can push her up against the side wall by the door. Her hands pull my hair as she drags my head down to her, and my fingers dig into her waist as I recognize this kiss is her final attempt to get me to stay. To verify my thoughts, she begins to tug at the side zipper of her dress. I grab her hand and fight the draconian desire to allow her to continue. "Lucy," I growl, preparing to open my fingers and drop her glass heart. It's that or lose this battle and hate myself in the morning. She doesn't understand she'd hate me, too. "Stop."

It's clear to me now.

"What?" Her voice raises as she slams her hands on my chest. "What is it, Stone?"

Lucy

My back presses against the wall, my hands flat on his chest like paddles prepared to initiate shocks to the heart if he doesn't say those three words.

"I can't. I can't love you, Lucy. I'm—"

"You're what? Afraid? Scared? Insecure? Want to run?" I can't control the volume of my voice as it rises to new elevations of high-pitched anger. "You kiss me. Everywhere. Slow and steady and full of sureness. Like I'm the woman you'll kiss for the rest of your life yet that still won't be long enough. Your hands have touched every part of me, and your whispered words have wrapped themselves around the entirety of my limbic system. You've made me yours, Stone. Yours!" Anger pulses through my veins as I strain to catch a wisp of a controlled breath. Within the battleground of my mind, I pray, no, beg, God not to punish me for my sins by taking this man away from me. *God, can we reinstate the earlier bargain? I'll do anything...*

"Yes. Dang it, Lucy! I'm terrified to love you." He slams his hands on either side of my head as he drops his own in defeat, eyes cast down so that all I can see is the top of his shaggy, blond hair. "I'm terrified to let myself melt into a puddle at your feet. To let myself become clay in your hands. To lose all sense of self in pursuit of your big, beautiful, hazel eyes. If I let myself love you, you will bring me to my knees, Lucy May. Straight to my knees in a position to beg you to love me for all my faults and failures, knowing there is no way in—" *curse* "—that I am good enough for you. You deserve more. So much more. You deserve someone who actually knows what love is!"

The fight I had evaporates at his blatant admission. Hearing those words outright makes all the fuzzy and confused feelings crystal clear. My stomach churns as I prepare my next words. I drop my hands from his chest and place a finger on his chin to tilt his eyes to me.

"When you figure out if you'll let yourself love me, come find me."

"Lucy," his voice cracks on my name. "Please be happy. Please find someone to help you out of this depression that's gripping you."

His request sends me reeling. I'm not depressed. I'm just... sad. And anxious. Who the— *curse* —is he to tell me to get help, anyway?! I swallow the bile burning up my throat.

"You need help," I bite before ducking out of his arms and standing behind him. He doesn't turn around. "Until then, don't contact me. If you aren't going to love me and help me out of this, then I need to pick up the pieces of my shattered life. And I need to do it alongside people I *know* love and care about me."

Though... who even does?

I'm so... alone.

Everyone leaves.

My eyes burn to cry, but I'm so numb. I wait a second. Five seconds. Ten...

Stone doesn't turn around.

"You should have just let me drown," I whisper. I will my feet to move against the desire to collapse into a trembling mess on his floor. One step. Another. Until my weakened, broken self is once again crossing the threshold of his door.

Defeated.

Bruised.

A shell of the woman who entered this house with determination and gumption a couple of weeks ago.

How did he do this to me?

How did I let this happen?

How is it ending?

As I close the door behind me, on the concrete porch, I collapse to my knees, feeling my skin split apart.

"Oh, God," I cry out in the smallest, fragmented voice I no longer recognize as my own. Tears finally break through. "Make it go away!"

Chapter 19

Stone

A knock at my door catches my attention, and I tell Stanton over my headset that I need to step away from our typical early Saturday morning round of *Call of Duty*.

"Hello," I say as I swing the door open to find... "Brother Johnny? What are you doing here? Is Mom here, too?"

He chuckles, wrinkles forming at the edges of his honeyed eyes. "No, no. She's home. Stella and Lucas are with her. I, however, would like to visit with you alone today. Sorry it's unannounced. Forgive my intrusion."

I motion for him to come inside. "It's no problem. You know you're always welcome."

"Do you have plans?"

"Not really. Going to a bonfire tonight with some friends, that's all."

He grins. "Wonderful. I'll be out of your hair after lunch. Don't want to get back home to my beloved too late."

My chest warms, and for a brief moment, I'm extra thankful my mom decided to let go of the feeling like she'd be cheating on Dad if she remarried. She needed someone like Brother Johnny in her life.

"Would you like something to drink?"

He scratches his balding brown hair. "Do you have sweet tea?"

"Would I be a southern man if I didn't?"

He laughs, and I point him to the couch while I make two glasses of tea.

"*Call of Duty*, huh? You like to game?" he asks as I hand him his drink.

"It's something my buddy and I do pretty much every Saturday morning unless we have other things happening. Just casual. This is really the only game I play these days."

Brother Johnny nods his head, and then suddenly, his happy-go-lucky pastor face disappears, in its place a stern—fatherly?—expression. "We need to talk about that girlfriend of yours. Now, don't be mad, but Lucas and Jared told me what was going on a couple of weeks ago after you visited us randomly, and I've been meaning to get up here to talk with you."

I clench my jaw but keep a smile pasted on my face. I haven't told my family that Lucy and I are done. So done that she never reported back to work. Instead, she sent my secretary an email saying she was resigning effective immediately three days ago. The day after she walked out of my house and wailed on my doorstep. I sat on the other side of the door, silently leaking tears and begging the God who everyone says is good but apparently hates me to change the prophecy He had set forth for my life. I said I was going to figure out this Christianity thing, but I've been too emotionally exhausted to even attempt to work through everything. "They did, did they?"

We both lean back against the couch as I fight to rid myself of the haunting memories of Lucy's broken cries.

"They're worried about you. And her. They like her a lot, you know?"

"Hm."

He continues. "And I do, too. Most importantly, I love you, Stone. I know I'm not your father nor could I ever replace him in your life. Furthermore, I would never try to do that. But I *do* love you as if you were my son."

That catches my attention.

"You—what? You do?"

He reaches over and places a tanned, wrinkled hand on my shoulder. Looking deep into my eyes, he says, "I really do."

Just hearing those words breaks something inside me that I didn't know was built. I've known friendship love. I've known romantic love. I've even briefly known fatherly love, though I think I forgot about it until this very moment.

Didn't know how much I needed it...

"Thank you, Brother Johnny," I say, fighting not to cry. What's with me? Only cried twice in my life but here I am, an absolute emotional wreck lately. *The way I cried over Lucy...*

"And because I love you like a son, I feel it is within my rights to talk to you like one, if you'll allow me. I drove all this way, after all."

I'm not quite sure I want to hear what he has to say since it obviously involves Lucy. I make a small mental note to sneak attack my brother-in-law and friend when I go back to Dasher Valley.

"Go ahead."

He doesn't skip a beat. "Stop running from the Lord, Stone. From what the guys told me, and after I prayed over what to tell you, it sounds like the issue runs deeper than you not wanting to open yourself up completely to Lucy. You can't love her well because you aren't allowing yourself to experience and know the love of your heavenly Father."

Dumbfounded and at a loss for words, I do the only thing I can do: shut up and keep listening. Because for some reason, I want to. I think—I know—it's what I've been running from.

"What's blocking you, Stone? You're a smart man. A kind and generous man. So why are you afraid to not only commit to Lucy but also to the Lord? And don't give me crap about it being because of Lacey."

"Pastor, you just said the word 'crap,' you know?" I ask with nervous laughter.

He only raises his bushy eyebrows, waiting for me to answer him.

I clasp my hands together and lean onto my knees, thinking. "I–I don't know. Lacey is the only thing that comes to mind. Being rejected by her hurt a lot. It made me feel like I would never be enough for any woman. If the one who knew me at my deepest level didn't accept me, then who else will?"

"I'm not saying she doesn't play a role. She does. But the problem runs deeper than that. It runs into acceptance. What else?"

A smidge of anger flares, and I stand to my feet. "If you know what the problem is, then why keep it from me? Just tell me already instead of making me read your mind."

Brother Johnny blinks, a frown forming on his face.

After a beat, I relax. "I'm sorry. I didn't mean that to come out as rude. But I'm at a loss—" *and emotionally unstable at the moment* "—though I'm sure it has something to do with running from the Lord or something like that."

"Bingo." He takes a deep breath and motions for me to sit again. I do, taking a sip of my sweet tea, relishing in the smooth taste. "From where I'm sitting, it looks to me like your problem is your lack of relationship with Christ. I have no doubt you're a Christian, but you've run far away. I think, and you can correct me if I'm wrong, but I think you blame God for taking your father away at such a young age. I think you blame God for giving your mother Rheumatoid Arthritis. I think you blame God for Lacey saying no to you when you proposed to her. I think you believe He's at fault for your inability to commit and love because everyone you do love somehow leaves or is punished."

I sit in stunned silence, unable to look away from him. All the emotions I haven't been able to name or process bubble to the surface and overwhelm me in my already fragile state. *That's exactly what's going on with me... How could I not see that? Lucy and her sadness and her fears were practically a mirror to me, her grief reflecting my own.*

I break down as raw guilt over my actions, sorrow over my life, consumes me.

As Brother Johnny holds me, I weep. He tells me to let it all out as he pats my back. He prays over me, and all at once, I know this is just the beginning of a long healing journey back to where I belong—in fellowship with Christ. Walking with Him. Letting Him lead so I can one day lead and love a woman correctly and fully.

I tell Brother Johnny what happened with Lucy three days ago.

"That's a tough one." He brings his fingers to his chin, deep in thought. "Lucy's an author, right? Words are important to her, and outside of your actions, your words have hurt her. Do you think you can use your words to help her?"

I think through the request as my eyes burn and ache from crying so much. My brain is mush at the moment, but I nod. "I think I can. I've read all her stories. I know what she likes. What she wants her leading men to say."

"Careful there, son. Don't say what you think she wants to hear. Speak from your heart. Be sure to take it to God first."

"Right."

"You know I'm a licensed Biblical counselor, don't you?"

I nod, standing to go fill up a glass of water.

He continues. "I understand if you don't want to talk to me about everything, but I am here for you. I can help you through this."

"Like, counsel me?" I ask, sitting back down with my fresh drink.

Brother Johnny nods.

"It might be a rough go at first, but I think—" I pause, taking a steadying breath. For so long, I've thought therapy and counseling was for weak-minded people. But honestly, if that's the case, then so be it. I'm weak right now, and I need help. "Okay. Let's try it."

"Glad to hear it, Stone. You're not alone, okay?" He stands and embraces me in a man-hug. "I'll call you tomorrow to set something up with you."

"Thank you," I say as we walk to the door. "Can I just call you Johnny?"

He grins, eyes alight. "I would love nothing more."

After he leaves, I hop on my motorcycle and take to the roads to process. I drive to Hartfield then down the Mississippi River, passing old antebellum homes and estates. I ask God questions, ones that I have zero answers to currently. I beg Him to fix me. I thank Him, even in the exit of my rebellious state, for sending Johnny up to talk with me today. I eventually find myself in front of the store, and go in and purchase a pink composition notebook.

Lucy is a lover of words and stories, and I want her to see my heart. Even if I don't know what comes next for us, if there will still be an us, I want her to know that I'm ready to change. To try. To wrestle with God and find answers.

I'm ready to learn how to love her best.

Swallowing the fear and resistance in my throat, I knock on Lucy's door.

"Who is it?" she calls in a strained voice from somewhere inside her apartment. I swear I hear her mention something about the audacity of receiving surprise guests as her footsteps approach the door. The urge to flee flickers at the edges of my thought, but I stand my ground, squaring my shoulders and clenching a small notebook in my hand. I suspect she's looked through the peephole and spotted me since she's said nothing else nor made a move to open the door.

"It's me, Lucy May. Can I come in?"

"Why? State your purpose." Her tone is indignant, but I can't control the small smile that flashes across my face at her word choice. She sounds like a detective bent on an accurate interrogation.

"I need to talk to you. And I have something to give you."

"I don't need anything from you. Nor do I have anything to say."

I place my hand on the door and bring my face closer to the peephole. Am I slightly nervous that some sort of needle may bust through it? Yes. "I have something to say. It's important you hear it."

After a long pause, I hear the deadbolt unlock and she slowly opens the door.

Taking in her beautiful face after not seeing her except in the pictures still saved in my phone, my eyes grow a little misty. My step-dad has counseled me a few times over the past couple of weeks when I've had something come up that I wanted to talk about with him, and I guess I'm a man who cries over small things now. Do I still sometimes feel like I'm not a man because of it? Absolutely. Do I now fight that internal monologue with scriptural truths? Yep. But I have a long way to go.

"What? You're the reason I'm like this." She gestures from her frizzy, unkempt hair down her stained t-shirt and then to her baggy basketball shorts

Wait a second, those are mine...

I press my lips together to keep from commenting something inappropriate, though I'm sure my locked gaze on the shorts says it all. *Man, I still have a lot of work to do...*

When I snap my attention back to her face, she's grimacing at me with her arms folded over her chest.

"You're beautiful as ever, Lucy. Now can I come in?"

"No," she says sternly. "Say whatever you need to say right here."

I guess I've earned that. I release a breath and remember the words that I wanted to say. "Apologies are not adequate for what I've put you through over the past four months, but I'm sorry. I've thought through many different ways I could show you how sorry I am, but everything came up short. I won't tell you the full story of what has happened since you walked out of my house, but I did write it down in this notebook, along with other things. I know you're a lover of words, so I wrote our story through my eyes, and I hope you won't criticize me too much for not being as talented a writer as you are."

The tiny pink composition notebook feels like a brick in my hands as I hold it out to her. She eyes it warily, but she takes it. As she begins to open it, I reach forward and snap it closed, my hand covering hers and sending all those electrical energies that I haven't felt in a while coursing through my system.

Our eyes meet, and I lean forward as if pulled by a magnetic force to kiss her. She doesn't smell like spicy vanilla right now. In fact, she smells like the old coffee stains on her shirt. Right before my lips meet hers, I halt, remembering this is not what I came here to do and it instead only proves that I need to tell her this final thing.

Sighing as I pull away, her face twists in confusion. And then disgust. She throws the notebook into her apartment and then spins to enter herself.

I grab her wrist out of instinct. "Wait!"

She turns and glares daggers at me but doesn't speak.

"I'm sorry. Again. Ugh!" I release her wrist and run the hand through my hair trying to control the frustration within my voice. "This is why I can't be with you right now. Because of no fault of your own, I can't resist you. You are heroin—without an 'e'—to me, Lucy May. I'm the problem, and the notebook will explain that."

She stares blankly at me, so I continue, bringing my voice to a calmer, albeit pleading level. "You almost used sex to keep me with you that night after the Halloween Bash. You should never feel the need to use your body in such ways. You are worth so much more than that. I was conflicted, going back and forth on whether to keep you all to myself while not giving you what I know you deserve or letting you walk away and thrusting my hand into my chest, ripping my own heart out. But the moment you reached for your zipper, I had my answer. I abhorred myself that I brought you so low."

Shame covers her face, and even though I've tried to make it clear it wasn't her fault, that I recognize that as the man, I led us to that moment. I have no doubt she's thinking if she wouldn't have done that then everything would be okay right now between us.

I cup her face in my hands, needing her to truly hear my heart. "Lucy May Spence. I love you. Most ardently." My lips twitch upward as her hazel-green eyes widen at my *Pride and Prejudice* confession. But I'm not done, and while I'd love to stop there and kiss her senseless, I can't. Not right now. "And it's because I love you that I cannot be with you right now. I've shown you lust, and now I am determined to figure out how to show you love. Genuine, pure love."

Her brows knit together, and I can tell she wants to punch me, so I hurry and continue. "There's no doubt in my mind that I want you. Lucy, no woman has ever had me like you do. Please, read my little book I wrote for you. See yourself how I see you. Understand that what I'm doing, though I know it hurts you as it does me, is *for* you. For us."

"Stone, I—" She opens her mouth, but I cut her off.

"I'm working on processing emotions that I've shoved down for a long time." I take a deep breath; all of this being one-hundred percent open stuff is draining. "Step one was surrendering my life back to Christ. Step two was realizing and admitting to myself that I loved you. And now I need to become a man worthy of you. I need to understand God's love for me so I can love you fully. But Lucy, I can't do that alongside you as much as I wish I could. And that's not your fault."

"So you're walking away again, right?" Her voice is tinged with franticness, and I can't blame her. Maybe I shouldn't have said I loved her before telling her I had some things to work on before I could be with her. But I couldn't wait to at least speak those three, honest words to her. Even if it's going to take a minute to figure out how to show her.

I drop my hands from her face and take a step backward. "This is not a cop-out or an excuse, Lucy. I pray you believe that. I will come back for you when I've worked on rebuilding my relationship with Christ. He has to come first. It's only then I can be the man you deserve. Be the man that can stand solidly by your side when you're feeling so low yourself. I understand you may not wait, nor will I ask you to. I can't give you a timeline as much as I wish I could. But if you're still here and will have me when the Lord gives me the green light, I would be over the moon."

The slim string of hope I had that she would understand me is cut when she spins on her heel, steps into her apartment, and slams the door, solidifying it with a lock.

Right then and there, I whisper a prayer that God will restore me quickly and that He will also heal Lucy. Tears burning in my eyes, I walk down the stairs and battle the urge from Satan to run back up there and beg her to take me as I am.

But I can't.

I have to be a better man for myself.

I have to take the time to be better for the woman I want to make my wife.

I'm learning to trust God again.

Chapter 20

Lucy

Darkness envelops me, but I can't complain. I never bothered to turn a light on when I arrived at the apartment earlier this afternoon after Thanksgiving lunch with Grandma Netty. I didn't even turn on the light when the sun set or when the moon casted shadows of the dead Bird of Paradise plant onto the white walls, painting them gray.

I sat down in the reclining chair, opened my laptop, and poured my heart onto a blank, white page using size-twelve, black Palantino font. A desperate plea to escape reality. An earnest attempt to live out my dreams and get the happily ever after I've always hungered for. I've built characters and worlds and conflicts that come with clear communications and healthy resolutions. At some point, I made coffee, and that was my dinner.

How many hours have gone by since I've sat down? I couldn't tell you. Seven thousand words have appeared on the screen, each one containing a piece of my soul until I was left with nothing. An apparition of a woman haunting her own safe space like a despondent ghost. That's where I am now—sitting in my reclining chair while the dim light of the laptop shines upon my face. If you were sitting in front of me, you would think I had glass skin. But not because of good skincare products.

I've cried a thousand tears, each one reminding me of *him*. Of the future I thought I was building. Of the hope that was shattered when he never turned around. Of the things I screamed in the midst of my anger. Of the time I slammed the door after he fed me lines about needing to grow closer to God. How low of him was that to use God as an excuse? How dare he say he loves me and then leave me!

This is why the whole "married in your heart" argument for sex outside of the marital covenant is not sufficient.

I stare at the plant's shadow on the wall, made visible by the orange glow of the apartment light outside my window. Loneliness lurks around every corner. It's found within every nook and cranny. But if I'm being honest, regardless of the hurtful things we've said to each other, I still love that man with everything inside me. I love him so much that I refuse to read that pink composition notebook he gave me. I can't bear to see myself through his eyes and shatter the illusions I cling so tightly to. He might have thought it was just lust, but for me, it was so much more.

It's why I'm writing tonight... because I can't cry to him. I'm cutting open the wound and bleeding out onto the page; my truest thoughts, feelings, and emotions ingrained in the dialogue spoken by dysfunctional characters in a reprehensible setting. The real me. *Ha*, I snort. *My readers would run for the hills if they read this.*

How do I even have readers? Why am I writing as if I have the experience to write romance? I'm unmarried. With no kids. No prospects. I can't be a good friend to those who love me because I'm obsessed with finding the man who will keep me warm on cold nights and carry groceries into our home while I put them away and hold me while I cry when melancholy strikes.

What grounds do I possibly have to ask people to buy any romance book I craft? I'm an imposter. A fake. I promote healthy relationships, characters who communicate clearly, flawed—but not *too* flawed—leads, and strong faith elements. But what if my readers knew who I truly was? What if they knew I've had sex outside of marriage? What if they knew I battled with intense sexual fantasies from time to time? What if they knew I let myself get blackout drunk after he left my apartment that day in order to avoid *feeling*, a secret not even my friends and twin know? What if they knew all of my relationships have failed because I demand too much too soon and don't know how to set and uphold clear boundaries for myself? What if they knew how desperate and starved for love and acceptance I am? What if they knew I'd do just about anything to be *liked?* What if they knew I questioned God at every turn and lacked the belief that He can do what He says He can do? What if they knew I questioned His existence?

They'd never pick up another one of my books.

Hypocrite! Liar! False Christian! Jezebel! Deceiving, wayward woman!

I can see it now. Hear it now. Echoing through my brain and etching into my heart like a scar. I'd be hanged by the Christian community like a witch in Salem, trending on social media as the next blacklisted Christian to be canceled. Do my questioning thoughts make me not a Christian?

I try to remember the time in my life when I surrendered to the Lord, recalling the peace and joy I felt.

Where is that now? Was it all a farce?

Here's the truth... The places, characters, and situations I create are a blundered attempt to pack the gaping chest wound left to expand after every failed relationship. They are a concoction of tropes, fantasies, and marketable content with a dash of my soul and spirit.

It's fiction. Not real life.

Real life is messy. Full of mistakes and failures.

Dark.

People miscommunicate and say hurtful things.

We all boast a little toxicity.

Sin creeps in slowly then consumes. Feeling desired feels *good*.

Unbelief is a very real thing.

And happily-ever-afters don't always happen.

My books are a means of escape, a medium to play god over my life. I create the perfect men and speak into the women I wish I were. I build towns where every single woman in a five-mile radius gets a happily ever after without the miscommunication trope or the third-act breakup.

But does anyone ever stop to think that those are tropes for a reason?

Because it happens all the time in this real, messy, complicated life we live.

What if I wrote something *real?*

Would I still find escape in it?

Would I still miss *him*?

Would I find myself in the process?

Would God forgive me for living a lie? For trying to play god myself?

I will and I do, I can almost hear Him whisper in the recesses of my head, and it stirs something within me.

Hope.

Hope that I can find peace and joy again. Hope that people may not accept the real me, and that's okay because others will.

Hope that God is real and He...

He desires me. He wants me to run to Him.

I watch the blinking cursor on the screen in front of me and I know I have a decision to make. I can choose to be honest and raw; I can let my readers know the real me and the very real struggles I face. Or I can choose to proceed with the image I've carefully curated.

I can choose to surrender to the Lord and turn to Him for healing, or I can continue trying to piece myself back together all alone.

My phone rings, and I dig around for it, realizing it had fallen between the siding and the cushion of the recliner.

"Grandma, is everything okay?" I ask when I answer.

"Lucy girl. Are you home?"

"Yes. Are you okay?" A smidge of fear works its way into my chest. Grandma Netty seemed fine earlier today when we had lunch.

"Yes, dear. But it seems I need some help with something at the house. Would you mind coming back over here?"

I glance at the time, realizing it is only eight at night. I thought it was much later than that. Ever since I sent my resignation email to the center, I've thrown myself into authoring full-time with the help of my sister's fiancé, Crown Prince Finley Andersson. He once offered to promote my books, and I decided I needed the exposure more than I needed my pride. Having a prince promote my rom-coms has definitely rocketed my sales. Anything to keep me from leaving the house and bumping into Stone. Grocery shopping is hard enough. He's in every shadow down every aisle.

Grandma clears her throat, and I remember I need to answer her. "Of course. Give me a few minutes to change my clothes and I'll be right over."

After slipping into leggings and an oversized Taylor Swift *Midnights* era t-shirt, I hop into the car and drive the short distance to my grandma's place.

The gravel driveway crunches under my tires as I arrive at the quaint cottage-esque home. Just around back, she has this lovely garden growing inside a collapsed shed that gives off a shadow fairy garden vibe, and it used to be one of my favorite places to sit and write before I secluded myself away to the confines of my personal prison—also known as my apartment.

I shut off the car and make my way toward the small white fenced-in porch and stand underneath the light. I knock on the oval-topped lavender door and shout to Grandma that I'm here.

But it's not Grandma that opens the door.

It's a person who looks just like me.

"Lorelei!" I scream, throwing myself at my twin who stumbles backward into the entryway. I prepare to tumble to the ground, but we don't.

I glance behind Lorelei's head and see Hadley grinning with her hands braced against Lorelei's back. She winks but that turns into a wince of pain. I drop my eyes to where she removed a hand from Lorelei's back and placed it on her ever-growing stomach. "I think little Anna Layne is excited we are all together again. She's ready to meet her two favorite aunties."

We laugh, and Lorelei peels me off her. I try to at least grab her hand, but she shakes her head and says, "I'm beyond overstimulated from the trip. We can hold hands and frolic through flowers tomorrow, huh?"

"Right." I nod, though I can't help the tiny prickle of hurt at her rejection. She's autistic and struggles with sensory overload, and well, sometimes it makes me feel alone when she can't meet me where I need to be met through no fault of her own. I shake it off and attempt to live in the moment. I mean, for the love of all things, she's here! "One, how did Finley's mother allow you to sneak away so close to your wedding and the coronation? Two, did you travel alone?"

Hadley, in her leggings and oversized t-shirt that I'm pretty sure belongs to her husband, wraps me in a hug. Well, as much as she can with her belly in the way. She whispers in my ear, "There are two very fine personal protection officers in the other room with Finley."

"Do you really think I would have let her travel alone?" A familiar sunshine-like voice says. I release Hadley and bound toward my almost-king-in-law. He wraps me up in a friendly hug. "It's good to see you again, Lucy."

Gabriel and Anders—Finley's PPOs who are dressed in suits—linger at the back of the room and wave gingerly. I wave back, and when Grandma comes to the doorway to call everyone to the table, my heart fills with genuine happiness for the first time in a while.

"Did you not get the memo that this was a leggings and baggy t-shirt sort of dinner, Finley?" I glance at Lorelei, whose outfit resembles mine and Hadley's.

Finley chuckles as he sets a plate of food down at the crowded table for six. Grandma always said she wanted to keep a big table at the house even though she lived alone so she could gather people together for food and fun times. "Trust me, you do not want to see this in leggings."

We laugh as he gestures down his polo shirt and blue jeans. We eat leftover Thanksgiving food and some new dishes that Grandma apparently whipped up in our short time apart. We catch up, crack jokes, and enjoy each other's company.

"Where are you two staying while you're here?" I ask Lorelei as we clean up dishes.

"I'm riding back with you, so I hope the apartment is clean."

A look of horror flashes across my face, and she rolls her eyes and mumbles, "Yeah, I thought so."

"What about Finley? Is he coming back with us?"

Lorelei shakes her head. "No, he's going to stay in Mason's vacation home. It'll be just like old times." There's a giddiness to her voice that makes me smile. "Tomorrow morning, Hadley and

I are taking you down to the coast, though, so we should probably leave here shortly to go get some rest."

"The coast? Why are we going there?"

She shrugs. "For fun. This is basically my bachelorette party, after all."

A smile stretches across my face as I rub my hands together.

"Don't get any ideas." She pins me with sharp eyes. "Nothing scandalous will be happening, got it?"

I feign a shocked expression. "Scandalous? Little ole me?"

She snaps me with a dish rag as I run away from her, right into Gabriel's arms. My gaze snaps up to the handsome brown-haired frenchman who I once attempted to date while my sister was going back and forth between allowing herself to date Finley. "Hi."

"*Bonsoir,* Lucy." He smirks at me, and I launch myself from his arms.

"Sorry about that. Running from my maniacal sister." I laugh nervously, though I don't know why I'm nervous. When I look at Gabriel now, and though he's objectively handsome with his chocolate curls, vanilla skin, and brown eyes, I feel nothing like I once did.

Because Stone still resides in my heart for better or for worse...

"It's all good," he says in a heavy French accent. "How have you been?"

"Uhh..." I'm frozen in place because my tendency is to overshare and answer honestly, but he is not the person I need to unload on. "I've been fine."

He looks me over with a skeptical gaze before shrugging it off. "You will be at the wedding and coronation, yes?"

I nod, and he grins.

"Good. Save me a dance."

"Ditto," I say, happy to know I will at least get to experience one dance where I'm twirled around a ballroom in a gown. I had small worries that I'd go and no one would dance with me.

Because Stone rejected me, everyone else must do so, too...

"Lucy girl!" Grandma Netty calls from elsewhere in the house. "Hold up before you leave. I have something for you."

I excuse myself from Gabriel and follow her voice until I reach her bedroom. "What is it?"

She stands up from bending over her dresser. "Here." She holds out a journal, and I gently grab the old, weathered leather book. "What is it?" I ask again.

"It's my personal journal from right before I married your grandfather. I would like for you to read it."

I tilt my head and scrunch my nose. "Why?" I don't question it offensively—I'm excited to read it—but I do wonder why.

She laughs. "You know my creative knack was painting, so please don't expect writing up to your caliber, but I feel like it could help you in what you're walking through right now. You told me everything regarding Stone." She pauses. "Right?"

My face reddens in embarrassment. I did tell her everything. When I left his house on Halloween night, I drove straight here and broke down in her arms. "Yes."

"Then please read this. I believe the Lord allowed me to find it buried at the bottom of a box I once thought I'd lost. As I read the words I'd written so long ago, I thought of you. Just return it to me when you finish, dear."

I hug her. "Of course. Thank you. I'll cherish every word."

We all chat together a little longer while finishing the last remnants of cleaning before heading our different directions. As Lorelei and I drive home, I reflect on the night, an overwhelming sense of gratitude for the perfect timing of it all. From sitting alone in my apartment, crying and bleeding onto the page, to having my soul filled with laughter and smiles and the people I love.

While her arms are still around me, a simple thank you rises in my heart. Not to Grandma Netty and not to Stone. Not to anyone but God. And even though I've done nothing but yell and scream at Him recently, I can't help but hope He hears my humble offering of thanks.

Chapter 21

Lucy

"I need more coffee," I complain as we finally reach the small Mississippi beach town of Willow Bay. Eleven hours in the car after leaving at three in the morning takes a toll on a girl.

"You've had like five cups," Hadley remarks, getting out of the passenger seat and stretching. Lorelei drove because she gets car sick easily while me and Hadley rode with her. Finley, Braxton, Gabriel and Anders followed behind us.

"Yep. Sure did. Got one every time you decided you had to pee."

Lorelei laughs. "Girls, girls. Behave yourselves. I know road trips make people hangry, so let's go eat some real food instead of the snacks we've consumed." She points to a colorful restaurant a little ways down the boardwalk.

The sun is shining hot and bright for a late November day, and the salty, gentle breeze rolling in from the brown coastal waters up ahead brings the temperature down to the perfect metaphorical "sunny and seventy-five."

We eat at a seafood restaurant that is raised on piles, painted in vibrant colors of blues and yellows, and overlooks the beach. Afterwards, we checked into a lovely beach house with an open screen porch, a beautiful view of the water, and enough rooms to where we can all sleep comfortably. The guys head off to do some fishing off the nearby pier while Lorelei, Hadley, and I hang behind to have some girl-time on the breezy, plant-filled porch.

"I might move down here," Hadley sighs with her head laid back on the cushioned rocking chair. I side-eye her, but she doesn't pay attention.

Lorelei is touching every plant on the porch, mentioning how she wished we would have brought Frannie with us instead of leaving her at Grandma Netty's place. At this point, I may let her take Frannie back to Korsa with her. Not only have I been an atrocious cat mom, but I know Frannie misses her twin, Frizzle, just as much as I have missed mine.

"Don't leave me alone, Hads."

I don't miss the sadness plaguing my voice. What was meant as a joke came out as a cry for help.

One that Lorelei heard loud and clear.

"Okay. It's time."

"Time?" Unease wraps me in a wool-like blanket as I sit up in the hanging egg chair.

Lorelei plops down on the other rocking chair. "We are here for my so-called bachelorette party or whatever, but mainly, I dragged you here to get you out of Juniper Grove and hold an intervention."

"An intervention? For what?" I look between Hadley, who is now perked up and rocking gently with her hands on her belly, and my sister who sits still as a statue.

"It's time you tell us what really went down between you and Stone. *The whole truth.*" Hadley raises her eyebrow at me, and I think she's already nailed down the mom look.

"Grandma Netty had a phone call with me a couple of weeks ago and told me the gist of what happened: you were fake-dating him until you weren't, and then you fell in love with him. He couldn't say he loved you. But then he did and said he needed time to figure out things regarding his faith."

I open my mouth to interject with something about Grandma sharing my secrets when Lorelei cuts me off. "And before you begin raging over Grandma telling me, she did it because she's worried about you. We all are. We tried to sit back and let you work through whatever it is depressing you, but I can't stop myself intervening any longer. Don't ask me to explain it, but I feel your pain, even across the world. You're depressing me, Lucy."

I sit slack-jawed while Hadley shifts her eyes between the two of us. She clears her throat. "What Lorelei means to say is that we both love you, your grandmother loves you, and we want to see you truly happy and bubbly and joy-filled like you used to be. And we don't want you faking it. We know it may take a long time to heal from whatever you have experienced, but we are on your side and are determined to push you through this."

"I'm fine, guys. Really, I'm—" Out of nowhere, I start crying. Attempting to speak through the snotty huffs and breathlessness that I feel, I manage to get out, "Okay, I'm not fine. Not fine at all. It hurts so much. And even when I think the pain gets better and I'm healing, another wave hits and knocks me flat on my butt, drowning me under the rough waters."

Hadley stands and wobbles over to me, making me scoot over in the built-for-two egg chair. She groans as I sniffle and snuggle close to her. She says, "I'll never get out of this chair without some help."

"That's why I'm staying right here," Lorelei says matter-of-factly. "The chair will not eat all three of us alive."

Hadley holds me, massaging my scalp as I cry. Once I don't think I can shed another tear, I tell them everything that happened. Including sleeping with Stone, which my sister didn't know about but Hadley did. I feel so much shame over it. Especially now that we aren't together. I am a dirty and used strip of rag. Soiled and rotten.

"Oh, Lucy," Hadley says, pulling me against her. "That feeling is the pits. I've definitely been in a similar situation before, and it takes a long time to heal. But it helps when you have people around who love you. Please don't keep us at arms length regarding these things anymore. We are the last people who will judge you, okay? You know my past. It's not pretty. But that didn't mean I wasn't worthy of good things. That's what Braxton told me. And it's what you and your sister told me, too. Now I'm saying it back to you. Lucy May Spence, you are worthy of good things."

"Did you read the book he gave you?" Lorelei asks.

I shake my head.

"That's the first thing you're doing when you get back, understand? While I'm not okay with how he went about everything, I still think you should read it. Maybe it will help with closure. It's good to have all the facts."

I nod, not sure if I'm going to listen to her or not. I have started reading one journal, however. "I did bring Grandma Netty's journal. I was reading it on the way here. This one line stopped me in my tracks: 'You were called to surrender. What you choose to give yourself over to is determined by you.' I was surrendering myself to him because of how bored and alone I was. I missed you, Lor. I missed—and still miss—Karoline. I didn't want to infringe upon your life, Hadley. I felt... rejected. And I think that caused me to cling to Stone. He was fun, interesting, and while we pretended, he showered me with so much attention. And when it became real, and we began opening up to one another, I knew I loved him like I've never loved a man before. I know I fall easily and quickly, but with him, everything was different. Regardless, he took the edge off my pain, and I don't think it was just because of our chemistry, though I realize I was most definitely addicted to sex with him. But ultimately, it's just *him*. I was stoned off of Stone."

I hold back laughter as I watch them roll their eyes and grin.

"There's a start. You're cracking bad jokes," Lorelei muses.

"Ha, you said 'crack'ing," Hadley echoes, and all three of us laugh like hyenas. It feels so good.

But then I start to cry again. "Saying goodbye... It hurts like no other goodbye I've said in my life. Deep down, regardless of the situation we found ourselves in, I think I started believing forever was attached to him. I don't know if it was the sex or loneliness or actually him. Outside of his slow emotional processing, I adore so many things about him. That's why it hurts so freaking bad."

"Did you know the word goodbye originally comes from the phrase 'God be with ye?' If you think about it, goodbyes aren't always permanent. Sometimes you just have to entrust another person to God because you aren't Him."

I stare at my too-smart sister, hope blossoming within my soul. Could that be the case? Will God give him back to me one day? Hope is a dangerous feeling, but I desperately want to cling to it.

After a moment, when no one responds, Lorelei speaks up again. "Have you considered seeking therapy for depression, anxiety, and sex addiction? Maybe it could help."

I sigh. "It's crossed my mind once, but I'm not even sure where to begin. Is there a Christian woman I could go to? I don't want a secular therapist who is just going to tell me to love myself more. That's a bunch of bull. But I also don't want a Christian therapist who is just going to tell me to pray more and try harder. That doesn't work very well, either."

"Actually, I know of a woman who might work for you," Hadley says, "if you're comfortable seeing Braxton's sister, Brandi."

Brandi? "She's a therapist?"

"Not practicing anymore, no, but I'd be willing to bet she'll see you. She does have a degree in counseling, and I know she stays up to date on everything."

"Huh, I didn't know that either," Lorelei chimes in. "Cool. She'd be perfect, Lucy. You both are already acquainted."

"Can I promise to think it over?"

"Absolutely," Hadley says while Lorelei nods her head.

"So, Hadley. You'll be birthing a human next month. How are you feeling? I'm sorry I haven't been there for you as much as I should have been." I stroke her hair, knowing there's no use in swimming in guilt over it. What's done is done. I can only do better moving forward. Confessing to them was like releasing the valve on a pressure cooker, and I kind of wish I would have done it sooner.

These are my girls. My people. I love them, and I need to allow them to love me.

"I'm scared, not going to lie, but the Lord has been good to me, reaffirming that I'm going to be a good mom. Even when I make mistakes, I'll still be a good mom. Braxton says that if I don't believe it then to leave it up to him to make me believe it."

"That's our Braxton." I laugh then shift my focus to my twin. "Are you ready for your wedding night?"

Lorelei's face doesn't flush red, even as Hadley begins to tease her. Instead, her brow creases as if she's in deep thought. "I'm nervous. I'm scared I won't be able to do it, you know? Because of my aversion to touch. It's still sometimes hard to kiss him even though I love it with my entire soul."

Hadley and I exchange a look before bursting out laughing. "You're sounding like me, Lor. Talking souls and such."

My sister mocks a laugh but shakes her head as if she's over us.

Hadley chimes in. "Finley loves you so much. He will wait as long as you need him to. He doesn't want to make you uncomfortable."

Lorelei smiles. "I know. He's kind of the best, right?"

We all nod in agreement because let's be honest, Finley Andersson is a gem.

The scent of my dark blend coffee refreshes my tired soul.

Brandi's confirmation text stares at me from my phone while Loneliness haunts me from the corner of the room. The beach was everything I needed with the people I needed it with, but now it's Monday, and everyone has gone back to their real lives.

On the bookshelf, stuffed underneath a stack of Lorelei's nonfiction books she left for me to read, is the corner of a pink composition notebook.

Stone's story.

It taunts me, begging me to pick it up and devour the contents.

Am I ready? Ready to see our time together through his eyes?

If I do, it will cut open the measly stitches I've threaded over my wounds. If I don't, I'll never know if what he was telling me outside my door that day he came over and gave me the journal is true or not.

Knowing I've made my decision by the simple fact that the book is still in the house and not in a dumpster somewhere, I get up from my recliner and snatch it before plopping back down. Frannie hops in my lap as if to be my emotional support animal for the duration of reading, and I stroke her mindlessly with one hand as I flip open the notebook with the other.

Chapter 22

Stone

"No Mississippi town does Christmas quite like Dasher Valley. And what a privilege it is to have a part of the Christmas festival hosted in the new Dasher Valley Community Center. Thank you all for coming out today, and don't forget to stop by the kitchen for a bowl of Mrs. Phyllis's Pineapple Jambalaya. Remember all proceeds go to support Hannah's Hope."

As the gathered crowd applauds, I exit from the front of the newly constructed gym and make my way to my family standing off in the corner. Mom embraces me. "I'm proud of you, son."

"I'm glad this place gives him a good reason to come home more often," Stella remarks. "But now I actually need to step away and go bug my constituents."

"Bye, Seester." I grin at the new District Four Mississippi State Representative as she grabs Gracie's hand and darts off toward a group of older folks gathered around and watching the Ring Rudy the Reindeer game. Seems President Marshall's endorsement of her really paid off and persuaded the people of District Four to vote for an Independent.

Jared's holding their son, Abram, while Lucas is chatting with Brother Johnny, and Mom is still looking at me like I'm the greatest thing in the world. And even in the midst of this sweet moment, a certain hollowness settles within my soul.

It's not because I'm without Jesus anymore. Though I still miss days and struggle, my prayer life is stronger than ever and I'm crawling through the New Testament, soaking in every word as if I've never read it before. Surrendering is hard work, but the peace and fullness that accompanies it is indescribable. Something you just have to experience for yourself.

But I miss Lucy. Everyday it's clearer and clearer in my heart and mind that she's the woman I want to marry. I'm still scared I'm not ready and I'll fumble her hard even though I've made insurmountable progress overcoming my fear of commitment and belief that God is out to get me. He's not. Just because things don't go the way I want them to doesn't mean that He doesn't care. He just wanted my surrender.

And just because you surrender doesn't mean that your fears dissipate.

It just means you've got help from the Creator of the universe to overcome them.

"Penny for your thoughts?" Jared asks. I realize he's handed off Abram to his mom, and Lucas has flanked the other side of me.

"Let's go for a walk around town," Lucas says. "I need funnel cake."

"Need?" I laugh, and then set off with the guys.

Not long after we reach the sidewalk on Main Street, Jared speaks up. "How's everything going, Stone? And be honest with us."

The resistance to share pulls at my thoughts like a phantom pain, but as of lately, it's not as strong as it used to be. "I miss her, you know?"

"Bet you do." Lucas smirks. "So you going to get your woman back or what?"

"What if I'm still not ready? What if the moment I'm in her presence again I fall into old habits? I still have *thoughts* about her."

Jared and Lucas crack up. Jared says through his laughter, "Dude, that is the most natural thing in the world."

"Don't get me started on thoughts I had about your sister before I—"

"Nope, stop it right there," I interrupt my brother-in-law. "I get your point."

Jared straightens up and claps my back. "Don't let fear win anymore, Stone. I've seen your hard work. You'll never be finished changing. There will always be something to refine. The thoughts won't ever completely disappear, and it's not about that. It's about what you do with them."

"I understand why you needed to step away from her in order to prioritize healing," Lucas joins in. "She was like a drug to you. But it doesn't have to be that way anymore. You have a stronger sense of who you are, and you have rooted yourself in Christ. There's nothing to be afraid of anymore. You're much stronger."

"That's what Stanton has been saying," I concede. "We do Bible study together now before our *Call of Duty* game sessions."

"And why haven't we been invited to play *Call of Duty?*" Lucas asks.

I shrug. "It's an open invitation. Most Saturday mornings at six a.m."

"Ah, too early. That's why," Jared comments, and we laugh.

We arrive at the funnel cake stand and order our own cakes of sugary, powdery goodness. We take them over to the picnic tables and chow down to the sounds of children laughing, parents hollering for their kids, and the occasional passerby who pauses to chat for a bit.

Once we start to walk back to the Dasher Valley Community Center for the outdoor bonfire starting soon, I ask for their advice on exactly how to approach Lucy once more. "She's leaving for Korsa in about a week as far as I know from when we were still talking. She's going to be there through New Year's. I was supposed to go, and we were supposed to dance a regency-style waltz to that Duomo rendition of 'Wildest Dreams' by Taylor Swift."

"Let me guess, you planned that, right?" Lucas jokes, and I punch him in the shoulder.

"I was on board with it. That dance meant holding her in my arms and seeing her wear a stunning gown. Of course I was in."

"Here's a wild suggestion. One I may have made to your brother-in-law here when he let Stella go back to New York City. Take a page out of Lucy's rom-com books and go after her. Meet her there. Walk in to that song playing. Hold her and dance. Then whisk her away to have an open and honest conversation with her. It's a palace; I'm sure there are plenty of places to talk quietly."

I grimace. "That's what I'm afraid of. Being alone with her."

"Don't be nervous about that, Stone. You may very well be tempted. It'd be weird if you weren't, but remember that you have learned how to have better control. Trust the Lord."

"Right." But I still frown. "What if she shoves me away and doesn't want to dance with me?"

Jared responds. "Wait it out. Catch her after the ball, then, and ask her for a proper conversation."

"And if she says no?"

"Respect it and tell her that you're ready when she is. Then come back home and do what you've had her doing—wait. You made a grand gesture. It'll leave some sort of impact on her."

"Good advice." Lucas nods. "You're a certified communication expert. How'd that happen?"

"Marriage is the best practice." He grins as Lucas puffs out air and agrees, tugging at the sleeves of his flannel shirt.

"I'll think about it," I say. "There's a lot I would have to do with both of the community centers to plan my absence."

"Plan your absence through New Year's," Lucas mentions with a wink. "Just in case the woman is stupid enough to keep a hopeless fool like you around." But as he says those words, he laughs and draws me in for a bro-hug.

"Love you, man," I say through my laugh, feeling a little more confident than I did before, though the fear is still lurking somewhere in the depths of my nervous system.

The next day, as I'm making the long drive back to Juniper Grove, I look up plane tickets to Korsa. I also take a huge risk, asking the mayor of Juniper Grove for Lucy's sister's phone number, since he used to be her boss. I reckoned if he didn't have it then it would be a sign not to go.

But he did have it.

And Lorelei answers my call.

"Lorelei Spence," she answers in a voice that's slightly deeper than her sister's. "Who am I speaking with?"

I swallow and release a breath away from the speaker of my phone. "Hi, Lorelei," I begin. "My name is Stone Harper, and I'd like to talk to you about your sister."

Silence ensues between us, just the rumble of the road beneath my tires. Finally, she clears her throat. "What about my sister?" *If a tone could cut and kill...*

"To be frank," my voice shakes. I try again. "I love her, and I would like to show her I love her by honoring an agreement we had regarding your wedding. I promised her a regency dance to a Taylor Swift instrumental, and I want to follow through."

Lorelei is quick as a whip to answer. "What are your intentions post-dance?"

"If Lucy May will have me, I plan to honestly date her with the intention of marriage."

She laughs, murmuring something about intentions of marriage. For a moment, fear grips me. She's going to turn me away. And if the bride doesn't want me at the wedding, there's no way I'm going.

Especially to a royal wedding.

"She told me everything, Stone. Did you actually do what you said you would do and work on your relationship with Christ? Can you truly love my sister?"

I vehemently nod though she can't see me. "Yes. I can. And I do. I want to prove it to her."

"You hurt her badly. I know—and she knows—that she allowed it to happen because of her own attachment issues. She's been working hard on overcoming her anxious attachment. If you show up to my wedding, which I am allowing you to do only because she sent me pictures of the little book you wrote her, and I found it to be honest and true, then you better be one-hundred percent sure that you will not play around with her feelings."

I take a deep breath, a smile breaking out across my face. I'm too relieved to care that Lucy showed Lorelei my story. That's her twin sister, after all. Of course they talk. "Thank you so much, Lorelei. I look forward to meeting my future sister-in-law."

BEAT SEVEN

CLIMAX // "DAYLIGHT"

Chapter 23

Lucy

"My baby, you are breathtaking," Mama blubbers, reaching out her hands as if to touch Lorelei's pinned-up, slicked back hair but remembering she shouldn't mess it up.

"I never thought this would happen to someone in our family," Dad exclaims. "You're royalty. Do I look good enough to walk you down the aisle?"

"Dad, you look snazzy in your suit," I comment.

"Very decadent, indeed, Mr. Spence," Mama coos, running her hand down his chest.

Dad beams. "Don't get me started on how attractive my wife looks in that navy blue dress."

"Okay, enough you two." Lorelei laughs. "You both look stunning."

I feign hurt. We won't touch the punch of actual hurt I feel at the fact that Lorelei and Finley will not be having bridesmaids and groomsmen per stupid royal wedding laws. "What about me, older-by-one-minute sister of mine?"

"Yes, Lucy." She rolls her eyes. "But you always look amazing, and you know that."

I shrug, smiling wide at my beautiful twin. Her hair is sprayed back so that not a single flyaway occurs. The bun on top of her head consists of little ringlets with white flowers pinned in at strategic places. Soon, a crown will be placed on top, denoting her as Crown Princess of Korsa, a title she will upgrade to Queen in two weeks upon returning from her honeymoon.

She looks every part the princess one would imagine my sister to look at the moment. Her wedding gown is made of silk, fitted around her chest and waist, then flowy until it drapes the ground. There are no sparkles or lace or rhinestones as I would choose. It's long-sleeve, the ends of each sleeve coming to a pointed "v" on her hands. The scoop neck shows off the Korsa family's crest that she wears around her neck in the form of a necklace. She only dons simple diamond studs in her ears and the silicone engagement ring. (She prefers not to have a gem or metal on her fingers.)

I twist my own silver ring, wondering why I feel so nervous right now when it's my sister walking down the aisle in front of the entire world.

"Can we have a moment?" I ask Mama and Dad, pointing between me and Lorelei.

"Of course, baby," Mama says, taking Dad's hand. "We will be right outside."

Once the large, arched door to Lorelei's room in Stjarna Palace closes, I take my sister's hands. "This is happening, Lorelei. Tell me your true feelings."

Her smile never dims as she gives my hands a squeeze before dropping them. "I would be lying if I said I didn't feel queasy. The thought of everyone inside the church watching, the cameras on me, the world tuning in... It's overwhelming. But I keep reminding myself that Finley will be right there beside me through it all, and that's a comforting thought."

"You guys are sickeningly sweet," I blurt as tears press against my eyes. "I'm so dang happy for you, Lor. Can I please hug you?"

Lorelei takes a step in her white sneakers and wraps me in a tender hug. "I love you so much, Lucy. Thanks for helping me get to this moment in my life."

"Whew, okay." I release her and step back, dabbing at the liquid gathering underneath my eyes. "I love you, Lorelei. You are so deserving of this."

She walks towards the door to let my parents back in as she says, "As you are deserving of good things, too." She winks.

Mama and Dad rejoin us. They dote on Lorelei for a few more minutes before the wedding planner arrives to move us to our places. We are all escorted out to a royal limousine that will transport us to the First Church of Korsa where the wedding will be held. Once we are in front of the massive medieval-style church, complete with stained-glass windows that tell various Korsan mythology stories, Mama and I are escorted into the church to take our seats on the front left dark-oak wooden pew. I sweep the crowd as I walk, and I swear I see Stone in the back.

But a second glance reveals it's just another tall, blond-headed man. Many of these Korsan men are tall with blond hair and blue eyes.

There I go, chasing shadows again...

There has to be over five-hundred people here, and I know my ex is not one of them. I briefly say a prayer that Lorelei will not panic and bolt (or pass out) the moment she lays eyes on this massive crowd.

As I sit, I wave to Finley who looks absolutely dashing in his princely attire in Korsan colors of navy blue, gold, and white. He waves back with a winning smile on his face, and then I briefly bow my head towards the King who is sitting in an overseeing position upon his golden throne. Above him is the Cross of Christ.

King Erik smiles gently and nods his own head in recognition, and for a brief moment, disbelief that I'm even remotely connected to this life washes over me. The urge to take notes throughout the ceremony for future books is strong, but I remind myself I'm here to enjoy this moment, celebrate my sister and Finley, and continue taking every passing scene in my life as it comes. My therapist, Brandi Kelly, gave me that advice, and I can't remember a time where I've felt so content.

Of course, mending my relationship with Jesus has been beneficial. Grandma Netty's note in her journal about surrendering to something stuck with me after I read it on the beach trip. When I got home, I made the conscious choice to surrender everything to God and see what comes of it. The next morning, I picked my troubles back up in the form of social media stalking Stone, but then God reminded me that I had surrendered it, so I gave it back to Him. Every single day has something that I have to give over to God. Even if I have to give it to Him every five seconds because I'm stubborn and anxious.

But I no longer feel defeated. I don't think of myself as used, dirty rags.

I am a daughter of God. I'm loved, cherished, and forgiven, even when I still stumble back into old ways. I'm not stuck there anymore.

I'm healing.

So much so that Stone hasn't been the sole object of my prayers lately. Instead, I've been praying over my literary future, my family, and my friends. I've started looking outward and upward instead of inward and downward.

And it's made all the difference.

Queen Sylvia arrives, and I catch my breath at how beautiful she is with her silvery white hair and Korsan blue gown. She's positively regal, and my heart stirs when I remember my twin will be in this very position one day.

She's going to rule the land in business-casual attire and tennis shoes, of course, but still.

Finally, Finley's siblings filter in, and I quickly wave at his younger sister, Astrid, as she sits on the opposite side of the aisle from me.

"Eternal Source of Light Divine" by Handel starts playing, and I nudge Mama, reminding her she has to stand as the mother of the bride before the rest of us can. Her blue eyes sparkle with tears as she smooths down her dress and stands, turning her attention to the back of the church where Lorelei will enter momentarily.

I stand along with the rest of the crowd as my twin and father enter through the dark, wooden-framed arched doors.

But I know there'll be a million videos surfacing of that moment.

So I watch my soon-to-be king-in-law's reaction as I bite my bottom lip to keep from shouting in excitement.

Love pours from his eyes; it's in the softness of his expression, the parting of his lips as he gasps. After a moment of pure bewitchment, a coruscating smile breaks across his face, and he leaves his post, bounding down the stairs and meeting Lorelei and Dad right where the seating begins on either side of the golden aisle. He hurriedly takes her hand from Dad, bowing to him then wrapping his arm around Lorelei's waist as he leads her up the five stone stairs.

Stone.

It's a shame I can't think about using that descriptive word in its adjective form without thinking about the person who makes it a proper noun.

Regardless of my healing journey, I still miss him.

And that's how I know there was something deeper than lust between us.

I wasn't lying when I said it.

I love him.

Presently.

A love that is a ghastly thing echoing around my heart.

As the ceremony begins, I find my thoughts drifting to the little story he wrote for me. After reading it, I cried and cried, attempting to determine if he meant the words he said or not.

Upon reflection, I remembered Stone never lied to me. He was always upfront and honest with what he knew to be true. He couldn't be honest about his feelings for me at the time because fear had him in a chokehold and the feeling that he could never deserve me was kicking him in the shins.

It was this one line he wrote from the male main character's perspective that gave me pause and pried open my heart to believing his reason for walking away: "I am choosing you in my rolling away for a moment, Lioness. I am choosing to better myself so I no longer stab you in the foot as you walk. I am choosing to shave off my rough edges and become something better for you. Become a pebble who doesn't cut you. Because I can't imagine my life without you."

The male character was named Stone and was depicted as an actual arrowhead stone. The female character was named Lioness and depicted as an actual lioness. It was cute and written more as a friendship story than a romantic story, but Stone did write a note from himself at the end that said it was because of our easy friendship that he fell in love with me.

I read it over and over for days. I allowed Brandi to read it in confidentiality. I talked to Lorelei about it and sent her images of the text. And we all came to the same prayerful conclusion: Stone had never lied to me, and it didn't look like he was starting now.

The crowd claps around me, and I blink to attention, kicking myself for zoning out so heftily. But it was simply the transition from the priest's scriptural reading to the vows.

I tune in completely, dismissing Stone from my thoughts, and watch my twin and the love of her life exchange holy and royal vows to each other and their country.

When the ceremony is over and we've all arrived at the ornate ballroom in Stjarna Palace, I watch for Gabriel to enter to dance with him as I promised on Thanksgiving. I search the crowds of women in stunning dresses, full of bright colors that counteract the long, dark days of the winter season in Korsa. The orchestra begins playing some unknown-to-me tune that has a happy, upbeat flow to it. Men are dressed to the nines in tuxedos, and all around me, people speak in a language I do not understand. Mama and Dad are somewhere, but I left them on my initial high of being at an actual ball. Now, feeling overwhelmed and a little lost, I make my way to the edges of the golden room in my silver stilettos that tie into a bow around my ankles. I lean against a cool, white column, recentering myself through deep breaths.

I watch as Astrid asks Anders to dance, then she catches my eye and throws a wink in my direction. I laugh, wondering when she got that grumpy man wrapped around her finger. I'll ask her about it tomorrow over tea in the royal gardens.

Suddenly, someone taps me on the shoulder, and I spin around, breathing a sigh of relief. "Oh, good. You're here. I was looking for you."

Gabriel flashes me a million-dollar smile, and in his french accent, says, "I'm promised a dance, yes?" He offers his hand, and I slip mine into his. He leads us out onto the polished wooden floor area meant for dancing. The song transitions into a waltz, and I follow Gabriel's lead. We are clumsy and a bit ridiculous, but I laugh through our errors, enjoying this moment and blocking out the haunting memory that me and Stone were supposed to do a well-practiced waltz to an instrumental Taylor Swift song that

Finley promised he would play when I asked him about it months ago.

As Gabriel begins to spin me around, my arm flies out, and someone catches hold of my wrist as Gabriel releases me, and I spin right into someone else's arms.

I snap my head around to complete the spin and see my new dance partner.

My breath hitches as I gaze into familiar, baby blue eyes and inhale Bad Boy by Carolina Herrera.

Chapter 24

Stone

Spicy vanilla invades my nose from her spin, and those beautiful hazel eyes—which look stunningly green with the help of her sage-colored gown—lock onto me in shock. She gasps, her fingers tightening around my shoulder as her other hand clenches mine.

A little too tightly, but I'm not going to complain.

She's not throwing herself away from me in disdain, so it's a win!

Right on cue, the music transitions to an orchestra version of "Wildest Dreams," and after shoving down my nerves for the millionth time since I've arrived and secretly gazed starry-eyed at her from a distance, I lead Lucy in our carefully rehearsed steps that we practiced during the evening hours within a small space in the center back in late September.

Her grip loosens in mine, her movements slowly melting into mine as we waltz in small, rehearsed circles around our dance space. She never takes her eyes off of mine, and not to be dramatic, but, I think I'm falling in love with her all over again.

When did it happen the first time?

Was it when we danced back in February? Was it when she put me in my place time and time again while I led with a boyish pursuit of her? Maybe it was when she slid into my family's lives like she's belonged there all along? Or when I found myself spilling my secrets over seafood?

One thing's for sure—the initial lust I had for her is absolutely nothing compared to this feeling of deep love. And it's love that commands me to work hard to keep my thoughts pure toward her, keep her protected, and cherish her like the strong, capable woman she is.

I spin her around and pull her in close to me. Her hand moves to gently brace the back of my neck as she tilts her chin to keep her eyes focused on mine. I see a million questions in her gaze, but we don't dare speak a word as we move in fluid motion while the rest of the crowd disappears into a hushed blur.

It's me, Lucy, and the music.

Her red hair, styled into perfect waves with two braids crowning her head right above the line of her bangs, flows with each spin I initiate. Somewhere throughout this dance, her shocked expression dissolved not into a smile but into a serious, contemplative look. Like I'm the study guide for a test she's about to take.

This moment is a test of sorts.

Will she accept me?

Kick me out?

Will I falter in my resolve?

Is it possible fear will freeze me again?

Most importantly, is she in a better place to have me?

It's something I never told her, but she needed me to walk away as much as I needed to. I could see the pain, the hurt, and the agony in her eyes with every passing day after she told me she loved me. Acting in lust and ignoring love, I took advantage. But she wasn't going to walk away from me. Not in her anxious state of loneliness.

I spin her out again as the song begins to draw to a close. Though her dress is loose, she does look healthier. Her freckled face is fuller, her skin warmer. She must be doing better; Lorelei most likely wouldn't have let me come if she wasn't.

God, don't let me slip up and break her again. Strengthen me so that I can be the man who loves her for all of her days.

The song closes and fades into an unknown number. Probably Bach or something.

Lucy remains in my arms, one hand placed on my shoulder as her arm presses against my chest at our nearness. My hand is on her waist, burning through her dress in my nervousness. Time continues to pass as we remain as statues staring into each other's eyes, breaths heavy from the dance. I feel the edges of my consciousness slip into inappropriate memories, so I lift a silent prayer of resolve and gently step away from her.

Dropping my hands to my side, I smile sheepishly and say the most epic "I've come to grand-gesture you" line in the history of forever: "Hi."

Kill me now. How did admitting I was in love with her turn me into an awkward specimen?

Her contemplative stare turns into... Is she hiding a smile right now? Fine. I'll remain awkward if it's impressing her.

"Mr. Notorious Playboy Boss has lost his edge, huh?" She crosses her arms and leans to one side.

"A pretty woman will do that to a man. Especially when he loves her." I smirk, metaphorically patting myself on the back for not having lost all my wits about me.

"Hm. So you love me?" She begins to circle me, carefully avoiding those dancing around us. I have half the mind to pull us away from the dance floor for this conversation, but the way she's eyeing me up and down like I'm prey is clue number one as to why I'm not going to get away with dragging her off anywhere.

Despite myself, I grin. There's my sassy, spirited, confident woman that I lassoed into fake dating me back in June.

"I do."

"And you had to fly to Korsa to tell me that right now?"

I shrug. She finally stops her circling and steps closer to me as if challenging my intentions. "We had an agreement, remember? You needed a date to this event. We even practiced a regency-style dance. How could I possibly leave you hanging out to dry?"

Lucy's face contorts into a grimace.

I probably shouldn't have said that...

She spins one-eighty and walks off toward the back of the ballroom, and I follow her, zig-zagging through dancing couples.

"Lucy," I call after her nervously as we walk past the table of food. She doesn't stop but heads for the large double doors.

"Lucy! Let's talk about this."

She continues marching forward, but she throws up her hand, motioning me to follow. Two men on either side of the door pull it open by the barred handles, and I follow Lucy out of the ballroom where we are immediately wrapped in a dampened silence.

The click of her heels continuing down the tiled floors echoes off the stone walls.

"Lucy, this is far enough. We shouldn't—" She rounds the corner of the hallway. I follow but then catch her wrists as her arm naturally swings backwards from her gait. "Let's not get too far away from watching eyes, okay? For my protection."

"Your protection? Do you think I'm going to hurt you or something? I—"

"No, Lucy." I drop her wrist and close my eyes for a brief second. When I open them, she's facing me, a challenging pout on her face that I'd like the chance to kiss off. I take another breath and speak slowly. "Not protection from you. Protection from myself. You plus me plus dark rooms equals our Lord and Savior arching His brow and turning His face away from us. It's simple math."

I watch her face flush in the dim candle lighting of the hallway. "You're too tempting, and I flew all this way to tell you that I'm done being afraid. I've strengthened my walk with Christ, and while I know there will still be plenty of moments of faltering, I'm not afraid anymore. He's taught me that love is selfless and looks after the other person. And because I love you, Lucy May, I will put you and your health first. I will look after you and cherish you. Forever. If you'll have me..."

In the middle of the spewed confession, my tone went from playful and mischievous to sounding like a golden retriever in need of cuddles. Lucy must pick up on it because she takes one small half-step in my direction, her hand lifting from her side as if to reach out to me.

But she stops mid-movement, stares at her hand, and then falls back into place as if she never moved in the first place. After a long breath, she cuts her eyes from the floor up to me. "I get why you walked away. It took me a while to wrestle with the idea. I thought you were using God as an excuse to run from me. But after I read your story, spoke with a few trusted individuals, and reflected for myself, I realized you had never lied to me before. But Stone, I only came to that realization a couple of weeks ago. Yes, it freed me. Yes, I believe you. But now, I've started focusing on my own healing. There are some things I've come to learn about myself, and in all transparency, I don't know if I'm ready for a stable, functioning relationship at the moment. And dang it, it hurts to say that to you because I love you, Stone. I love you so much that now I have to be the one to say 'I need space to figure things out.'"

Her words are a thousand bees stinging my heart, and I feel the now-familiar push of tears behind my eyes. Lucy's are already falling, trailing down her freckled cheeks, leaving a line of black streaking both sides, evidence of our twin flame bruise. Taking the two steps that were needed to close the distance between us, I enclose her in my arms, tugging her face close to my chest as she breaks herself apart in my arms.

I can't tell you how many minutes pass by as she cries in my arms. Silent, tearful floods pour from me, streaming into her hair. She never said it was over between us, so why does it feel that way? I don't resent her, nor am I upset at her for this extremely difficult choice she's making (I mean, I had to make it a month ago myself).

"I want this for you, Lucy. I want your healing. However long it takes." She tries to catch her breath through her receding sobs. After a second, she pulls away from me, but I don't let go of her. Instead, I fix my gaze on her glistening eyes (why are eyes the prettiest when they're tear-filled?) and say slowly and surely, "I will wait for you, Lucy. Take your time and do what you need to do."

"But what if—"

I cup her cheeks, placing my thumb over her mouth. "No what-ifs, Lucy May. You're it for me. If you don't want me after you've taken the time you need, then so be it. But as for me, you're the love of my life."

She nods her head, takes a small step into me, and kisses my cheek. "If healing doesn't bring me to you, Pebbles, then I don't want it."

I chuckle and kiss her forehead. "I'm ready to heal together when you are, my little lion."

"I like deadlines, Stone. That's something you didn't give me when you walked out, so I'm giving a deadline so you're not left wondering when, where, why, and how like I was. The coronation is in two weeks. I'll be home a few days after New Year's. We will talk then about where we stand with each other and what we want. Let's take these next couple of weeks to really pray, talk to those who love and care about us, and listen to the Lord's guidance?"

My jaw comes unhinged at the straightforward suggestion, and suddenly I'm swimming in guilt. "Thank you for that. I'm sorry I didn't offer the same assurity to you. In the future, I will make my intentions better known and with clearer operating boundaries, okay? Thank you for teaching me that just now."

For the first time tonight, she genuinely smiles at me, teeth and all, and I say a prayer right then and there for the Lord to help—and selfishly, move quickly—Lucy with whatever she sees in herself that she wishes to work on.

BEAT EIGHT

JOYFUL DEFEAT // "CLEAN"

Chapter 25

Lucy

"Don't what-if yourself into the grave, Lucy. Stop the intrusive, spiraling thoughts as soon as you realize they're happening." Brandi pegs me with a stern look, repeating a phrase she's said often in our sessions. Her face softens after seeing my expression of genuine fear over the scenarios I've expertly crafted inside the confines of my head. "I understand you are worried you'll mess up again and sleep with him. I understand you're scared that he will go cold on you and walk away one day because of your anxiety and battle with anxious attachment. But if you do sleep with him, does that mean you are condemned to hell and are no longer worthy of the love of Christ? If he does go cold and walks away, does that mean you'll never smile again?"

"Yes," I say immediately. Mostly as a joke, but I think there's some truth to the singular word, which is what terrifies me the most. I huff out a breath and cross my arms, leaning back on her sofa in her living room. "That's why I don't think I'm ready to go back to him. When the plane landed back in Mississippi two days ago, all I wanted to do was run to him and hug him and start over with him. But instead I texted him and told him I was back and I wanted to wait one more week before talking. I'm obviously not ready to see him."

Brandi doesn't miss a beat. "Not ready to see him or not ready to put yourself out there again because you have dug yourself a 'what if' grave?"

Somewhere, deep down, I know she's right. The fear is loud, though. The ghost of the pain and heartache lingers like an unwelcome house guest. What if he— "Ah, shoot. You're right," I cave, catching myself hopping and skipping down another trail that leads to desolation.

"So what do you think is the next appropriate course of action for you to take?"

I think over her question, chewing on my bottom lip and fiddling with the silver ring on my thumb. "I don't know. I'm supposed to reach out in a few days, I guess. I'm still scared, though. It's not like I don't want to jump into his arms, smiling as he sets me on his bike and rides me off into the winter sunset. I want that more than anyone could know. But how do I know if it's the lust talking, the attachment issues talking, or if I'm truly meant to be with him?"

Discovering I have anxious attachment issues was eye-opening. Combing through my childhood with Brandi, I discovered my parents didn't give me the attention I needed. It wasn't their fault; I had a twin sister, after all. When Lorelei showed signs of not wanting to be touched and held, that led to a lack of touching and holding on my end, but I needed it. It's not my sister's fault, either.

It just is what it is. It's the fallen world we live in. My parents loved me well. But when people started leaving my life (not intentionally, of course, and I keep reminding myself of that), the attachment issues really came out. It's why I've cycled through men. It's why I use sex to keep a man, even if I don't understand I'm doing it

I just want to be truly known and loved.

But now I know I am truly known and loved by the One who formed me. No earthly love could top that.

My therapist and friend leans forward, taking my hands in hers. Her green eyes hold mine as she smiles. "I'm not going to tell you what to do. Love him or leave him, that's your decision. It's between you, him, and the Lord solely. I'm here to support you. I'm here to give you practical and functional ways to help overcome the anxious attachment you've formed with him because no matter what you choose to do in regards to him, there's no room for that in any relationship you may find yourself in—romantically or otherwise. I'm here to help you stay true to your morals and values because much of our self worth stems from our personal systems of belief."

"So much for your help." I jokingly roll my eyes.

"But," Brandi begins, grabbing my attention again, "if no one has told you this before, allow me to be the first to. And if someone has, let me reiterate good, Biblical advice that would do you good to remember: Love does not start out as some mythical tether binding two souls to one another. The *choice* to love someone forms a tether. The choice to follow God and keep Him at the center of your love strengthens the tether. Love is emotional and physical, but it is also a choice that is actively demonstrated."

I press my lips together, nodding thoughtfully as she releases my hands and leans back. Hadley told me something similar before regarding her and Braxton. Yes, they had chemistry out the wazoo, but Braxton kept choosing to love her. She had to choose to believe herself worthy of love in order to accept the love he had to offer.

Karoline had to choose to forgive Mason for an act that scarred her. It was her love that allowed her to forgive him.

Finley had to choose to constantly pursue my sister without any evidence that she would eventually say yes to him. A blind choice. A selfless choice. He loved her through her own journey of self-awareness.

Choice. Worthiness. Forgiveness. Self-awareness. Selflessness.

Love.

That's what it is... a choice to see someone's worthiness, assist them in their daily journey of self-awareness, give selflessly, and forgive when wronged.

Stone and I may not be perfect, but we are chosen by God, deemed worthy of love, forgiven of our wrong-doings, and constantly being made self-aware through a lifelong process of sanctification only given to us by God's selfless sacrifice of Himself.

Chance after chance, we fall and mess up. But sometimes we get it right. And maybe, *just maybe,* we can get it right together.

Typing 'the end' has never felt so satisfying.

The merman and vampiric urban fantasies in my projects folder give me the bombastic side-eye as I sheepishly smile and remind them that I will complete them soon.

They don't speak back, of course, because they are documents on a computer and I may be a little insane.

But what writer isn't?

An idea resonated in my soul back in November, a thought to be more intentional and honest in my writing and on my social media. I've hinted at things to come to my readers, but today is the day I announce that I've put my urban fantasies on hold in favor of another romantic comedy. But this rom-com will be different. It's my blood on a page. It's my sins laid bare. It's my head and heart split open for all to examine.

As they dissect the evidence I lay before them, will my readers resonate or will they hang me? Will they relate to the two very broken characters I've poured my experiences into, or will they deem me unworthy of calling myself a Christian? Will they understand that sometimes breakups are necessary and can actually bring two people toward a state of healing and reconciliation? Or will they burn the book because the happily ever after took a little too long to materialize?

Speaking of materializing my new book's ending...

I really hope there's something to this manifestation stuff.

Just kidding, folks. Don't come at me with your pitchforks.

I close my laptop, pick up my phone from the armchair, and scroll through social media for a minute before posting the announcement that I have a new rom-com book coming out on the first day of spring. I mention it's different from my previous works and has a darker undertone of sin represented, but I don't say anything more. Not yet, at least.

After I hit post, I do the opposite of what the algorithm would suggest and close out social media. I check the time, which is almost five in the evening.

Stone should be home now.

Nervous energy swirls inside of me as I stand from my trusted brown recliner chair and head to the bathroom to freshen up. As I swipe mascara on my lashes, I send a silent plea that it won't run down my face later. More like a prayer that there won't be a reason for it to. I style my natural curls half up-half down, and just to look my cutest, I add a simple white ribbon to the back. Taking one last look in the full-length mirror, I compliment my simple torn boyfriend jeans and off the shoulder floral crop-top with a brave smile.

"You've got this, Lucy May." I wink at myself for good measure then spritz my perfume on my neck, in my hair, and down my body. Once I'm back in my bedroom, I say three kind words to my new purple orchid Karoline bought for me during her last visit.

Thankfully, Frannie has yet to eat this one.

Feeling a little more confident with my dolled-up armor in place, I grab a water, my purse, smile at the now-thriving Bird of Paradise plant beside the door that Lorelei revived during her visit over Thanksgiving, and exit the apartment.

Once I'm in the car and heading down the road, I contemplate too long on whether to listen to the *1989* album by Taylor Swift, an audiobook, or a podcast, so I end up driving in silence, whispering small prayers as I turn down his short driveway.

I wish it were longer...

His massive black truck is in the driveway alongside his shiny black motorcycle, so he must be home unless he's off with someone else. I eye the pink leather jacket and helmet in the back of my car, and then I say a prayer that I'll get the chance to wear them again.

Taking a deep breath, I turn off my car and get out. I wore my sneakers today, so I don't make a sound as I walk down the cobblestone path to his front door. I stare at the mahogany door, feeling like I may come unhinged at any moment the longer I wait. My hand is raised, and I'm ready to knock.

If only I can make myself move...

Closing my eyes and inhaling through my nose, I grumble to myself, "Just do it—"

"Lucy May."

My name is spoken in a rough but feminine voice that belongs to myself, but the sound is mingled with a masculine voice. One full of shock.

I peek through one eye, seeing the most handsome man I've ever met standing in front of me in joggers and a t-shirt, his blond hair unkempt and blue eyes dazzling.

He laughs, and I realize I'm standing there with my fist raised and one eye opened. *Not* how I was planning for things to go...

Popping my other eye open and dropping my hand, my body begins to buzz as I bask in his bearing; he's the confident man I've come to know, but now there's a certain humility to him that didn't exist before. The confidence is in the strong set of his shoulders that promises to protect and guard me. The humility is in the softness of his expression that vows to love me despite his struggle to feel worthy of it.

Or maybe Romance Writer Brain is still turned on from finishing that first draft earlier and I need to knock it off.

I also should say something...

"Hi." I recall his first word to me after dancing at Lorelei's wedding reception.

A flashing smile crosses his face. "Hi, Lucy May."

My insides melt a little under his gaze, and I have to shake my head to clear the thoughts. I'm here for a reason, and it's not to swoon over this man. "So, I've been thinking, and I'd like to see us start over. Try again. Have a second chance or whatever." I shrug, trying to play it off casually because the fear of rejection is still as present as the stories I write in my mind.

His smile somehow widens, however, and it's not his cocky one that denotes a snarky, flirty line. It's genuine. And beautiful. And all for me.

"Yeah?" Stone questions, surprise in his voice. "I'm not dreaming, right? You're really here?" He reaches out his hand, taking strands of my hair between his fingers. I grab his hand and weave our fingers together.

Stone kisses my hand. "I still don't feel worthy of you, Lucy May. But I pledge to love you. Even when I'm afraid, I'll love you." He kisses my forehead. "Even when I stumble, I'll love you." He kisses my cheek. "Even when I don't see my next step, I know it'll always include loving you."

Not able to stand it anymore, I blurt through my tears, "I love you so much." And then I release his hand, snake mine behind his neck, and drag his lips to mine. This kiss is drenched in passion, but there's something different in the way he lightly holds me, as if he may break me if he's not careful. His lips move softly against mine, cherishing every second they dance together. He laughs against my lips, and we stand there smiling into each other's souls.

"I didn't know allowing myself to love you would feel so good," he says, taking a step back. "I really should have surrendered to this sooner."

"Who are you and what have you done with my cocky, playboy former boss?"

He cocks his head, shaggy blond hair falling to the side. His smile turns saucy as his voice lowers. "Oh, don't worry, Little Lion. I'm still my charming self." He runs his hand down the side of my cheek. "It's just all for you, now and evermore."

Stone drops his hand and clenches it into a fist. He rocks his jaw, his expression changing from flirty to full of desire. Stormy gray-blue eyes and all. "And maybe not until I put a ring on your finger. The temptation of you hasn't changed."

I gulp, a swarm of hot desire mixed with guilt swirling in my stomach. I look him over, wishing I could glue myself to him. "The temptation of you hasn't changed either, Onyx."

"We should set physical boundaries to help us if we're going to start over," he says, running a hand through his hair. "Like not being here at my place—or yours—alone."

I glance behind him at his open door and hurriedly nod, visions already filling my mind. But I will fight against them because Stone is worth more than my sexual desires. He's worth my honest love. "Agreed. Or not being alone anywhere, really." I can't help the heat that rises to my face. I wish I was the woman who could remain tame in a vehicle alone with him out in the middle of nowhere, but that's not me. And since I know I'm nothing more than a feral animal sometimes, it's best to stay out of those scenarios.

Suddenly, Stone smiles. "How about a bike ride to Books and Beans for dinner? Do you happen to have your jacket and helmet? If not, we can take separate vehicles. Or if you're comfortable with a short drive alone, we can ride together in my truck."

His rambling is adorable, and pride swells within me. He's going to meet me halfway in this. He's going to take each step carefully like I am. The fear that something will go wrong and I'll mess up again is still present, but it's dimmed after this encounter with him. Something has changed in him, and I know I've changed.

And I can't wait to explore our transformed sides together.

We can do it. With strong wills, boundaries, and the help of God... We can really start over and finish healing together.

"I just so happen to have my jacket and helmet, and I'd love to go on a ride with you to Books and Beans for dinner."

He presses his lips together to hide his smile and tucks his head down shyly, rocking back on his heels. This shy side of him, the side that's acknowledging his vulnerability, is the hottest thing I've ever seen. It beats Flirty McFlirter Pants, hands down.

I turn and bound to my car and secure the goods, noticing my journal on the floorboard. I pick it up and turn to the latest entry, smiling as I recall writing it last night. Flipping through previous pages, my heart constricts at the evidence of my depression, my fight with God, and the heartbreak of a lifetime. Those are memories I should probably hold on to, but also, I don't ever want to remember that place. I hated it there. My new book will be enough evidence of the fight.

I start to rip out the pages when Stone places his hands on my waist. "Whatcha doing?"

"Starting clean." I spin in his arms, holding up the ripped pages that contain my darkest, depraved thoughts. I eye the bike over my shoulder and envision letting the pages set sail in the wind. *How freeing...* "Would you judge me too harshly if I littered? I promise these pages will decompose one day."

Stone smiles crookedly and places a kiss on my forehead. "You do whatever you need to do."

I slip into my jacket and put on my helmet as we walk to the motorcycle.

After he helps me on, he lifts my face shield and puts his face to mine, our helmets stopping our noses from touching. "Thank you for giving us a second chance. There's something different about you." I notice crinkles around his eyes, indicating he's smiling as big as I am right now. "You're like an orchid. Sensitive and picky, but when you're in the right environment, you absolutely thrive. I'm excited to create an environment for you to bloom within. I love you, Lucy May."

I could not possibly wipe the smile from my face if I tried. How did he know I now have a thing for orchids? *God, thank you for speaking through this man. My man.*

Stone chuckles and lowers my face shield, then in a very Stone-like move, he slaps the back of my helmet before hopping on the bike. I'm still laughing in disbelief at it all as he cranks the motorcycle. I wrap my arms around him and hold him tight, the torn papers clutched in my fist. Part of me clings in fear that he will walk away from me, but I know it's the anxious attachment talking. The other part of me clings to him out of love, feeling prayerfully thankful that the Lord is providing the two of us another chance at choosing each other. This time for love, not for lust or out of loneliness or running from God.

Stone revs the bike, and then off we go. As the wind encloses around us, I feel it's God wrapping us in His arms, looking after us and protecting us from ourselves. I open my fists, and I let go of the past once and for all.

Epilogue

Lucy - Two Years Later

"Stone!" I shout, zooming around the house like a crazed banshee looking for my husband. The Banshee effect is heightened by my all-black purifying charcoal face mask. "Stone! Where are you? Granite!"

"Babe, what is it?" He emerges from the bathroom with only a towel wrapped around him, his shorter hair damp and torso glistening from stray water droplets.

"Er, I—"

He smirks, takes the two steps toward me, and kisses me breathless. Ladies, get you a man who will kiss you while you sport a face mask. Even if it causes your mask to crack and crevice. "You had something to tell me, Little Lion?"

"Did I?" I shake my head clear of him, then I remember the email on my phone that now resides on the floor since I dropped it when he kissed me. "Oh!" I pick it up and shove the phone in his face. I already had one thing I was going to tell him before we left on our date, that way I could also tell my best friend, but now *this* news has taken center stage. Can I shock my husband twice in one night?

I analyze every nuanced expression flickering across his handsome features as he reads the email to himself, mumbling the words under his breath. I bounce on my toes, awaiting his response while tears press against my eyes.

"Lucy. This is real?"

"I think so! I mean, I need to research her and stuff, but she seems legit." Tears build in my eyes as he pulls me in for a tight hug.

"I'm so proud of you, Lucy May. I knew your stories were special."

"Special enough for the big screen?" I choke out, disbelief and excitement tinging every word I speak. We read the email again, noting the producer's name, her passion for Christian-based content produced by Christian women, and the offer to meet to discuss the possibility of the book I released two years ago becoming a feature film.

"This is our story, Stone. It's the book I wrote about us!"

I follow him to our bedroom, continuing to gush as he gets dressed for our double date with Braxton and Hadley tonight. Oh, I can't wait to tell Hadley!

"Do you think they'll want to produce my story next?" He shaves his face while I wash my mask off.

"It can be the kid-friendly version of mine." I chuckle to myself, remembering the precious story he wrote for me when he needed to step away to get his relationship right with the Lord. And let me tell you. It paid off. Everything.

Together, we are constantly learning to take our fears to the Lord. We have learned to love each other with an unconditional love, and even when we struggle to like each other some days (like when he struggles to open up about what's bothering him, or when I lose myself in my stories when he needs my affection), we fall back onto our deep, unwavering love that seems to be growing more and more as each moment passes. And it's the perfect time to add more love into our family of two.

As I do my makeup, Stone showers me with praise, and I preen under his love and affection. When we got married two years ago—a simple wedding with only family and friends in attendance since it was an extremely short two-week engagement—he slipped a little phrase into his vows that he has honored and upheld every single day of our blissful union: Lucy May, I promise to make sure you know how desired and wanted and loved you are each and every day.

And man oh man, he has done just that.

Whether it's words of affirmation, like he's doing now, or building me a writing desk, or cooking supper when the depression I still occasionally struggle with hits, he always looks after me, treating me like I am his queen.

Which we joke about all the time since my twin is a literal queen and all.

"Are you ready?" he calls from the doorway, and when I walk out of our bathroom wearing a floral skirt and an off the shoulder puff sleeve top, I realize we once again match. I don't think we've ever intentionally matched our outfits, but somehow, we end up doing it anyway. The red in my skirt is brought out by his red button down. My khaki-colored top matches his khaki pants (that I still can't get enough of).

Stone takes three prowling steps before stopping in front of me and trailing his fingers down the nape of my neck and across my exposed shoulder. "Mm, I think we should stay in tonight. Let Hadley and Braxton have their own date night."

"We've rescheduled twice on them, Onyx." But even as the words leave my mouth, I bring my fingers to play with hair at his neckline, giving it a little tug. He moans and captures my mouth with his.

I blame it on the hormones.

"Third time's a charm," he mumbles against my neck. And I'd have to agree, but I also have exciting news—two exciting things, now—I want to share with my best friend that is out-tempting me at the moment. Stone is a real temptation, however. Sex is not something we struggle with inside our marriage. In fact, it's so much better than it was before we married. Now, guilt and shame are absent from our midnight tangles. It's pure love, devotion, and, well... It's fire, that's for sure.

My face heats and desire pulls as I think of last night, and right as I'm on the verge of caving and having a repeat, he steps away from me wearing his signature smirk. "Okay, Lucy May. You are thoroughly kissed, so we can leave now. Just don't think about what happens when we get back from our little double date, okay? We don't want to make Hadley and Braxton jealous of our childless sex lives."

He's joking, but he's also provided me with the perfect segue. I love a good transition in a story.

"Come here." I motion for him to follow me into the bathroom where I'd taken one more test today just to be sure. I pull the covered stick from where I stashed it in the wicker basket full of my things under the sink. "Film optioning rights aren't the only thing we are celebrating tonight."

I hold the double-pink-lined test out in front of him, watching his expression filter through confusion, realization, shock, and finally, joy. His blue eyes sparkle brightly, his smile captivating as always. "I don't think my heart can take any more good news today, my love." He places his hand on his chest. "We're having a baby?"

I nod, tears spilling from my eyes. I really should have announced this before I fixed my makeup. He picks me up and spins me around, setting me down after my feet accidentally hit the bathtub. "Sorry about that," he says.

"You can massage them later," I jest. Then I blot my tears and straighten out my clothes. "So you're excited about this?"

"Are you kidding me? I'm—" He pauses, tears prickling in his eyes. "There are no words. I'm thrilled, Lucy. We are going to be parents! I'm having a baby with you." He runs his hands through his styled hair and blows out air. I reach up to fix his hair before planting a kiss on his cheek.

"We are going to be parents. That's kind of scary if you think about it." I now understand that fear Hadley had when she found out she was pregnant. There are so many things you don't think about until you know there is a child growing in your womb.

"The Lord will lead us." Stone plays with my hair. "You're going to be an amazing mother. You are so full of life and love."

"What if we have twins?" I ask jokingly.

Suddenly, I remember our first kiss and the vision I had. Everything has come to fruition. From Lorelei's wedding ball to our wedding night. To the desk I now draft most of my stories at. To the movie deal. And now... A certain coldness sweeps over me.

"Stone. What if we have twins?"

"Good thing there are two of us," he says with a shrug. "Think they'll be boys?"

If that last piece of the vision comes true, then yes.

I shake off the worries and concerns, silently giving them over to the Lord. Whatever He brings our way, He will help us handle it.

"Ready to go, babe? We are going to be late." I walk out of our room, already feeling the unsettling weight dissipate.

"Let's go." He follows me out, grabbing our leather biking jackets and helmets. He helps me onto his bike, and I do my little tuck thing so I don't flash anyone because of my skirt. Before he gets on, he leans down and kisses my stomach, sending butterflies and blissful happiness throughout my body. "I can't believe how blessed we are."

I smile at my husband. He hops on the motorcycle, and I wrap my arms around him, unabashedly feeling his abs.

As the engine revs and we set off toward Perry's Seafood, I grin as the wind kisses my skin. The Lord has been so gracious and patient with me and Stone. He has freed us, redeemed us, and is now using our story for His glory.

I silently pray the movie is made and impacts every single Christian woman who struggles with strong sexual inclinations and depression, the same way I prayed the book would.

But as with everything in my life lately, I give it all back to Him.

LOVED THE STORY?

Consider leaving a review on Amazon and Goodreads!

Catch Emma Jane and Knightley's story in *Emma Jane's Guide to Matchmaking the Mayor* today!

Read the book that started it all, *The Politics of Christmas,* starring Stella and Lucas!

Dear Reader

If you made it this far, you have all my love and support. I know this wasn't the easiest book to digest. Will you trek with me for one moment longer? Grab a cup of your favorite tea or coffee and sit down with me. Let's talk as friends, shall we?

This story is the first book I've written based on a theme alone. If you didn't catch it, it's redemption and revitalization from sexual immorality. Why? Because I'm a twenty-eight year old woman who has struggled with unhealthy sexual boundaries for years. Let's get two things straight: sex outside of marriage is a sin but your sexual inclinations and desires are not sinful. Furthermore, your sexual desires are not your identity.

I know what it's like to feel like you have no one you can talk to about it. No one you can talk to about how you have a high sex drive or that it's super-duper hard to curb said drive. It's a dirty and shameful topic, right? Of course you can't openly talk to other Christian women who seemingly have it all together. Ones who don't struggle with desiring sex. Good heavens! You definitely can't go to your own mother! What would she think about her little girl?! You're all alone, stuck in dark, depressing midnights that never seem to end. Sometimes you think you're doing better, but when that man comes into your life, or ovulation hits, or you just want to *feel* something again... you slip up. Maybe you slip up in your mind, alone, with a screen, or with a willing man. And you do it again and again and again. No matter how hard you pray. No matter how often you read your Bible. No matter how much you beg for forgiveness on your knees. No matter how hard you try to fight the Beast...

You can't seem to break free.

I get it. I see you. I feel your pain, confusion, and hurt. I know you have to put on that mask at church and hide your struggles. I know the fear of someone finding out about you is terrifying. It's numbing. It's suffocating. It's isolating. I know you want to stop... That you wish you didn't crave it.

I'm not here to tell you it will all be okay. I'm not here to tell you that you have safe people in your church or home life that can help you through it. I'm not God, and I don't know for certain where He has you or what He has in store for you.

But, I am here to say that He HAS you. If you have surrendered your life to Him, if you declared Him Lord of your life, He will not run from you because of your sexual sins. He will not discard you like a used rag. He will not mock you or make fun of you or scowl at you. He will not tell you to just try harder.

God will reveal your sins to you. He will bring you a breaking point. He will get your attention one way or another. And when your world comes shattering down around you, He will be there to pick up the pieces. He will hold you, love you, and plan your steps. He will show you just how much you need HIM. He will remove the labels you've welded to your heart. It will hurt like nothing else in this world has ever hurt, but sweet woman, you will be FREE. Redeemed. Restored. Revitalized. Renewed.

Run to Jesus. Run to Him over and over and over again. If you mess up, He will be there to restore you. He will clean you up and forgive you as many times as it takes. You are not too dirty, too used, or too far gone for Him. We are fallen sinners living in a fallen world. Of course we are ALL dirty and unclean. He knows we can't course correct or cleanse ourselves on our own. Given the choice, we will always choose sin.

That's why Jesus came to this earth, experienced but did not fall victim to all of sin's temptations, and then defeated it once and for all on the cross. Why? Because He LOVES you. He wants to sit with you in your brokenness. He knows what it is like to be tempted. He knows temptation is not something we defeat on our own.

Run to Jesus and surrender to Him. It's a daily thing we must do. He will lead us away from sin through the guidance of the Holy Spirit. Step by step. It may take weeks. It may take years. You may never completely defeat your sin in this lifetime, but with Jesus going to battle for you and with you, you CAN experience freedom and joy again.

I want to encourage you to find a trusted woman you can share your struggles with. Find someone who can pray for you, mentor you, and hold you accountable. Sexual issues root in loneliness and isolation. It thrives in darkness and depression. God created us for community—that is one of the biggest steps you can take outside of prayer and allowing God to search your heart. Speaking your struggles aloud to someone is an action that must be taken in your healing journey. If you struggle with finding a trusted woman who is already in your sphere you can talk with, I encourage you to find a Christian therapist.

You don't have to fight this alone. You are not (and never have been) alone. Surrendering to the Lord is a daily action. Sanctification is a never-ending process. Don't give up. Don't throw in the towel on your fight simply because you *feel* too broken or used or dirty. Feelings lie to us. Trust the truth of the Word of God. I'd like to end with a historical account found in Mark 5. This story has stuck with me for years, and it's a constant reminder that if I just reach out to Jesus, I can be made clean:

> *And a great crowd followed him and thronged about him. And there was a woman who had had a discharge of blood for twelve years, and who had suffered much under many physicians, and had spent all that she had, and was no better but rather grew worse. She had heard the reports about Jesus and came up behind him in the crowd and touched his garment. For she said, "If I touch even his garments, I will be made well." And immediately the flow of blood dried up, and she felt in her body that she was healed of her disease. And Jesus, perceiving in himself that power had gone out from him, immediately turned about in the crowd and said, "Who touched my garments?" And his disciples said to him, "You see the crowd pressing around you, and yet you say, 'Who touched me?'" And he looked around to see who had done it. But the woman, knowing what had happened to her, came in fear and trembling and fell down before him*

> *and told him the whole truth. And he said to her, "Daughter, your faith has made you well; go in peace, and be healed of your disease."*

Reach out to Jesus, acknowledge your sin, surrender it daily to Him, and speak your struggle to a trusted woman or Christian counselor. You might not be okay, but you will SURVIVE.

All my love,
   Drew Taylor

Resources

Disclaimer:

Below are resources I have read and recommend or have come recommended by trusted people in my life. If you are in the throes of depression, please use caution before diving into books outside of scripture. As with everything in life, use the guidance and conviction of the Holy Spirit. The scripture verses chosen are not an exhaustive list but are ones that I personally turn to. Please search the scriptures and allow the Lord to speak specific verses over your life.

BOOKS

> *Sex and the Single Christian Girl: Fighting for Purity in a Rom-Com World* by Marian Jordan Ellis
> https://a.co/d/0wTwZYk
> *Bad Girls of the Bible: And What We Can Learn From Them* by Liz Curtis Higgs
> https://a.co/d/44kwQTS
> *Passion and Purity: Learning to Bring Your Love Life Under Christ's Control* by Elisabeth Elliot

https://a.co/d/gjPpWa3

Holding Hands Holding Hearts: Recovering a Biblical View of Christian Dating by Richard D. Phillips & Sharon L. Phillips

https://a.co/d/i7UE3Xq

Finding God in My Loneliness by Lydia Brownback

https://a.co/d/8ejXudk

The Path of Loneliness by Elisabeth Elliot

https://a.co/d/0WTzZ1o

Christians Get Depressed Too by David Murray

https://a.co/d/j1DKOEG

Spurgeon's Sorrows: Realistic Hope for Those Who Suffer from Depression by Zack Eswine

https://a.co/d/cBL7Ffn

Overcoming Fear, Worry, and Anxiety by Elyse M. Fitzpatrick

https://a.co/d/djTqnSj

Gentle and Lowly: The Heart of Christ for Sinners and Suffers by Dane C. Ortlund

https://a.co/d/6NiFOvA

A Gospel Primer for Christians: Learning to See the Glories of God's Love by Milton Vincent

https://a.co/d/hkGQL8y

SCRIPTURE

Sexual Immorality:

Ephesians 5:1-21
Galatians 5:16-26
1 Corinthians 1:12-20
1 Thessalonians 4:1-8
Psalm 119: 9,11
James 1:14-15

Redemption:
Ephesians 1:1-14
Romans 3:21-26
Galatians 2:15-21
John 3:16-21
Isaiah 44:21-28

Depression:
Psalm 34:17-18
Philippians 4:4-9
Matthew 11:28-30
Proverbs 3:5-8
Romans 5:1-5
Psalm 102:7-11
Psalm 143:8-10
Hebrews 13:5

ALSO BY

DREW TAYLOR

Sign up for my newsletter where you will receive access to bonus scenes, additional chapters, extended epilogues, and much more! New content added at random!

Scan the QR code or click on the link to learn more about Drew Taylor's books!

www.drewtaylorwrites.com

ABOUT THE AUTHOR

Drew Taylor writes modern closed-door romance stories from a Christian worldview. She believes faith-based romance can be full of heart, humor, and hope while showcasing the reality of our fallen human condition. Her redemptive and engaging stories point to the One who embodies true love–Jesus Christ.

Drew lives in the great state of Mississippi where she teaches high school English. When not teaching or writing, she enjoys reading, baking, researching conspiracy theories, and spending quality time with the people who mean the most to her. Sign up for her newsletter for important updates in case Social Media decides to kick her off one day:

https://mailchi.mp/61fed5b940fb/drew-taylor-author

Follow Drew:

Instagram: @authordrewtaylor

Facebook: Drew Taylor, Author

Pinterest: @authordrewtaylor

YouTube: @authordrewtaylor

Acknowledgments

So many people worked very hard on this story, but ultimately, this story belongs to Jesus Christ, my Lord and my Savior. I think those who worked alongside me would agree. Thank you, Jesus, for your sufficient grace, constant pursuit, and unfailing love.

Printed in Great Britain
by Amazon

62830819R00198